BLINDSIDED

A NOVEL

BLINDSIDED

CALVIN MILLER

PUBLISHING GROUP
Nashville, Tennessee

ISBN: 978-0-8054-4348-6

Published by B & H Publishing Group,
Nashville, Tennessee

Dewey Decimal Classification: F
Subject Headings: TERRORISTS—UNITED STATES—FICTION
                   SUSPENSE FICTION

Scripture quotations are taken from the Holman Christian
Standard Bible®, copyright © 1999, 2000, 2002, 2003 by Holman
Bible Publishers.

07 08 09 10 11   10 9 8 7 6 5 4 3 2 1

PROLOGUE

Two Western men collided in a rush of greetings. Both were tall and attracted the attention of the crowd. Peter, the older of the two, was angular and crowned with a thin spray of hair that would not cover his expanding baldness. Ned, on the other hand, was burly and fringed with a dark beard. He didn't look Arabic, but his appearance seemed to win more instant approval with the Yemeni men who witnessed the greeting.

The two men smiled, glad to see each other. But their smiles lasted only a moment before their faces reclaimed their sobriety. Each took a folding chair and sat down, the warmth of their greeting fading into solemnity.

"I'm glad you could come, Peter," Ned began.

"I would have it no other way," Peter replied.

"Any trouble coming through customs?"

Peter shook his head as he mopped the sweat off his brow. "How do you stand this heat?"

"Well, it's tough," Ned conceded, "but I've endured it out of concern for my friend there at the front of the jury box. He's been through a lot of scrapes, but this time, he isn't going to make it."

Ned Baker and Father Peter said little else as they sat in the burning market square in Aden. The equatorial humidity was oppressive, and the sun scalded the dull gray paving stones of the city square.

It was early March, and the temperature was already insufferable. Aden, like hell itself, was always hot. Desperately hot. The flies were thick. Both men brushed them away from their faces while they talked.

They were not tourists. They were on urgent business and dared not, even for a moment, forget why they were there. They were there on a day set by the Yemeni government for public execution. The jury box was sheltered from the sun by a dull green tarp stretched over an aluminum lattice-work. Behind the elevated stage was a sun-weathered fence behind which was the penal area for the immediate sentences the court decreed.

The first two criminals to be tried had been found guilty of stealing electronic equipment from a parochial sheik, according to the charge read aloud in Arabic. Ned and Peter averted their eyes when the swordsman chopped off the thieves' right hands, noticing how the men's screams pierced the souls of onlookers who had gathered for the public trial. There were surgeons standing by who immediately began to staunch the bleeding. Still, for the first few minutes, there was an unbelievable flow of blood. Neither Peter nor Ned could see how the punished men could keep from bleeding to death.

But the third man facing the executioner was clearly a young Westerner—an infidel, as the jury had labeled him. His crime was announced: he had encouraged a young woman in his small Christian academy to appear in public without her mandatory burka. The young woman, said a turbaned jurist, had been remanded to the safekeeping of her parents. But the man—who had been prevented from entering the U.S. embassy to seek sanctuary—was about to be beheaded.

"This was the man I was telling you about," said Ned, nodding toward the accused. "His name is Francis Serrano, a young man of Italian descent from Hoboken. He's been working with rural schools here in Yemen and doing a great job. He's only twenty-seven and has been with the Peace Corps for six years. He was friends with that Baptist doctor, Martha Myers, who was assassinated up in Jibla four years ago. He's innocent, Peter. He was dragged from his bed around midnight two nights ago. The embassy has no knowledge of his arraignment, and before they find out, he'll be in eternity. He's a Catholic man, single, with no prospects of marriage. He told me in his e-mails that he is interested in entering the monastery when his term is up next April."

"Can you take him early if I manage to get him off the hook?" Peter asked.

"Of course."

Once the offense was read and the punishment announced, the young man's head was covered with a black bag—one that clearly had been used several times before . . . and had not been washed between uses. The flies were clustered thick on the dark stains of the bag as the man was led to the block.

"Pay attention to the man with the scimitar," said Ned. "His name is Ishaq. The Arabs call him the White Jackal."

"An albino Arab?"

"Apparently," said Ned.

The albino man was striking—handsome, pale, and muscular. A trimmed, white Vandyke beard rested on his rugged jaw, and beneath were sharp neck tendons that stood out like steel girders supporting a marble head. His red eyes were piercing, seemingly colored by an inner inferno.

"An albino Arab," repeated Peter. "That can't happen very often."

"No, only once in every century of Muslim terror, I believe."

"He's not the one who cut the hands off the thieves."

"No. He only handles capital offenses. He likes being an executioner for the state. He volunteers for these executions and finds himself eager to take care of his business."

"His business?" Peter queried.

"Yes, he feels called to rid the world of infidels and purify the earth for the reign of Allah, thereby paving the way for sharia law and Muslim caliphate."

"His grudge runs deep, then?"

"Very. He is wealthy in his own right and has no family. And our poor Peace Corps friend has only till the end of the next drum roll to live. Unless, of course . . ."

"Of course," said Peter.

Ishaq the albino executioner approached Francis Serrano, who was now kneeling with his neck on the block. Francis's legs were strapped to the platform, while his upper chest was harnessed to the block to prevent struggling during his execution.

"Excuse me, Ned," said Peter, rising slowly, "I must make my way to the scaffold to the work of God. It's odd how the best work of God seems ever to be done on scaffolds. As James Russell Lowell said, 'Truth forever on the scaffold, wrong forever on the throne. Yet that scaffold sways the future and above the dim unknown standeth God within the shadows keeping watch above his own.'"

"A good poem, a great truth," said Ned, "but we haven't enough leisure for poetry." He quickly extracted a small envelope from his pocket and jammed it in Peter's pocket. "Here's a little gift for you, Peter."

Peter reached toward his pocket to examine the gift.

"No time for that now, Peter. You can look at it later. Scaffolds are no better for gift-giving than for poetry. Now, to your work."

Peter strode to the front of the crowd and up the stairs to the raised scaffold.

"Excuse me, followers of the Prophet. I can allow this no more," said Peter, in Arabic.

A wave of restlessness moved through the crowd.

"Who is this old man who dares to interrupt the flow of justice?" Ishaq demanded of the jury.

"I am sent by Allah, who raised prophets and thrones. Read of him in your own holy book. I am sent to offer you two proofs that the man before you is innocent of all charges. And Allah will confirm the signs I give you. First, I will count to ten, and the fire that once fell on Mount Carmel will fall again on this scaffold. And when the burst of flame is past, there will stand on this platform a beast like you have never seen before. With his silver fangs, this beast will unleash the leather straps that bind the prisoner and set him free. Then all of you must bless this good man's innocence."

Peter began to count to ten in Arabic. At ten, an intense flash of fire seemed to consume the oxygen in the air. Winded, Ishaq collapsed unconscious. As the fire died, a silver wolf leapt from the vanishing flames and fell upon the scaffold. He began at once to gnaw the buckles and straps of the condemned man. In a moment the fetters fell.

Ishaq lay silent before the drama.

"Stand, Francis Serrano," said Peter. The man stood, and Peter ripped the bag from his head. "Ladies and gentlemen," he began, acknowledging the few women present, blinking in bewilderment through the slits in their burkas. "I give you Francis Serrano, whom Allah has judged to be innocent and free of all charges brought against him."

Though still stunned, the crowd broke into applause.

"Now, Francis, you are free."

Francis stood shakily. Peter dropped his voice to a whisper: "There's your friend Ned. Go to him now. There's a car waiting to take you back to the airport. It's time you began your year of approval at the monastery. If ever there was a good time to go into the ministry, this is it."

Peter and Francis hugged, descended the scaffold, and parted. Francis hurried from the square with Ned. The silver wolf followed Peter in the opposite direction. The crowd departed warily. They had just disappeared down a hot, treeless street when Ishaq began to regain consciousness.

■ ■ ■

Ned and Francis were at the Aden airport and lifting off the runway within the hour. Meanwhile, Peter remembered that Ned Baker had slipped something into his pocket. He retrieved the object.

It was a folded envelope crumpled around a hard, metal object. Peter tore the paper away to reveal a small medallion on a gold chain. Nine words were printed on one side of the medallion: "I have tested you in the furnace of affliction." On the other side was "Isaiah 48:10." The gold gleamed in the hot Yemeni sun.

"Well, Kinta, my friend," Peter said to the wolf, "we may be about to enter Gethsemane. But if so, I will need your help more than ever." He slipped the chain over his own head, letting the medallion rest above his heart. The cold medallion suddenly felt as hot as the furnace it spoke of. It burned momentarily, but when the burning faded, the man and wolf walked on. They had one more chore to do before they could leave Yemen. Peter decided to do it in the dead of the night after the hellish heat of the day had cooled.

■ ■ ■

It was two o'clock the next morning when Ishaq went to the roof of his flat-topped house to relieve himself over the edge of the cool stucco wall. When Ishaq turned around, he saw two sets of bright eyes glaring at him from the corner of the roof.

"Is it you, old man?" asked Ishaq. "You caught me by surprise today, or I would have put two heads in that basket."

"Never forget whom you are talking to, Ishaq. It is I. I am not put off by your reputation of slaughter and death. I have come for one final reason. Now that the young man you would have killed is free, there is one final request I should like to make of you. I want you to agree not to come to Seattle. For Seattle is not the proper place to pursue your hatred of Christians. If you do, you will face the greatest warriors you have ever met. They will not seem like warriors to you, but I guarantee you, they hold a power within their circle you cannot conquer. They don't want to kill you. In fact, as of this moment, they do not even know that you exist. All they want to do is to live. But their lust for life is so powerful within them that your lust for jihad must face their faith."

"I fear nothing and no one," Ishaq retorted, moving slowly toward his foes. "I have a great purpose for living. You're in my way, old man. All who want to live without honoring Allah are in the way."

"Don't you want to live, Ishaq?" Peter asked, also methodically closing the distance between them.

"What is life, but the service of Allah? I will serve him by cutting his enemies out of his world. I have no vengeful feelings for this. I kill only to make the best of life possible. When infidels die, the world is always better and Allah is freer to be praised by the true people of faith. In spite of your warning, Father Peter, I will come to Seattle. May Allah be merciful to the infidels who live there. And if they all must die, they will leave the world a better place. They have spoiled the earth long enough. We have cried at the hands of America; now it is time for Allah to drop the sword of justice. You cannot stop me, Father Peter. No trick like the one you used today to save Francis Serrano will work again. Your city will pay for its Christian values."

"Ishaq, the God I know was the father of a carpenter. He is in love with you and all your people. He would call your nation to mercy and teach you that—while he is no stranger to dying—it is living in peace that was the point of his death."

"Please, none of your Christian theology. This is not a seminary debate we are engaged in. It is jihad. It is holy war for a holy cause. Many in America have already died. More must. It is jihad alone that purifies the earth. It is jihad that will wash away America's secular disease of sin. It is jihad that Allah ordains to pave the Prophet's way."

"Then you are committed to this march of folly."

By this time the two men were face to face. Kinta prowled by his master, ready to defend him should Ishaq attack. But Ishaq seemed to relax. Then, without warning, Ishaq whipped a vial from under his nightshirt, uncapping it and throwing its contents directly into Peter's eyes. The stinging liquid sent Peter staggering backward until he fell flat on Ishaq's roof. The stinging gave way to a burning that cut a dark flame across his vision, and the darkness settled permanently upon him.

"Cobra venom, my friend. Whatever war you seek to wage against me in Seattle will be a battle you must fight in darkness." Ishaq raised his hand to seize his fallen enemy and throw him over the edge of the roof. But no sooner had he lifted his hand than Kinta struck him like a cannonball. Ishaq reeled and fell, hitting his head on a steel railing and falling into a quiet, gray stupor.

When he awoke, he was alone. Peter and Kinta were gone. He had no doubt they would meet again . . . in Seattle.

CHAPTER 1

A thin blind man and his sentry animal walked briskly along State Highway 99. The man wore black trousers, a cassock, a clerical collar, and a Seahawks ball cap. They were close to Riverton, and the highway was busy with traffic. Airplanes blended their thrusting whines into the melee of sounds that filled the morning air. Three miles later, the busy world of noise calmed itself against a quieter backdrop of urban sounds. The blind man could tell he was getting farther from the airport.

The great dog, sensing his master's fatigue, directed him from the shoulder of the road to a shaded patch of grass. A score of yards from the pavement was a convenient tree the priest could lean against. The morning rain had dried sufficiently for the grassy tuft to be hospitable, and in this pleasant spot the two sat down.

The great animal seemed as weary as his master. After the old man loosened his grip on the harness, the two of them lay down in the grass, the animal on his stomach and the old man on his back. To all those driving by, it appeared that he was staring up into the sky, but in truth, he was unable to stare at anything.

He ran his thin fingers through his friend's thick fur. "It's you and God who keep me honest, Kinta, old friend," said the priest. "You are my eyes. God illumines the darkness within me, and you light up the darkness outside me. I should have called you Faith, for it is my faith in you by which I navigate the sharp edges of the world."

The great animal looked at him, and somehow the old man could detect the hurried glance. "I feel the weight of your eyes, Kinta. I know you're looking at me."

He lay in silence for a long time then took his friend's shaggy head in his thin blue fingers. He tousled the fur and laid his own face alongside the animal's snout.

"The last time I visited Seattle, I had my eyes but no mind," he mused. "This time I have my mind but no eyes." He paused once again and patted his companion on the head. "The last time we came, the world needed a lesson in ecology. This time it needs to know how to become secure in an unsafe age. These are dangerous times, Kinta. Poor world. People will do almost any dastardly thing to control it. There are those gathering in Seattle right now who want to take this beautiful city and blow it to bits. And what's to be done? What can one blind man and one very capable beast do to stop them?"

Kinta snuggled close to the old man's leg.

"Do you know why they want to do this, old friend? They believe God wants them to do it. And why do they think God wants them to do it? They suffer from a common human notion that God feels as they do about every issue. It is a naive soul who brings the mighty mind of the Maker down and clothes it with such tiny biases that it can fit in with the most pitiable human prejudices. Yet so much of the world does it. Once people create God in their own small image, God can become their ally in the most awful ventures. Of course, in doing this they create a picture of God that most people would rather not see altogether. God sure gets a bad reputation from those who invoke his help in their own willful need to destroy things."

At length the old man joined his sleeping dog and dozed into silence.

He napped to the lullaby of distant traffic and large planes, cloud-snipping their way onto sunny runways. Eventually, he abruptly jerked awake. "Well, I suppose we'd best be about our attempt to protect God's reputation. The statehouse in Olympia is full of law-makers who are unaware of terrorists living in their midst, plotting their destruction. I guess we'll spend the next few days walking a hundred miles to tell them what we know. These are desperate days, and what we know is too important to keep. We've got to get the word out."

They rose and walked back to the highway. The powerful animal continued to lead his master down the same road as before. The old man struggled to keep up with the canine's stride. "Whoa there, boy. Pace yourself. It's a long way to Olympia, and I've got only half as many legs as you."

CHAPTER 2

Lieutenant Gary Jarvis saw a State 99 sign and his wandering mind came back to a sharp focus. *After all*, he reminded himself, *life has to stay on course.* He needed to pay attention to his driving and think about safety, not his destination. He gave tickets to people who didn't give their entire focus to driving. But he couldn't keep his focus; his mind was elsewhere.

He kept thinking about the meeting he had just attended at the capital. He went to Olympia a lot, but it was never to his liking. This particular time was especially distasteful. The Board of Border Security had wanted to gather what the local police knew about the rumors rampant in Seattle, yet Gary had had no information to give them. The press did, however; they circulated rumors that a terrorist cell or group of cells were operating right under the nose of the authorities, and yet no one knew any details about them.

Gary approached the outskirts of Seattle. He fingered his Starbucks coffee cup, lifted it as though to drink, then set it back in the cup holder. It was cold.

Gary drove on, glancing at his watch to check the date. Monday, July 9.

He couldn't remember when the rumors had started about an expanding group of Arabic terrorists filtering into the city and mingling with the homeless, attempting to spread their influence out of the al-Jabar mosque. This mosque was just a refurbished ware-house in the docks area of the city. The two or three terrorists who had been picked up for vagrancy were connected with the same group of Garcia Coyotes that were responsible for smuggling illegals across the Southern California border.

But Gary wasn't the only one frustrated. The entire West Coast branch of the National Security Agency was also in a perpetual state of uproar. The local police and the NSA were holding joint meetings, intent on making the search for terrorists a group project. With the mayoral elections less than a year away, the city's political candidates were also working to keep the city safe, while simultane-ously doing all they could to assure themselves of the election. Gary himself wanted to do whatever was necessary and was taking no chances of missing significant leads, hoping also to assure the chief that he was keeping his eyes and ears open.

He kept wondering how a West Coast port could have become a stopover for such a menace. He recalled that the NSA had inter-cepted several calls between al-Qaida cells in Afghanistan and six public payphones in Seattle. There was only one reason public phones were being used instead of cellular—to avoid monitoring of their call recipients. If these were terrorist cells, these Arabs—or Yemenis or whoever they were—were taking every step they could to avoid detection.

Still, all the telephone surveillance hadn't led to specific arrests or even suspicious characters whom they might watch to gain an entrance into this supposed plot. Gary and his colleagues were baf-fled. Actually, Gary was more than baffled; he was obsessed about finding any key to confirm the street gossip. He longed to set him-self on some real course of action.

There was one observable arena of action—street people. Constant surveillance was leading the police to crack down on vaga-bonds, as they were the perfect community to embrace and dis-guise foreigners. They were hard to keep track of since their lack of addresses and social identities kept them from being rounded up and investigated in any systematic way. The key to solving this puz-zle seemed to be hiding with the street people, which is why Gary intended to probe among the street people of Seattle. If there were any answers, they would best be revealed in undercover work. But even though he could easily get the costumes for the undercover job, the way of life would be much harder to arrive at. He would be instantly exposed because of their lingo, values, and even their smells. How would he ever be able to pull it off?

He struck the padded dash of his unmarked squad car in sheer frustration. And he was still twenty minutes away from the station—a long way out on State 99.

While occupied with his thoughts, he spotted a tall priest wearing a Seahawks ball cap and dark glasses, walking a huge guard dog. He was hitchhiking down 99, apparently headed out of town. More important, he seemed to be the very candidate Gary needed to begin his trek into the seamier urban side of Seattle. Wondering why this particular vagrant was so far out of town, and heading even farther, Gary turned back to intercept the priest and his dog. He soon pulled up on the shoulder just behind them. Gary braked to a stop and quickly leaped out of his car, slamming the door shut and yelling, "Hey there!"

The priest stopped and turned to face the voice. His huge dog made a suspicious rumble in his throat.

"Easy there, Kinta," said the man.

Gary, realizing his prey was blind, announced, "I'm a policeman."

"I'm not," replied the blind priest congenially.

"What are you doing out here on the highway?" Gary asked.

"Any law against walking down the highway?"

"No, but there is against hitchhiking and another against vagrancy."

"Have I got my thumb out? Did I ask you for a ride?"

Gary realized he was losing control of this conversation. "But you're headed out of town."

"Any law against heading out of town?" asked the man.

"Nope. It's just that most people like—"

"Like me stay downtown and sleep under interstate bridges," the priest finished helpfully.

The lieutenant decided to take the conversation down another road. "You from Yemen?"

"Not from Yemen."

"Where are you from?"

"Not from Yemen."

"You Arabian?"

"Does my clerical garb look like a turban?"

Gary tried yet another tack. He reached out to pet the animal. "What's your dog's name?"

Kinta growled and showed his fangs.

"You don't recognize him, do you? Ah, Kinta how quickly they forget us."

Then the light came on in Gary Jarvis's brain. "Kinta? Father Peter? What are you doing down here hitchhiking?"

"How else does a blind man without a car get places?"

"Blind! How did you become blind?"

"It's a long story; I can tell you later."

"This is unbelievable. I'm happy to see you. Things always seemed to go better when you were around. Maybe you can figure out a way to help the Seattle Police Department untangle its current maze of terrorist reports."

"Maybe," said the old man.

Gary turned his right hand palm up and offered it to Kinta to make sure they were still friends after their long separation.

Kinta licked his hand then paused.

"He must not like my taste," said Gary.

"He doesn't like men's cologne and particularly Chrome Azzaro."

Gary was dumbfounded. "He must have quite a nose."

"He's got nose enough to know he doesn't like men's cologne," said Father Peter. "And I'm the one who knows it's Chrome Azzaro. One of the traits of the blind is that we have pretty good smellers."

Gary smiled. "Look, I had a cup of coffee going in the car, but it got cold. Can I buy both of us a hot one and we'll start this conversation over?"

"Well, I'm headed to Olympia, but I'm in no real hurry. Sure, I'd appreciate a fresh cup of coffee."

■ ■ ■

The old man soon found himself seated across from Lieutenant Jarvis in a McDonald's. Kinta rested on the floor just beside his master. Two tall cups of black coffee steamed in front of the men.

"Do you spend much time . . . no, let me start over. Do you mind if I ask you why you're going to Olympia?"

"I don't mind at all, but since when does an investigator ask if he can ask anything? You sure you're a policeman?"

"Pretty sure," Gary smiled.

"Can you keep a secret?" asked Father Peter.

"Definitely."

"So can I." The old man grinned.

Gary smiled again. "When I last saw you at the Shapiro cabin a year ago, you and Kinta just walked off into the night. We all thought we'd never see either of you again."

"Well, you were wrong. Here we both are."

"Are you really . . . ," Gary hesitated.

"Blind? Yes, my friend, I really am. It happened to me in the Middle East, but as I said, it's a long story. Blindness is an inconvenience, but it has an upside or two. You see, nobody suspects a blind man. I can walk in and out of heavy traffic, and everybody stops for me . . . so far. And it has taught me a thing or two. For instance, I have to do something myself I have told others to do for years."

"What's that?"

"Have faith in something beyond myself. I have always loved Kinta, but now I must trust my life to him. It's not all bad, you know. I hear things and know things that people would never tell a seeing man."

"You know it's only a matter of time until people figure out that your guard dog is really a wolf, and you'll be in trouble for harboring a wild animal."

"I guess I'll cross that bridge when I come to it. In the meantime, I've got an assignment to take care of."

"What assignment?" asked Gary, bent on getting some straight answers from the priest. "Where do you get your assignments? Who are you? Who assigns you your assignments?"

"One question at a time. Actually, you'd never believe who I work for, so why don't we just put that aside for now?"

"OK, then, why are you headed to Olympia?"

"That's the second thing I wanted to tell you. But Gary—may I call you Gary?"

"Sure."

"Well, you're probably not aware of this, but there is a terrorist cell operating under the radar of the Seattle police."

At first Gary bristled at the intimation that a blind priest might be seeing more than the Seattle Police Department. "Father, if you know anything at all about this, I would be grateful to hear you out. We have heard the gossip from a handful of homeless vagrants, but it's all been hearsay—nameless and faceless and tough to assemble into hard conclusions."

"It's not hearsay; it's real. And I want to tell you all about it. But first, could you get a couple of Sausage McMuffins for Kinta? He's not been eating much lately, and we've a long walk ahead of us to Olympia."

Gary jumped on the chance for more time to grill Father Peter. "Yes, I'll get him the McMuffins, but let me drive you to Olympia."

"Can't have that!"

"Why?"

"You'd blow my cover if anyone saw me riding in a police car."

"My car is unmarked."

"Hmm," the priest considered the offer. "Are you wearing a uniform?"

"No."

"Well, OK then."

"Shall I get Kinta the McMuffins now?"

"No, you can wait, if you don't mind his eating in the car. He's neater than I am when he eats."

"Tell me what you know about these terrorists." Gary grew suddenly urgent.

"I wish I knew more so I'd have more to tell the authorities at the capital. But the center of the cell seems to be the al-Jabar mosque."

"Have you been there for any of their services?"

"A few."

"And they let you in dressed like that?"

"Don't seem to mind. I do have one of those Arafat head shawls. It's black and white, they tell me. It must go pretty well with my priestly garb since nobody seems to mind my being there. It was there that I got the first clue of Seattle being in danger."

"Tell me about it!" Gary demanded.

"Hey, slow down. The coffee is good. No need to hurry. Anyway, I overheard two of them talking about their loyalty to Scarlet Jihad and their plan to wake the city to the glories of Islam. They used the words *Talabani* and *Qwest Field* in the same sentence but were speaking too softly for me to get all things connected."

"Father," Gary interjected, "could I possibly deter you from your mission to Olympia? I will drive you there if you insist on going, but I would like for you to show me all you know and introduce me to the street people where all of this could be building under our noses. Instead of going to the capital with so little to report, you could help me go undercover. We could keep the edge of secrecy and perhaps avoid driving the assassins underground."

"Well," said the priest, "I guess there's a better way to spend my time than blowing the whistle on a situation that might best be looked into with surveillance. Have it your way. I will work in the city and wait for you. Meanwhile, I think I'll have another cup of coffee."

"You're hitting the caffeine awfully hard for a man who used to not drink coffee."

"True, but I'm acquiring a touch of civility. Seattle is no place to live if you don't glug a bit of caffeine now and then. Sure is ugly stuff. Bitter too. Smells good though."

CHAPTER 3

Al-Haj Sistani woke as he always did, well before daylight. He slipped into a thin white nightshirt, placed himself in the rapt position, and then bowed in the general direction of Mecca. He always prayed five times a day. Today, he felt a sense of deliberate intention not just about his life but also the day. It was Tuesday, July 10.

When his prayers were over, he showered and put on a pair of Levis, a white dress shirt, and a dark blue Windbreaker. He fixed a cup of instant oatmeal and ate it, then left his apartment. He drove his old, red Honda Civic to a modern office building and warehouse east of the I-5. He entered the corporate edifice through an unlocked side door.

"Salaam, al-Haj," said his boss and mentor, Zalton al-Zhabahni, with a brisk embrace and a kiss of peace. "Al, good news! Let me show you something." Zalton walked him to a stack of new cardboard barrels. "These have just arrived from the Cartel for Islamization." He gestured toward the barrels, each with "Strategic Weapons Development Corporation" stenciled on it.

"Is that what we've been waiting for?" asked Al.

"All that and more." Zalton grinned.

"More?"

"Look at these babies!" Zalton said. He drew a stainless steel cylindrical object the size of an aluminum soda can out of a woodmitered box atop the barrels. "Here!" he said, handing one of the objects to Al.

Al weighed the object in his hand and then made a pretense of nearly dropping it.

"Careful, friend," Zalton warned, "even in pretending, that is not funny. These little jewels cost $17,000 apiece."

Al started to hand it back to Zalton, who refused it, saying, "No, you keep this one. I still have a half-million dollars worth of them in the box. I'm going to stash them in the corporate safe in my office. But I want you to take this one and measure the laser reach of the device. I want you to become a real expert on these detonators. Everything must work and work well when the time comes. Study their intricacies, Al. Then be ready to take off the jeweled cap and set the distance-to-monitor mechanism inside. We want to be sure these are performing just right. How else can we teach all Seattle to say 'Allah' and mean it?"

Both men leaned back against the barrels and smiled with some satisfaction. "These barrels will stay in security bay E-5 until we need them," Zalton continued. "They'll be locked in and no one will be able to get to them but you and me. I want to give you two combinations. One is for the laser-sensitive lock that seals off E-5. This one is a simple combination, but the letters are all Arabic, so only our company people would be likely to know the combination. But the combination to the corporate vault is in plain old arabic numerals. These you will have to write down and memorize. Here." He thrust a paper in Al's direction. "Commit this to memory as soon as you can."

Al took the paper and stuck it in the pocket of his Levis. He put the stainless steel detonator in the same pocket. Then he followed Zalton out of the dispatch section into the office area of Spratton Laser Technologies.

"Al, I want you to stay for a bit this morning," Zalton began. "In a minute or two, three other members of Scarlet Jihad are coming in, and we're going to finalize the plans for using all the stuff we've been stashing in E-5. Can you stay?"

"Sure, I've got time. You're the boss."

"Akbar!" Zalton yelled over his shoulder as he and Al entered his open, well-appointed office. "Set up a tray with coffee and food. I've got a big meeting in my office. And Akbar, once it gets started, I want no interruptions at all."

"What if the big dogs call from Yemen?"

"Nobody! Not even anybody from Sanaa. If they call, tell them I'll just call back. And while you're setting up the tray, bring Al and me an early cup . . . both black, OK?"

Akbar nodded and left.

Al and Zalton were barely seated when Akbar reentered Zalton's office with two cups of steaming coffee and set them down, filling the whole area with a wonderful aroma.

Zalton took a sip. "Al, you know what I was thinking when those barrels came? I was thinking how gullible these Americans are. They hire a Yemeni corporation to protect themselves from terrorists. They have a saying over here that hiring your enemy to protect you is like hiring a fox to guard the henhouse."

Both men laughed.

"How's your Christian slut?"

Al flinched a bit. "If you mean Carol, she's fine."

"You know, Al, she's not Muslim. The Hadith says you gotta be nice to her, but you can be nice and still have your way with her, and it won't be counted against you in heaven."

Al flinched a second time.

"What's the matter, Al? Are you two getting too close? It's OK if you end her 'infidel status' and convert her. But a man needs a woman when a man needs a woman, if you know what I mean."

Al nodded, reflective.

"Now, take my wife Clarisse. She's beautiful, and as infidels go, she's quite an infidel. She's just a real classic."

"Zalton, were you ever really in love with Clarisse?"

"To quote Tina Turner, what's love got to do with it? She's mine and she always will be. She doesn't know it, but when this is all over—when we're back in Yemen—I've got another wife. I know two are only a poor man's harem, but two are better than one."

"I don't want two. I want one. And I think I want Carol. And I don't think I could ever lead her on and let her believe she was my one and only if I still had a woman in Yemen. Somehow it's just not fair."

"Fair!" Zalton fairly bellowed. "What's not fair? Mohammed had thirteen women—or maybe more—till he just quit counting. He was a holy man too. Nobody talked to him about what was fair."

"Does Clarisse know your feelings about women and wives and—"

"She knows everything, and she gets kind of loudmouth about her 'repugnance,' as she calls it. But I bust her in the side every once in a while, and she forgets her Western ways for a moment or two."

"I don't think I could ever hit Carol."

"Well then, she could give you a lot of misery, even if she does convert. The Prophet said at least figuratively in Surah 2:223, 'Wives are playthings, so take your pick.' I've picked and picked and picked. That's probably your problem, Al—you need to pick a little more. And you need to pick without being so picky if you're gonna find the right woman to make you happy. Honor the Prophet; he knew best."

There was a rap at the door. Akbar opened the door and three of Zalton's friends entered.

"Salaam!" they said, embracing Zalton and Al. Then the attendees took their chairs around a long, mahogany table at the far end of Zalton's office.

"Rasul, how are you doing?" asked Zalton.

"I am very fine," said Rasul with a thick Arabic accent. "But, Mr. Zalton, I have some very bad news. Someone in the outer circle of our jihad lost a bomber's belt, and it has fallen into the hands of the local police."

"How do you know this?" Zalton asked.

"I know this because one of the plainclothes men came to the warehouse door the other day, holding it in his hand. He asked if anyone in the company had lost the belt. I asked what it was. I can only hope I convinced him that I didn't know."

"Well," Zalton said, "this means we must all be very careful in the future. If we lose our edge of secrecy and surprise, our plans will be very much curtailed."

"Jibril," said Al, "did you bring the plans of the stadium?"

"I did. Fresh out of the library at city hall," he replied, pulling out a large sheaf of blueprints from a black portfolio. He plopped them on the table, and the whole group gathered around them.

"If there was anything I learned in Aden back when we bombed the *U.S.S. Cole*," Jibril continued, "it was that we can achieve a lot more destruction by carefully placing charges than just by hitting structures at random. The upper tiers of the stadium rest on the second level of steel beams. If we alternate tiers—say thirteen, fifteen, seventeen, and so on—the whole of the stadium could collapse with half the amount of explosives."

Zalton looked pleased at Jibril's thorough study of the matter and complimented him, while noting the steel joints circled in red on the blueprint.

Ishaq spoke. "I am pleased to report that I got a job at the stadium in maintenance and now have a uniform and badge that would admit me to any part of the stadium. In just two days of work, I have marked those junctions that Jibril had circled. Further, I have studied the matter of which beams would be easiest to charge without being seen. I also know which would be most difficult."

Zalton smiled as the group talked of their plans, though much would be required to keep those plans on schedule. His smiled faded when Ishaq spoke up.

"I received a bill today from al-Qaida for more than we have in our treasury," Ishaq said. "They said to send it quickly if we love the Prophet."

Zalton cleared his throat. "Men, maybe we've got more going on than al-Qaida does. I wonder if we want to go on financing al-Qaida with funds that Scarlet Jihad needs. We must complete our service to Allah here in Seattle. Should we take the money we need to supply a group of patriots we never see? I say, let's use our dollars to do our work. We can then finance their work with what we've got left over."

"Amen," said Akbar.

The others agreed.

They talked further of the details of their scheme, settling that coordinated timing was best if the mass attack was to be effective. As the meeting drew to a close, they did their salaams toward Mecca. When their prayers were past, Zalton asked each of them if they were living purely, and each of them said that they were.

Al made reference to Carol Jones, asking each of them to remember her in their prayers. "Keep your head on straight," said Rasul. "This is no time to lose your way. Our cause is too great, our plans too requiring."

Zalton spoke up. "I would like you to recant the idea of developing any serious relationship with the psychiatrist's nurse."

"I will keep my head," said Al, "but I like this woman. I cannot abandon her. Surely Allah knows my heart. Surely he will protect me and preserve all our dreams and still keep me from abandoning my love."

"It is the word *love* that most troubles me," said Zalton, rather sternly. "A woman is a woman, that's all. Love is what we give Allah. It is in Surah 2: Allah is the only essential; all women are playthings, that is all. Do not speak of love of women. Speak of loving Allah. Put your love where your love must be."

Al grew quiet. So did Rasul, Akbar, and Jibril.

They all agreed to meet again on Thursday, just to keep their jihad on course.

"Sacrifice yourself for the love of the Prophet," said Zalton, patting Al on the shoulder as he left the room.

"To love Allah is to love all things," said Al.

Zalton saw a hint of defiance in his eyes.

Al shook his hand, but when Zalton reached to pull him into an embrace, Al turned on his heel and walked away.

"Watch him, Jibril," said Zalton. "There is too much riding on his life for him not to be a team player. Watch him very closely."

CHAPTER 4

Mary Muebles pushed her chrome shopping cart into the circle of light. She hated arriving late at any meeting. But late was better than never, she reasoned.

In some ways she didn't seem like one of the street people. She wore a crisp pair of black oxford pumps—never mind that they cost seventy-five cents at the Salvation Army Store. She was striking in her black Lycra pants that she bought at the Veterans Thrift Store. She had gotten her low-cut gypsy blouse out of a mission barrel at St. Vincent's House. Her hair fell in dark, black cascades of curls to her shoulders. Her large, Jennifer Lopez earrings accented a strong but beautiful face. She reached down into her shopping cart and lifted a clean, white shawl out of it. She draped the shawl over her hair and let it fall in tassles of yarn down to her waist.

In her cart was also a mostly used bottle of Estee Lauder's Beautiful and a plastic bag over an old King James Bible in Spanish. She drew up a steel chair and fit her lithe body into the circle of students that had come to the al-Jabar mosque for the Qur'an studies that al-Haj Sistani led every Tuesday night. She found herself mesmerized by the strong young Muslim who worked hard to help his circle of students understand the Qur'an.

Most of the students were motivated by the enticements as much as the study. Those who stayed till it was over were always given a five-dollar gift card to McDonald's—a ticket to at least one good fresh meal for the day. The homeless liked the burger certificates better than the free bowl of soup they got for attending services at the Inner City Mission. But Mary was motivated by the chance to learn the Qur'an from the handsome young teacher who attracted more women to his studies than men. This was highly unusual since Islam was a man's religion, and the women had very little to say in any of the meetings. Very little chance was given to them even to take part in the class discussions.

This particular night, Mary sat down by Wanda Williams, who had her own shopping cart with very little in it. Wanda always dressed in slouchy clothes spotted with bits of this and that. Her shoes were old, yellowed Nikes. Her hair suffered from a want of curling, and Estee Lauder was never on her shopping list.

Still, Mary liked Wanda. She was an eccentric who was now on her twenty-second reading of the Christian thriller *Left Behind*. Wanda Williams was conversant on two topics: old politicians and '50s movie stars. She was an alcoholic but, thanks to the Salvation Army's Adult Recovery Centers, was making her way through life with some sobriety.

Wanda was a Wiccan and would have continued meeting with the covens, but Wiccans have their pride, and the poorer witches never seemed to find acceptance among those who were better off.

"Those Wiccans who drove in from the suburbs for the covens were snobby about their witchery," Wanda would say. She could laugh about her rejection, but inwardly she was lonely, which is why she was meeting with the Tuesday night Qur'an study group.

Occasionally she hallucinated. She admired Shirley MacLaine and was convinced (like Shirley) that in her previous life she had been a Hebrew prophetess. As a Hebrew prophetess she had foretold the fall of Jerusalem in the seventh century BC, but since it didn't actually fall till the sixth century, she never made the list of prophets who got things right.

Mary also knew Carol Jones very well. In fact, they met from time to time not only at the Qur'an studies but also at the Pathway of Light Cathedral's soup kitchen. Mary had tried often to talk Carol into seeing if she could persuade her boss, Paul Shapiro, to give Wanda counseling pro bono. The last time she asked the psychiatrist, he had actually agreed to do it. In their one counseling session, Paul had discovered that Wanda often fell into a trance and prophesied things such as the rise of Arabic terrorism in Seattle. He realized that Wanda's odd fixations on Muslim terrorists made more sense than the psychiatrist wished they did.

Mary felt that Wanda was wrong about al-Haj Sistani. Wanda saw him as nothing more than a Muslim zealot who was trying to make converts among the street people of Seattle. It was Wanda's wild speculations about Al that had led Paul Shapiro to meet with his old friend Gary Jarvis. He told Gary that he believed there might be a strain of subterfuge that was gathering itself among street people in Seattle. Gary had listened intently and decided that someone on the police force needed to go undercover. With or without the permission of the chief of police, he decided to see what he could dig up.

Melody Jarvis, eight months pregnant, was reluctant for her husband to live unprotected on the streets but eventually agreed to his plan.

Then there was Joanna Nickerson, Carol Jones's pastor at the Pathway of Light Cathedral. Initially introduced by Paul Shapiro, Carol had grown to love Joanna in the time she had spent listening to her sermons. Joanna was feisty yet full of a desire to serve God.

Joanna was also uneasy about the new wave of street Islam that seemed to have the poor of the inner city so spellbound. She had advised Carol against forming a relationship with Al, but Carol was falling hard and fast. To Carol, Joanna's advice made her seem prejudiced against Muslims.

Carol squeezed in between Wanda and Mary at the Qur'an study. She hugged them both. They were clearly from different societal strata, but Al had cautioned Carol several times not to give it a thought. One thing was clear: both Mary and Wanda cared enough for the Islamic way of doing things that they each wore a shawl across their face when speaking to the men of the mosque. It wasn't required, but it was something that they did.

Carol didn't do it. She was keeping her place in a world where it seemed to her Muslim women had no place. Still, she didn't feel all that great about appearing insensitive to what the men of the mosque required.

Everyone could tell that Carol was not a street person. Nor was she the kind who automatically accepted all that she heard the young imam say. She was so much her own person that it rankled some of the Muslim men who attended. They often looked at her most disparagingly. Al was not critical of her apparent obstinacy and was instead compassionate, telling her she didn't have to learn everything all at once.

Carol had informed Mary, Wanda, and Al that she was a Christian and that she was committed to helping Sister Joanna at the Pathway of Light soup kitchen. And Carol reminded the poor who attended the mosque that they were all welcome to eat with Sister Joanna at either lunch or dinner on any day or night they chose.

Everyone could see that Carol had a thing for al-Haj, and Al clearly reciprocated. Mary knew that right after they met Al gave Carol an illustrated copy of the Rubaiyat of Omar Khayyam. She also knew that Carol and Al had often shared a dinner together at Ivars.

Their romance was clearly budding, and Carol found herself more and more drawn to Al. But she did not feel the same about Islam. It was just too great a leap for her. As they sat in the circle of those at the al-Jabar mosque's study group, Carol found herself sniffing the jasmine sachet he had given her. In the wake of the delightful odor, she looked over the heads of those in the study class and admired the dark-skinned, sensitive man who had captured her esteem. His masculine magnetism and sincere faith added to his intrigue.

The Qur'an study session was drawing to a close. Al finished his final prayer of the evening and began greeting the attendees, while Carol walked to the back door to wait for him. Al was a man who cared about people. He helped Mary Muebles up from her chair. She didn't really need any help, but she did enjoy his attention. As for the several older men who had come just for the McDonald's certificates, even to these Al showed a special compassion in touching them and helping them to stand. He was not a Christian pastor, yet that was the closest comparison Carol could make.

Carol watched Al greet a man she'd never seen before. He was whiskered and tattered, yet he was clearly playing some kind of role. Somehow, he seemed familiar. It was the small tattoo above his wrist: "USMC." He had once been a military man. Al welcomed him warmly and gave him a five-dollar McDonald's card. Carol was unaccountably intrigued. Who was he? Eventually, she abandoned her curiosity with the man and took her place just outside the door of the mosque to wait for Al.

When everyone was finally gone, Carol and Al walked toward the McDonald's where some of the tenuous Islamic students went as soon as the service ended to cash in their good fortune. Al asked Carol if they might talk a bit over some coffee. She agreed and they went into the McDonald's, ordered a cup, and sat down.

"Al," Carol began, "I so much enjoy learning about Islam, but I just don't think I could ever become a Muslim."

Al reached out and touched her hand. "You don't have to make up your mind about this right now, Carol," he said, stirring a bit of half-and-half into the dark coffee. He stared as the white swirled into the dark, retreating from the headiness of their conversation.

"Carol," he said, returning to the issue, "I really wish you would visit the monthly meetings of the Order of Muslim Women. It meets in one of the women's homes out in Bellevue."

He patted her hand, but Carol drew away from him. She was more than resistant. She seemed utterly closed. Al dropped his attempt at persuasion, and Carol eagerly changed the subject.

"You know, Al, I can't help admiring you. I think everybody does. I guess I even envy you, because you have something you believe in. I'm not sure I've ever really believed in anything. And when those of us who believe so little run into someone like you, it's hard not to want to be like you. I can see it in the eyes of everyone who studies with you."

Al stared again at the surface of his coffee then lifted his eyes. "Carol, could I change the direction of our conversation for a moment? There's something gnawing at me that I must say to you."

"Sure, Al, anything."

"I've had two friends now who have died detonating suicide bombs."

"Oh how horrible!" Carol was repulsed.

"Well, the odd thing about it was that it didn't seem all that horrible. I mean, nothing of their bodies was ever found, and they died so fast they didn't feel anything. They were just here and then they weren't here—one minute on earth, the next in heaven."

"You sound as though you admire that sort of thing," Carol said cautiously.

"Carol, you've told me so often that you admire my zeal. You think it gives meaning to my life and even to those I live among. Well, these two guys believed in what they were doing. They paid the ultimate sacrifice to prove it. And they weren't any kind of hero in their own eyes. They were simple men who found the pleasure of life in sunshine, a good meal, and deep friendships."

Al paused, working up his nerve. "Carol, I know you think I have faith, but I really don't. What have I ever done to prove how much I love Allah or the Prophet? I'm thinking about joining a group called the Martyrs' Brigade."

"Al," Carol said, disbelieving, "you're starting to scare me."

"I don't want to do that. But can I confess to you that for all that I admire about America, I see in the country a lot of superficiality? In the country I come from, people are poor. Like those in most Muslim countries, 80 percent of them can't read or write. There's 60 percent unemployment. Poverty is rampant. Maybe people who own nothing on earth develop a need for God that just doesn't happen in rich, self-sufficient countries like yours.

"Have you ever known a Christian martyr? I mean, who do you know who loves Jesus so much they would die for him? Yet you Christians generally criticize Muslim martyrs as cowards who kill others in such a way that their killings require their own life. I cannot see the cowardice anywhere in such a notion. They are truly men and women of Allah. I think they are lovers of God—

true lovers who demonstrate their love by the seriousness with which they treat the issues of their lives."

Carol was stunned. "But if they blow themselves up and die as fast as you say, is there anything particularly heroic about that? Wouldn't it be better to live and minister for Allah than merely to kill others? That's the one thing I don't get about Islam. Why does everybody want to kill everybody else? If they can't find a Westerner to behead, they will kill their own people—maybe even in suicide bombings—just to make a point of some sort. Wouldn't it be better to give their lives in serving others instead of always trying to make some life-and-death statement? You don't see suicide in the lives of Jesus' followers, only in the lives of Mohammed's."

"I don't know, Carol. A lot of people have died for Jesus over the years."

"Yes, but they didn't die trying to kill others. That's the weird thing about Muslim martyrs—even when they die for God, they're thinking about how they can kill others in the process. Consider my friend Joanna. She loves God, but she spends all her days trying to help others. Martyrdom hasn't occurred to her, I guess, but neither has mass murder."

"I see what you're saying. But we Muslims believe in helping others and in doing good deeds and all that stuff too."

"I guess," Carol said, but it was clear she disagreed with him on the subject. She couldn't see suicide bombers as real people of faith. She seemed convinced that to die for God when you could live for him was a bad trade. Although she loved Al for his zeal, she had to admit she was both attracted to and repulsed by it at the same time.

As they got up to leave, she noticed a paper tract sticking out of his pocket. The first line was visible: "Eternity: the Reward of Jihad." She didn't comment on it but it burned in her mind as she returned to her apartment and later got into bed. As much as she loved Al, he was from a world far separate from the Iowa where she had been brought up. She needed help sorting through her emotions. She would love him for all eternity, but *eternity was the reward of Jihad*, or was it? She couldn't sleep for trying to answer the question. Weary with concern, she finally almost drifted off then suddenly sat straight up in bed. She remembered where she had seen the man with the tattoo. She knew who he was. But what on earth was *he* doing at the mosque?

CHAPTER 5

Gary Jarvis left the Qur'an study just as everyone was leaving the mosque. He was in a bad mood because of one little item he had forgotten to take care of: his marine tattoo. It was a tiny mistake, and he had tried to remedy the situation as soon as he noticed the error, pulling his tattered sleeve over the tattoo the moment he noticed Carol eyeing his wrist. She had "made" him. Or had she?

Gary and Carol knew each other casually because of his wife's friendship with both Joanna and Carol's boss's wife, Rhonda Shapiro. They didn't know each other well, so he was hoping his undercover disguise had worked. But he left the gathering chastising himself for not having been more discreet. The whole purpose for going undercover was to keep his identity concealed while he sorted through the street gossip on terrorism.

Still, all was not wasted. At that very lecture, Gary was able to put together a picture of the ardent hallmark of Islamic devotion. It was so easy to see, especially when he considered the boring services that often occurred in Christian churches, that there was a heady intrigue about Islam. He had felt it almost from the very moment al-Haj began his lecture. Something in the glistening eyes of the zealot lecturer marked him as a man of passion—a man who never said things he didn't believe. Gary also observed Carol Jones' fastidious interest in the speaker.

When the lecture ended, Gary pushed his shopping cart for three blocks to his SUV. He threw the cart in the back then drove back to within half a block of the al-Jabar mosque. Through binoculars he scrutinized Al and Carol as they left the mosque and walked to McDonald's. He followed but kept a very respectful distance till they were inside. Then he watched them as they drank coffee and talked, wishing he could overhear what Carol and the Muslim zealot were discussing.

They talked for what seemed a very long time before they stood. Al embraced her—nothing passionate, but evidently romantic. They parted company, and Gary noted Al's disappointed demeanor as he left the restaurant and retreated down the shadowed sidewalk. He followed Al in his SUV at a discreet distance. Al walked for a mile before he turned into a side street leading into a condominium complex. Gary parked his car and walked silently to the building's entrance. *Blast it!* The condominium complex required security access. Gary jotted down the address: 4213 Compton Street. He looked across the street. At 4212 there was an Apartment for Rent sign in the window.

He turned back to Al's building and saw a light come on. Bingo. Al's condo.

Nothing much happened that evening. He watched Al say his final prayer for the day, the *Salat al-isha*. When the lights in Al's condo went out, Gary got into his SUV and left.

As he drove, he sorted though the images and impressions of the evening: the Qur'an study, Carol Jones, and al-Haj Sistani. He thought about how normal terrorists could appear. They seemed so warm and kind even as they measured their steps into the very heart of whatever holocausts of terror they planned.

Lost in such thoughts, he approached his own apartment. Melody was asleep when he got home, so he undressed in the dark, snuggled in beside her, and was soon fast asleep himself.

The next morning the SPD sent a plainclothes policewoman to rent the apartment Gary had spotted the night before. Later that night, Gary, dressed in the blue coveralls of a maintenance man, walked up to the front door of Al's complex. He pulled his ball cap down over his eyes and waited till a young woman exited the secured door of the building. She smiled pleasantly at Gary, who nodded his head, adjusted his ball cap, and walked into the building. She courteously held the door for him to enter.

It was easy getting into Al's condo. Although Gary had no warrant, he knew these suspected terrorists would never go to the police to protest his unwarranted search, and time was so much of the essence he decided to take the fastest way to work on his suspicions. Gary carefully sorted through Al's personal effects, searching from his dresser drawers to the medicine cabinet. Nothing. Disappointed, he began planting a telephone bug and a couple of micro-relay cameras with remote digital feedbacks to monitor any conversations inside the secured condo. When everything was satisfactorily installed, he left the condo and walked around the block to covertly enter his stakeout position across the street.

He set up a tripod and mounted a digital camera with a zoom lens that could separate the threads on a silk suit. Then he picked up a pair of binoculars and, focusing on the condo across the street, smiled at how well the contents of the room came in. Al had left his drapes entirely open. The slats of his plantation-style blinds were also open. It was a practice investigators called the Exhibitionist Male. Such egotists made voyeurism a snap. Whether this passionate Muslim could have a flair for thinking so well of himself, Gary didn't know. But it appeared that he might. If so, such a trait could be his Achilles' heel. At any rate, it would sure simplify Gary's surveillance.

Nothing much happened that evening. The hours crept on so slowly that Gary cursed his vocation and wished he'd gone into something more exciting—like monitoring bacteria or studying mushrooms. But his luck was to change by evening on the next day.

On Thursday night, July 12, he saw Zalton enter Al's condo. He had his suspicions about the high-level nature of terrorist cells, and seeing the CEO of Spratton Laser Technologies made him wonder if Zalton might be the power person of the plot. He knew for sure Zalton was Al's boss. How convenient that he was at the center of Seattle's corporate esteem.

A little later, three other Arabic men approached Al's complex. Apparently, a meeting was being held. Gary managed to photograph each of the men with a full frontal shot before they were buzzed in. As they entered Al's condo, they were greeted, thus identified to Gary—Rasul, Jibril, and the startling albino, Ishaq. Al seated the men, passed out several cans of beer, and began the meeting.

Gary observed their habits and mannerisms. But more compelling than their mannerisms were their plans, relayed to Gary through the hidden audio system. He discovered that they called themselves the Scarlet Jihad and that they had a huge cache of explosives somewhere in Seattle that they intended for murderous purposes, but he could not discern where it was hidden. However explicit the men were about their murderous intentions, they were frustratingly vague about specific names and locations.

Then a terrible, tiny tendril of smoke began rising from the light fixture where Gary had hidden the audio bug in Al's condo. Apparently the heat from the halogen bulb was frying the microphone. Almost as soon as Gary spotted the smoke, he heard a pop from his speakers and the sound went dead. All five men halted their conversation and peered intently at the smoking light then, inexplicably, looked across the street toward the window of Gary's apartment. But Gary's lights were dimmed; he knew he couldn't be seen.

Unfortunately, the miniature microphone then fell out of Al's light fixture.

Gary cursed his luck. The five men launched out of their seats and charged Al's door, hurrying toward the secured entrance. They rushed out of the building and started to cross the street.

Gary grabbed the camera from the tripod but hadn't time to take the binoculars. He bolted out the back door of the apartment and down a dark alley, sprinting down a serpentine arrangement of alleys and side streets until he reached his van, panting.

He cursed again. He had managed to escape without revealing his identity but had lost his stakeout and the element of surprise. Now they knew they were being monitored. Worst of all, he still had no clear details of the ploy the Scarlet Jihad group was planning. He knew the players but not the rules of the game or even where the deadly game would be played.

■ ■ ■

On Friday, Gary dressed in his coveralls and ball cap and drove to Al's condo. Once more his disguise as a building super got him quickly past the receptionist. The apartment was empty. Al was gone. He could think of little else to do but wait till the Tuesday Qur'an study to have another peek at al-Haj Sistani while wearing his homeless disguise. It would probably not be possible to tail him to find out where he had moved. They would be watching for any sign of surveillance. Still, there was much to be done, and he wasn't sure how much time he would have to get it done.

Back at his office, he printed the images of Zalton and the other members of Scarlet Jihad. He called the chief in and they agreed to go back to the vacant condo and see if they could find any fingerprints, but the search was useless. All the doorknobs and windowsills had been carefully wiped down. Gary fumed again about his clumsy surveillance techniques. The chief wasn't too thrilled about his errors either. "That was an amateur's mistake" and "You're too much of a lone ranger" were the constant refrains of the chief's reprimand.

Then they got a break. They asked the building manager for a key to the disposal unit and searched through Al's can. Luckily, Al's garbage had not been picked up yet. They told the manager they were taking the can and heaved it into the back of Gary's SUV for a trip to Forensics.

Bingo. There were fingerprints everywhere. The beer cans held all sorts of prints, presumably from all five men who had frequented the apartment.

Zalton's prints yielded no previous terrorist activity. However, his clean record made sense, as it would have been impossible for him to have the kind of clearance he needed to work at Spratton Laser Technologies if there were anything dirty on his portfolio.

Al was also clean.

Jibril and Ishaq, however, had a traceable history. Both of them had clear links back to the *U.S.S. Cole*. Both of them were listed on the "suspicious list" at the CIA. But both of them had bona fide visas, granting them free passage into the country to work for Spratton Laser Technologies.

The problem was there was nothing on the recordings of his brief surveillance to indict them with. It was clear they were up to something, but Gary needed more details. And now that he had blown the whole surveillance attempt, the group would go further underground to do all their future planning.

Forensics was still investigating the trash can items when Gary left headquarters. They might come up with more evidence, but it looked like the fingerprints on the beer cans were their best lead. His mind circled like a restless hawk above the things he knew and the things he didn't.

On Saturday he and Melody crossed Puget Sound and drove around it toward the north of the Olympic Peninsula. On Sunday they went to church to hear Joanna, ate at their favorite Italian restaurant, then went home and read the Sunday paper.

Monday brought no news from Forensics. On Tuesday Gary replayed all that he knew and didn't know about Al and Zalton al-Zhabahni. Gary knew Zalton was not only dirty but dangerous. Yet there was no way to prove it with the information he had gathered so far. The workday dwindled. He called Melody to remind her that he had some undercover work to do and wouldn't be home till quite late. He looked at his watch as he cradled the phone back onto the hook. It was 4:45 on Tuesday, July 17. Qur'an study night. He hit the office men's room, dressed in his homeless costume, threw his shopping cart in the back of his SUV, and took off for the mosque.

The study itself was less inspirational than its predecessor. However, there was an interesting addition: Ishaq the albino came in late and sat looking bored. Only once did Ishaq look his way. Gary knew he didn't recognize him. As the study group broke up, Gary moved as close as the dissembling crowd would allow toward Al and Carol, who were talking quietly with each other. Carol was telling Al that she had come across great news. The U.S. Attorney General was speaking at some sort of Christian rally at Qwest Field in August. She wanted Al to go with her.

Al suddenly became agitated. His hands trembled a bit. "No, Carol, I can't go and you shouldn't either."

"Of course I'm going. I'm going and I want you to go with me."

"Carol, I don't want to go that particular event. And I don't want you to go either."

"Why not? Why not me? Why not both of us?" Carol quizzed.

"Because . . . I'll . . . I'll . . . be out of town."

Gary watched their faces. Al was lying. More than that, Al's lie was suggesting some truth: the Seahawk stadium was at least one of the terrorist targets.

CHAPTER 6

"Good afternoon, Mrs. al-Zhabahni. Pardon me, but did I get that right?" Paul Shapiro asked.

"Very good," said the woman, managing a weak smile.

The faint smile was meant to portray a surface pleasantry that Clarisse al-Zhabahni wasn't really feeling. Her heavy makeup did not entirely conceal a huge bruise covering the left side of her face. Paul Shapiro could tell she was uncomfortable in his office. He could also tell she was afraid.

"Shall I have Miss Jones bring us some coffee?" asked the psychiatrist, trying to diffuse the stress his new client felt.

"Coffee is just what I need to get me through this. I . . . black." She bit her lip.

Paul Shapiro walked to his office door and opened it. "Carol," he said to his assistant, "bring us two cups of coffee. Black."

He returned to his chair opposite his client. She was a beautiful woman. Her blonde hair and light complexion were as stunning as the white blouse and gypsy earrings she wore. Her tight, white denim skirt stopped just past her knees. She wore pantyhose— something most liberated Western women had given up. And her stiletto shoes were clearly high couture. Her glamorous face was taut with an anxiety Paul Shapiro could not account for.

Paul Shapiro was himself handsome, but without accompanying arrogance. He had a kindness and ruggedness that invited his clients to be open with him. He was instantly likeable and safe—excellent traits to have as a counselor who hoped to invite a confessional openness among his clients. He adjusted himself in his chair and leaned toward the woman.

"While we're waiting for the coffee, may I ask you, Mrs. al-Zhabahni, what brings you to my office on this warm July afternoon?"

"Would you mind calling me Clarisse?"

"Clarisse it is."

"I am married to Zalton al-Zhabahni, the CEO of Spratton Laser Technologies, a Yemeni firm," Clarisse began, hoping to restart the conversation more coherently. "Are you familiar with it?"

"I've heard of it," Paul replied.

"Well"—Clarisse decided to dive in—"I need to get a divorce. But my husband, Zalton, would never allow it. He is Islamic and just doesn't believe in divorce. And," she added, looking nervously about her, "I need this to remain absolutely confidential."

"I promise this office is like Las Vegas: what happens here stays here. You may depend upon our professionalism."

"Well, Dr. Shapiro, I am sure you've noticed the bruise on my face?" she asked candidly.

Paul nodded.

"I have a couple more beneath my clothes. What worries me is that when Zalton loses control, he might one day seriously injure me or even . . ." She buried her head in her hands and began to weep. At that moment Carol Jones rapped on the closed door and entered. She set down a tray containing two steaming mugs and a small crystal dish of chocolate sticks. She quietly left.

Paul reached for one of the cups of coffee and stirred it with the chocolate stick. Clarisse regained her composure.

"Go on," Paul gently urged.

"Well, I need help . . . a place to go where I'll be safe."

"I can arrange that," the psychiatrist said. "Shall I call and set up an appointment with Seattle Social Services?"

"Not today . . . not just yet," said Clarisse. "Doctor, do you know what this is?" From her purse, she extracted what looked like a titanium soda can, except that there was a red sensor on the larger end of the object. Paul took the object from her and turned it over in his hand, unable to make heads or tails of it. He finally shrugged his shoulders and shook his head.

"I believe it is a RLD," said the woman, "a remote laser detonator for a bomb."

"Where did you get it?"

"Spratton Laser Technologies imports these things from Japan. I found it in the pocket of Zalton's denims."

"Well then, why bring it up? Wouldn't that be a natural thing to find if his company imports them?"

"But these are all supposed to be counted and classified and kept in the company safe. And they are very expensive. This single unit would cost thousands of dollars. The question is, Why is he carrying them around in his pockets? This is not just a breech of company policy, it's illegal. He has flown to Yemen six times this year, so it could be just a part of his company business. But some things just don't add up. Like this."

She pulled a narrow envelope out of her purse and handed it to the psychiatrist. "This also fell out of his jeans," she said. "I found it lying on his prayer mat."

"He has a prayer mat?"

"Yes, he's very devout. He prays five times a day toward Mecca. From the angle our house sits on, he's really facing Vancouver, not Mecca. But if I tried to correct him, he might take a whack at me. I don't understand his need to control my life so viciously."

Paul opened the narrow paper sleeve. "This looks like microfilm inside," he said. Paul kept a microfiche viewer in his office for special research projects he found necessary for publishing articles in career journals. He stood up and walked to a library microfiche decoder and turned it on and laid the top celluloid strip out of the sleeve on the light stage of the magnifier. "Wait a minute. It looks like some kind of stadium blueprint. Might even be the one for Qwest Field." He turned to face Clarisse. "Why would your husband carry this around?"

"I have no idea," Clarisse said automatically, though her face betrayed some dawning suspicions.

Neither of them spoke for quite a while.

"Dr. Shapiro, when the *U.S.S. Cole* was attacked in the Gulf of Aden, Zalton was not only in Yemen, he was in Aden . . . Do you remember the attack? I think about twenty U.S. sailors were killed."

"Yes, I do remember. But are you saying that Zalton was involved in the attack on the *Cole?*"

"No, he is far too clever for that—at least, not overtly. Had he been overtly involved, he would never have gotten the top-secret security clearance needed to work for this country. But I believe he might have been complicit in the disaster. I have a photo of him standing at the pier in Aden, and the date scribbled on the back of that photo was just three days before the attack occurred."

"What are you trying to tell me about these objects?" asked the psychiatrist, pointing to the detonator and the microfilm.

Clarisse ignored the question, additional clues swirling in her mind. "I have another photo of him in front of a huge aircraft hanger at a flight school in Florida with none other than Moussaoui, the front man for the 9/11 terrorists. Do you remember when all of those Saudis were enrolled in flight school to learn how to fly planes but not to land them?"

Paul nodded.

Clarisse looked like she was going to break into tears again. She bit her lip, paused, then said, "I don't know who I am married to, but I can't stand thinking about what he could be. You know all the hijackers on 9/11 were into pornography. They found all those books and videos among their personal effects after the towers came down. I found a similar cache of that stuff in the back of Zalton's corporate files . . . the files he keeps at home."

"Clarisse, there are plenty of men into pornography these days. Pornography is as close as the drugstore or Internet."

"Even if you're right, how would you account for these detonators?"

"But think about it, Clarisse," said Paul, feeling he needed to balance out the circumstantial evidence with other possibilities. "The detonator could have a lot of practical explanations. It doesn't have to indicate that your husband is up to something clandestine.

Actually, I'm far more concerned about the battering you've been taking. That's something I can do something about. If you want to file for a divorce, I can also help you get started on that."

"But what should I do? If he knew that I was here today . . ."

"Is there anything that keeps him riled up all the time?"

"No, it's just his nature. Oh, he's always upset that I won't convert to Islam. He calls me his infidel . . . well, I won't say, but it rhymes with 'witch.'"

"Clarisse, there's something we psychiatrists call *psychic intention*. It means that clients can't be helped until they become proactive in solving their own problems. You have a problem that could cost you your life. I can help you with it and protect you but . . ."

"Protect me? Doctor, there is no protecting me, and if my husband finds out that you know about the detonator, there's probably no protecting you either. If he really is connected with the *U.S.S. Cole*, the whole West Coast could be in danger."

"Well then, why did you come, Clarisse?"

"Frankly, I can't handle it alone anymore. I didn't want to implicate you in any vendetta my husband might have going, but I'm tired of living alone. I'm tired of always being afraid. I'm tired of being battered. But I'm still more frightened than I am tired."

Paul listened without interrupting.

"You want to know what I want from you? I want you to be my friend. Isn't that what they say on the streets? Psychiatry is paid friendship. I just want you to be there, because the day is coming when I may have a need so great that it will put all of our necks on the chopping block. When or if that day comes, I just want you to be there for me. I just don't want to deal with the answers till the questions have become so demanding that there's no putting aside their importance. I won't deal with this till I have to."

Her eyes were full of tears.

Paul Shapiro was aware of the distant sound of the office telephone ringing in the reception area. Things were so quiet he could even hear Carol taking the call. She was saying, "No, I never reveal the names of the doctor's clients . . . No, he may not be interrupted now . . . No, you may not talk to him now . . . Hold, please."

In a moment Carol knocked on the door. Paul stood and opened the door a crack to speak with her, while shielding the weeping Clarisse.

"Dr. Shapiro," Carol began, "there's a Zalton somebody or other on the phone. He wants to know if his wife is here. He says he had her followed. He says he knows she's here. He says he wants to talk to either her or you right now!"

"Carol, tell him that if he wants to talk to me, he can make an appointment for next Thursday. Then hang up. If he calls back, just don't answer the phone."

Carol swiftly returned to her desk, and Clarisse was standing when Paul turned toward her. "I've got to go," she quaked. "I've already implicated you far too much in my affairs. Good-bye, doctor!" She fled toward the door.

Suddenly she stopped, retraced her steps, and grabbed the detonator on Paul's desk. She jammed it into her purse and left the room.

A whirlwind of confusing thoughts swam in the doctor's mind after her exit. He wasn't sure he was glad she had gone. He already knew more about her than it was safe to know, and yet he had failed to give her the clearest course to protect her in her troubles.

He had two more appointments that afternoon. One was a compulsive neurotic whose phobias kept him installing extra locks on his door, which was already burdened with dead bolts. The other was an agoraphobe who had been trying to work up the nerve to go to Macy's on sale days but kept dropping before she actually went shopping.

Shapiro was glad when both appointments were over and he could go home. He put his client files into his drawer and stood to leave the room. He turned off the office light then noticed the microfiche machine was still lit. He froze. The microfilm was still there.

Clarisse's husband was sure to discover that it was missing.

CHAPTER 1

"Wednesday, July 18, 2007" read the Thomas Kinkade calendar on the wall of the soup kitchen. To Rhonda Shapiro, facing the awful paintings on the calendar was the worst thing about helping out Sister Joanna at the Wednesday luncheons.

Joanna, seeing Rhonda looking at the calendar, remarked, "He sure is a 'painter of light,' isn't he, Miss Rhonda? You know nobody knows how he gets so much light on his canvasses." Joanna was beaming.

"He mixes yellow, white, and red and tells everybody it's some kind of magic, Joanna," said Rhonda, turning back to the buffet to ladle out more soup. "The man could improve his painting with a roller and pan."

"My, aren't we being critical!"

"Not really, Joanna. It's just that you've also got a Thomas Kinkade mouse pad, a Thomas Kinkade nightlight, and Thomas Kinkade placemats."

"And don't forget about my Thomas Kinkade afghan, and it sure is pretty, except one of the homeless people spilled chili on it one night while watching HBO boxing."

"Well, good for the chili eaters," Rhonda said.

"Hey, you two art critics, how about helping me in the soup line?" interrupted Mary Muebles, her smile drawing them back to the work at hand.

Mary Muebles was the newest helper to Sister Joanna. She was especially good at helping the homeless—probably because she had lived among them for so long, being homeless herself. Mary had a touch of elegance about her that kept a lot of street sleepers coming to the free luncheons. She was fond of reminding her friends that she had once been a flamenco dancer on the *Noche del Rio River Show* in San Antonio. But that had clearly been a long time before she showed up at the Pathway of Light Cathedral.

Wanda Williams, the poor Wiccan, was also there. Near her was her shopping cart, filled with all three of her dresses and two heavy blankets that kept her warm on cold nights. It also held a giant tarp to keep the rain off during damp Seattle nights. Her kindness issued from a desire to give herself away, for she had nothing in her shopping cart that would have enriched any of their lives.

"I am reading *Left Behind* for the umpteenth time," she said. "I sometimes get the shakes while I'm reading it. It sure makes the Second Coming exciting!"

Mary smiled and continued ladling the soup.

The servers had barely gotten into the second course of hammy beans and cornbread when the rear door of the kitchen opened to reveal Father Peter and Kinta. All the homeless broke into applause out of respect for the old priest. Walking with a stiff, stately gate, Father Peter followed Kinta's lead to the serving table.

Rhonda was amazed to see her old friend again. And Kinta held a special place in her heart. Kinta saw her immediately and stared at her as though their friendship was still intact. He might have run to her, but the old priest's hand was on the harness, and Kinta was obedient to the trust that had been put in him. He never flinched, though the tiniest whimper issued from his throat when he stared at Rhonda.

Rhonda glanced at Joanna and saw recognition of the priest in her face as well. She wondered briefly where Joanna had met him, then noticed that Father Peter didn't seem to be looking at either of them as he approached. One of the homeless men called out to Father Peter, who turned toward the voice. The man left his seat and strode quickly to the priest, offering to seat him and get some food for him. The priest accepted and sat where directed.

Though bursting with curiosity, Rhonda focused herself on the task she had volunteered to do. But as soon as her service behind the steam table was finished, she quickly made her way to the table where the old priest was. "Excuse me, Father Peter," she said, "I'm so excited to see you. I want to go get Barney to show you how big he has grown."

She darted off to the church nursery to get her two-year-old before he could reply. She returned with her child and placed him before Father Peter.

■ ■ ■

After Father Peter played with Barney, Rhonda took him back to the nursery. When she returned to the conversation, Mary Muebles was introducing al-Haj Sistani around the room. Al was well-dressed, except for the slightly scuffed backpack on his shoulder with a "Spratton Laser Technologies" logo emblazoned on it.

"Rhonda"—Mary gestured toward her—"do you know Al?"

Rhonda shook her head.

"Hello, Al," said Rhonda, extending her hand.

"Hello, Rhonda," said Al, shaking the offered hand.

"Are you just Al? No other name?"

"Actually I'm al-Haj Sistani. I'm from Yemen, but I'm over here working for Spratton Laser Technologies. We're the research arm of the Strategic Weapons Development Corporation. I'm over here on a work visa."

"He's a Muslim and he reads the Qur'an," said Joanna. "He says we have the same God, but I don't believe it."

Joanna usually had a semisweet way of being abrasive, but this remark came out so flatly that it shut off all conversation for a moment or two. Finally Al broke the awkwardness. "Well, Sister Joanna, you believe in Jehovah, right?"

"Right, but I don't call him Allah." Joanna was still being a little snippy.

"And you believe in Jesus, right?"

"That's right, that's very right, that's mighty right!"

"Well, so do we, we believe in him too. We just call him Isa."

"Well, why don't you call him by his right name? His right name isn't Isa!"

"It is in Arabic."

"Well, it still looks like you Arabs could bend a little and learn to say it like it is written in the Good Book."

"In whose good book?" asked Al. "Our good book is the Qur'an, and in our good book he is called Isa."

"Well, you'd best get you a better good book!"

"Isa is Isa, whatever you call him. Mary Muebles, how do you pronounce Isa in Spanish?"

Mary looked very uncomfortable. She could see where the conversation was going and wasn't altogether sure she wanted to go there. "Well," she began tentatively, "we call Isa, *Hay-sous*. Yes, that's right—*Hay-sous Christ-o.*"

"So you see—whether it's English or Spanish or Arabic, it's just all Isa."

"Or Jesus!" said Joanna.

Rhonda decided to take the conversation in another direction. "Father Peter, tell me all that's been going on with you since we last saw you." She paused. "Do you mind my asking how you came to lose your eyesight?"

"It happened when I was in the Middle East. But it is a long story, and I'm sure of little interest to anyone here. I am content, for I have Kinta, whom I have learned to trust, and trust is the basis of all great relationships. He has bright eyes, keen enough for both of us. He has never yet misguided me. He is the only guide I need."

Joanna interjected, "See, Al, that's just how I feel about Jesus. But I don't see how you people can just bomb everyone you don't like. How can you just blow up everything and then say God told you to do it?"

"Whoa, now Joanna," said Rhonda. "I'm sure Al doesn't blow up people. Does he look like he would? Let's let that go."

"Yes," said Wanda Williams. "In *Left Behind*, Jesus comes back before anybody gets blown up, but Arabs could have the mark of the beast. Do you have the mark, Al?"

"No, I'm not the beast!" said Al.

"I didn't think so," said Wanda. "You don't look like a beast, so you won't get left behind, will you?"

"I don't think so," said Al. Turning to Rhonda, he then said, "No, it's OK, Mrs. Shapiro. Joanna has brought up a very valid point."

Rhonda was instantly wary. How did this complete stranger know she was Mrs. Shapiro? She didn't have time to dwell on it very long, for Al continued speaking.

"Joanna," said Al, "all Muslims aren't like that. We don't all blow up things. We are often as normal as everybody else. There are always a few terrorists that make the rest of us look bad. We are not all out to exterminate Jews and Americans."

"I do hope not," said Rhonda, "We're Jews, you know, Mr. Sistani. I mean, my husband has only lately become a Christian, but through most of his life, he was Jewish. I'd like to think you have nothing against us."

"Of course not," said Al.

"But you do work for Spratton Laser Technologies. Don't they manufacture weapons, detonators, and the like?" inquired Father Peter.

Al carefully picked his words. "Yes, but our products are manufactured mostly in the West and purchased almost entirely by Western nations."

"I understand," said Father Peter in a tone that conveyed some disbelief.

Father Peter's distrust left Rhonda even more unsettled. "Al," she said, trying to sound casual, "how did you know my last name?"

"I've met a nurse at our Islamic study group who works for your husband the Jew." Al's face flushed.

Rhonda could tell his prejudice had slipped out, but decided to let it pass. "So you know Carol Jones?"

"She's a beautiful Christian," said Al.

Joanna caught the slightly dismissive tone in "Christian" and answered with a bit of nip in her voice, "Would she be any better of a person if she were a beautiful Muslim or even a Jew for that matter?"

"I didn't mean that," backtracked Al, attempting some damage control.

"Will Muslims go through the tribulation?" asked Wanda the Wiccan.

"Wanda," Mary nudged her, "pipe down. We're not talking about that right now."

"Well, I didn't mean any harm, Mary, I just didn't want Al to have to go through the tribulation and get hailed on or have to live with all the frogs that are gonna come up out of the Euphrates, and if there are frogs, there will probably be snakes and—"

"Wanda," said Mary, more insistently, "stop it with the frogs."

Wanda clammed up and went back to reading *Left Behind*.

Joanna said nothing. Rhonda said nothing. But Al went on against the tide of resentment that seemed to be gathering against him. "Well, all I know is that Carol has shown a lot of interest in the subject."

It wasn't clear whether Carol was showing interest in Islam or Al himself. But just in case it was Al, Joanna took a final volley at him: "Does she know about your view of the afterlife—how Allah rewards faithful men who enter into paradise with a harem of seventy-two virgins? What do dead Muslim women get besides the right to wear a burka and take a number and wait in line if they're not at the top of the list and if they want to see their dead husband at any future century when he gets around to their number?"

Joanna was obviously antagonistic. Rhonda was increasingly suspicious. And Father Peter was, at best, tentative. Only Mary Muebles attempted to keep things civil.

"When does your Qur'an study group meet . . . and where?" she asked, though she already knew. She even winked at him—a gesture seen only by Al and Rhonda.

Al handed Mary a card and smiled warmly at her. "You'll come?" he asked.

"I might," she smiled, "but I'll warn you ahead of time. I'm a Sonoran Catholic—'Soy Catholico,' as we say. It's hard to surrender all that the generations have taught me. 'Viva La Virgin!'" She smiled. "In Mexico, that's not just our religion, that's our identity as a people. It's really our whole sense of patriotism."

"Did you know," asked Al, "that the Virgin Mary is the most venerated woman of the Islamic faith? She was the mother of Isa, you know."

"Do you believe this too?"

"Of course. Every good Muslim believes that—doesn't every good Catholic?"

Mary Muebles smiled, but she was the only member of the group doing so.

Al excused himself to go, saying farewell to a mostly unfriendly audience. He rose and turned toward the door. A copy of the Qur'an was sticking out of his Spratton Laser Technologies backpack. It tumbled out of the pack and fell on the floor, splaying its pages. A photo of a familiar face slipped out. Nobody said anything, except for the blind priest. "Bin Laden?" he asked the young zealot.

All eyes turned toward the blind man who spoke as though he could see. Rhonda was completely puzzled. How could the priest have seen the image on the photograph?

"Such sight is a momentary gift," said Al then added, "I really must be going," to deliberately change the subject. He rose, stuck the Qur'an into his backpack, and walked out. The book still protruded above the corporate logo on the backpack. To Rhonda it seemed a foreboding sight—an Arabic holy book above the emblem of the Northwest's largest weapons development company.

Wanda returned to the group, wheeling her shopping cart. Noticing that they didn't greet her, she turned to look at the person they were watching. "Do you think al-Qaida could be the great horde from beyond the Euphrates?" she asked as Al shut the door behind him.

"Get your things together, Wanda," said Mary, "we've got to get going. Hurry or I'm going to leave you here."

"I will hurry," said Wanda, arranging her stuff in the shopping cart. "I sure don't want to get left behind."

"That's good, sweetie," said Mary.

"There are snakes in the Euphrates," said Wanda.

"I'm sure," said Mary.

CHAPTER 8

O n Sunday morning, July 22, Paul and Rhonda Shapiro found
themselves engaged in Sister Joanna's sermon. On one side of
them were their close friends, Gary and Melody Jarvis, and on their
other side was Carol Jones, whom Paul had invited.

Melody Jarvis wasn't altogether sure she liked Joanna's sermons.
They tended to go on a bit long so that everyone was late getting out
of church. But Joanna never cut her sermons short. Sermons were
things the Lord gave his messengers so they could give them to the
flock. It was important to take time for God, which for Sister Joanna
meant that they had to take time for her sermons.

While Joanna was getting worked up over the fruit of the Spirit
in Galatians, Melody was working up an appetite. When Joanna
said that "someday we're all going to be sitting and eating at the
Marriage Supper of the Lamb," Melody wished they could all get
out of church and go eat.

Melody was not alone. While the congregants admired Joanna's
service to God, her sermons sometimes challenged their patience. On
this particular Sunday, attention in the Pathway of Light Cathedral
was not as good as it usually was.

Paul Shapiro, however, was engrossed in Joanna's sermon. She
had befriended Paul in some of his life's most desperate moments,
and he felt a sense of duty and admiration for her. He owed her at

least a good hour of listening because she had helped him through a crisis when his friends were few and scattered.

The women, however, felt no such allegiance to Joanna. Rhonda and Melody were thinking about the kind of lunch they would order, and Carol was thumbing through the hymnal, back to front and front to back. Mercifully, Joanna finally closed her sermon with a Helen Steiner Rice poem, and at 12:30 Henry Demond, who had the occasional gift of prophecy, delivered everyone with a short benediction. Usually his prophecies never came to pass, but on one very dramatic occasion one had. "Everybody in God's service has something given to them by God," said Sister Joanna, "and for Henry that gift was prophecy."

No one ever considered that Henry had been given the gift of short benedictions, but for Rhonda, that was perhaps God's most compassionate gift to him.

"Paul, dear," Rhonda began, "would you go to the nursery and pick up Barney? I'll get his safety seat buckled into the car."

Paul nodded and headed toward the nursery, eventually finding his happy baby. "Barney," he said, picking the boy up, "let's go find Mama, so we can go to dinner. Are you ready to go eat?"

Barney clapped his chubby little hands to let Paul know he was more than ready.

So was Janie Nickerson, Joanna's daughter.

"Mama," Janie pleaded, "can I go to lunch with you and Rhonda and Paul and baby Barney?"

"*May* I go to lunch with you and Rhonda and Paul and every-body?" corrected Joanna. "And no, you may not. Mr. Demond is going to take you home and fix you some macaroni and cheese."

"Aw, Mom," Janie protested, "I don't wanna go home with Henry. I wanna go with you and Rhonda."

"That's enough, Janie!" said Joanna. "Henry!"

Henry walked up and took little Janie by the hand and led her, stiff-legged with resistance, out of the church.

■ ■ ■

The rest of the group met up at the Skipjack. When they were finally stuffed into a booth, Paul said, "Well, Carol, it was good to have you sit with us in church. How did you like it?"

"It was OK, I guess," said Carol.

"Such enthusiasm," said her boss.

"Well, the service was awfully long," said Carol.

"Now, honey, did you mean 'sermon' when you said 'service'?" asked Sister Joanna.

"Now, Sister Joanna," said Carol, "you know I would never criticize your preaching. It's just too wonderful!"

Joanna smiled and turned to peruse the menu.

■ ■ ■

During lunch, they talked about the church, the clinic, and the shadows of long-ago events that had first drawn them together (excluding Carol). Eventually the check came, but after paying, the group was still enjoying each other's company and didn't want to part. It was a beautiful Seattle afternoon, and the sunny July day inspired them all to do something else together, rather than just go home. They wound up driving to the Market District, enjoying the warm walk and the Market's endless stairways. They watched the "fish pitchers" wow the crowd and then strolled along the tourist pier before splitting up and heading toward their cars on the wharf.

They hadn't walked very far when they came upon a group of street people involved in some sort of row. Gary Jarvis was the first to spot the reason for the uproar. There at the center of the struggle was none other than Father Peter and Kinta. Some PETA activists were trying to manhandle the old priest into an animal sanctuary van. Kinta didn't like the way they were treating Father Peter and was snarling and showing his teeth. This further angered the animal activists, and they were shouting that he had to give up the wolf. "You can't keep a wild animal in the city!" they cried.

Around the group were street people carrying signs that said Street People for Allah. Carol Jones suddenly became very distracted. Al was marching among the street people. Rhonda instantly picked up on Carol's altered behavior, noting its source in Al's activities.

Obviously, Carol's interest in the handsome young Muslim involved more than just his Qur'an studies. Carol broke away from her friends and ran to his side.

Al seemed to be on Father Peter's side, as were the Shapiros and Jarvises. Only the Shapiros' baby seemed to have no opinion. The young Yemeni man grew instantly defensive as some rough street kids tried to force Father Peter closer to the shelter van. He positioned himself in front of the van's doors and pressed himself between Father Peter and the ruffians, managing to shield him enough to move him ever farther from the van. In the struggle, Al's backpack hit Father Peter in the chest, providing an opportunity for a sleight of hand that would change the destiny of Muslims in the Northwest. When Father Peter attempted to pry away Al's backpack from his chest, his hands fell on two things. He initially grabbed them to keep them from being spilled out, but in the confusion, he neglected to mention to Al that he had taken them from his backpack. He simply felt them in his hand and then stuck them in his pocket. The exchange was over.

The riot subsided as quickly as it had begun.

The Jarvises left almost as soon as the hubbub subsided, but the rest of the party continued on down the pier. Kinta, who had been at the center of the uproar, moved peacefully out of the turmoil as though he found the whole riot uninteresting. But the Shapiros and Joanna Nickerson were not quite ready to let their bubbling emotions settle. They all walked back toward the Shapiro van.

"That was a very nice stand you took, Mr. al-Haj Sistrani," Joanna said.

"That's al-Haj *Sistani*," said Al, a little defensive about how she had pronounced his name.

"Well, I'm not all that good at Arabic," Joanna said, "but needless to say, we're all most grateful. You're welcome into the Cathedral anytime."

"Well, thank you very much, but I attend the al-Jabar mosque," said Al.

"Well, I don't know nothing about mosques, but I appreciate what you did for Father Peter and . . . well . . . you'd always be welcome in our church."

"'Course," she finished, "you couldn't come in bringing any weapons. You ever beheaded anybody, Al?"

All Al could do was shake his head.

"That's good that you haven't. I don't think we would want any beheaders in our church. Is that a part of your doctrine?"

Everybody laughed except Carol, who thought Joanna was being crude and insensitive. "That's a rotten thing to say, Joanna."

"Well, Al-Jezeera covers that kind of thing all the time; it's all on Fox News, and I for one don't approve of it!"

"Well, Al doesn't either," said Carol.

"Well, anyway, you're always welcome to worship Jesus with us, only we never let anyone into the soup kitchen with explosives. You can come. You don't even have to be born again, but you can't carry weapons."

Carol bit her tongue to keep from telling Joanna to be nice.

Father Peter thanked Al for his rescue and said, "Kinta and I had better lay a bit low for now." He then took out a Muslim prayer shawl and put it around his head. Joanna questioned him about this, but he assured her that he really liked the folks at Al's Qur'an study. He often had frequented these meetings. The prayer shawl helped him find acceptance and freely mingle among the Muslims.

It had been a long day, and Joanna's after-church lunch had left her exhausted. She asked the Shapiros to drive her back to the church and the party broke up.

Rhonda asked Father Peter if they could drop him and Kinta somewhere, but the old priest declined and walked away from the riot area. Carol decided to go for coffee with Al, who promised to get her a taxi back to her apartment.

Only one person left with a renewed sense of purpose. It was a blind man, who felt in his pocket and pulled out a folded piece of paper and a small cylindrical object. He didn't know what the object was, nor did he know what was on the paper, but he stuck them both back in his pocket. He felt they must have some significance, for what one grasps accidentally in one's hand may be only an accident, or it may be a gift from heaven for whatever purposes God has. He would have to get someone else to identify the two items.

■ ■ ■

Later that night Al was in his apartment, sorting through his backpack, when he found two important objects missing—a remote laser detonator and a piece of paper inscribed with some very significant numbers.

CHAPTER 9

After six o'clock that same Sunday evening, Joanna was dozing in front of her television when a knock at the door woke her. It was difficult to tell if the door was really hers or the front door of her dreams. She moved through a mist and opened the door. There stood Isaiah the prophet. She was immediately grateful that he didn't have Spotty the owl on his shoulder.

"Come in, Ike," she said.

He did.

"Sure glad you didn't bring Spotty," Joanna said.

"He left me a few months ago for a lady owl up north of Vancouver."

"Well, that's good. He was awfully cheeky."

"Joanna," Isaiah ignored her remark, "we need to talk."

"OK, shoot."

"Father Peter needs thy help," said Isaiah in his typical King James manner.

"He knows I'll help him no matter what."

"Well, he's gonna ask thee to go to the al-Jabar mosque with him."

"Now, wait just a minute, Ike. I don't like going to mosques."

"That works out perfectly because they don't believe in female imams."

"Female what?"

"Imams. You know, *women preachers*. So thou shalt have to wait outside till he gets through with his prayers."

"Well, I ain't the type that cottons to high-falutin' imams who think they're the loftier gender."

"Now, thou shalt not have to join the mosque. Just go with him and wait for him outside the mosque until the prayer time is over. He'll have on his Arafat head rag, and thou shalt be comfortably disguised in a loose flowing garment, so as far as anybody knows, he and thou will look like man and wife."

The doorbell rang. Joanna, confused at how it could ring when Isaiah was standing in the doorway, excused herself. "Pardon me, Ike, but I gotta get the door." She turned to look for another door and found herself locked in her recliner, almost paralyzed. She had been dreaming and the real doorbell was still ringing. Prying herself out of her chair, she went to the door. Behind it were Father Peter and Kinta. The old priest was wearing his prayer shawl and carrying a very large box.

"What brings you out this evening?" Joanna asked, still shaking her dream out of her thoughts. "You can't be all that lonesome to see me; I just got home from our trip to the Market."

"Joanna, I need you to help me do a couple of things."

"What are they? You know I'll be glad to help."

"Promise me you won't get angry or anything like that."

"I promise, but why would I?"

"I don't know, but I just felt you might."

"Put that out of your head," she comforted him, "and come in. What are you carrying here?"

Father Peter and Kinta came in. He handed her the cylindrical object from Al's backpack. Joanna turned it around in her hand.

"I have no idea what this is," she said, "but it's heavy."

"I could have told you that," he said. "But when I turned the thing over in my hand, I touched some words etched into the metal. Can you tell what the etchings say?"

"Nothing much," said Joanna, "just letters: *RLDS*. Could it be this is something made by the Reorganized Latter-day Saints?"

"That's not very good logic, Joanna."

"Well, you asked and I was only trying to help." Joanna huffed. "And, you promised not to get mad."

"I'm not mad," she protested, then muttered, "I'm just trying to find out why you would ask me to help you and then criticize me when I did."

Peter ignored her and stroked his chin. "Is there anything else on the cylinder?"

"No, just a little green light that keeps blinking. On the thin end of the cylinder there is a lens. It's very small—about the size of a bean." She pushed the green flickering light and a thin burst of red light shot across the room. "Well, I'll be."

"What? You'll be what?"

"I won't be nothing but confounded. When I pushed the green light, a bright red laser beam popped out of it. Oddest thing I ever saw."

"I've heard about these laser detonators," said Father Peter. "They think that terrorists might have blown up the nightclub in Bali with one of them. That must be what we've got, Joanna— a remote laser detonator of some sort. Maybe that's what the *RLD* of *RLDS* stands for."

"What about that *S*?" Joanna asked.

"I don't know. Maybe it stands for *systems* or *services* or *surveillance* or . . ."

"Or *Satan*," Joanna interrupted. "This just sounds like the devil to me, Father Peter."

"Here's another thing I want you to look at," said the priest, pulling a piece of paper out of his pocket. "Is there any writing on this?"

"Some," she said.

"What does it say?" he asked.

"There's the word *television* and some numbers."

"Television?"

"Actually, it says *TV*."

"What are the numbers?"

"Looks like 14, 37, 52, 19. Could these be television channels?"

"Is that all? Just numbers?"

"Well," offered Joanna, "there are some little letters by the TV channel numbers."

"What kind of letters?"

"Little *r*'s and *l*'s."

"It sounds more like a combination to a lock or railway station locker or a vault. Maybe it's 14 right, 37 left, 52 right."

Joanna was amazed. "That fits. You can see more than any blind man I ever saw. But what about the *TV* part?"

"I don't know that. But we may find it out. I want you to go with me to the mosque tonight, and after it's over, I want us to do a little 'tailin'.'" A determined look spread across his face. "We're going to tail al-Haj Sistani. I got these things from his backpack. We'll take Kinta with us; he's got a very good nose."

Father Peter handed Joanna the big box he had brought with him. She tore it open and saw a huge robe—a burka.

"I'm not wearing this. Isaiah told me you'd be bringing it. And I'm not wearing this. I don't mind helping you—I know you're blind and all—but I'm not wearing this. No way. Got that, Father?"

"You can't just go waltzing up to a mosque and be seen like you are. You're black and you're not a Muslim, Joanna."

"Why not? It worked for Mohammed Ali. Anyone who's black can be a black Muslim. Everybody's doing it. I can too. "

"Yeah, but it won't work for you. Remember, you're a woman who's known all over downtown Seattle. So you've got to put on the burka. Everything will be covered but your peepers, and nobody will recognize you. I don't know exactly where Al will go after work, but he often goes straight to the Spratton East facility. If he goes in there, we're going to follow him."

"But will they let us in? I mean, even if you wear your Arafat head rag and I wear this mud-ugly burka, will they let us in?"

"I believe they will. Every guard at the front gates at Spratton is Yemeni, and most of them have seen me at Al's Qur'an studies. I think they will let us in. I think they'll greet me with a triple kiss."

"Yuck!"

"It's the Muslim way."

"Whatever." Joanna shrugged. "But why don't you get Gary Jarvis to help you? He does this kind of stuff for a living."

"I didn't ask him, but he couldn't go tonight anyway. He's got an early morning briefing tomorrow on all this terrorist gossip down in Olympia. He doesn't know about the stuff I just showed you. Joanna, I believe that this terrorist cell is committed and that al-Haj Sistani is not only involved but near the center of the operation. So—"

"We're gonna do a little tailin'," she finished. She thought of calling Gary Jarvis but felt there were other conclusions to be made before she did.

Reluctantly, Joanna slipped the burka on over her street clothes. "I wish I didn't have to wear this. I look like a tank under a tarp." She paused, remembering. "I gotta call Henry Demond. He lives just down the block. He'll be here in a jiffy to look after my little Janie."

While they waited on Henry, Joanna took time to arrange Father Peter's head shawl. "Muslim men always look kind of funny in these things," she said.

"Any funnier than Muslim women look in burkas?"

Joanna was silent.

In a few minutes Henry showed up. He broke into gales of laughter when he saw Joanna. She shushed him. "You'll wake Janie."

"Where are you two going dressed like that?" Henry recovered. "You look . . ."

"Fat?" she offered.

"Ample," answered Henry.

"Come along, Kinta," said Father Peter.

The great wolf rose regally and walked to the priest and brushed against his leg, signaling his master to take the harness. Father Peter grasped the harness and Joanna's hand and left.

They walked down the hill, past Seattle Pacific University, and then another mile to the warehouse that was the al-Jabar mosque.

All heads swiveled in their direction as they entered, but since the study was already underway, no one spoke. Kinta and Father Peter and Joanna all sat near the back.

"Is Carol Jones here?" whispered Father Peter.

Joanna looked around, seeing mostly men, except for a veiled woman or two. There was even one other woman in a burka. "I don't see Carol," she whispered back. "Mostly guys in head rags."

Al was lecturing on Surah 3:71, apparently on the sacredness of the Holy Qur'an. Joanna had to admit he was a dynamic speaker.

When the study was over, Al came running up to Father Peter and gave him the triple kiss. "It is good to see you so often at our studies, Father Peter! And who is this?" said Al, gesturing toward Joanna.

"It is a Libyan woman," said the old priest. "She lost her husband who ran a taxi cab in Watts before she moved up here." Father Peter hated lying but knew that he must protect Joanna's identity at all costs.

"Ah, so she is a widow?" asked Al.

"Yes."

"She is . . . heavy?"

Joanna was not one to hold her peace. "I am ample," she said, "not heavy!"

Father Peter tried to cover for her insolence. "She is heavy of heart since her husband's death."

"She must be from a very conservative mosque."

"Yes," said the priest, "her husband was *Talabani* in Libya."

"I see," said Al.

Al and Father Peter bussed each other a second time, then Joanna, Father Peter, and Kinta left the mosque. Joanna used her cell phone to call a cab. Soon the cab arrived, and all three of them climbed in the back seat. Joanna could tell the cab driver was uneasy with Kinta in the car, but that was too bad. There were city ordinances protecting seeing-eye dogs.

"Are we well hidden? Is the cab visible from the front doors of the mosque?" Father Peter whispered.

"Yes," answered Joanna.

"Good, wait till Al leaves, and then we'll follow him. Keep out of the light and stay far enough away from him that he doesn't see us."

Joanna waited and waited. It seemed to Father Peter that they had waited too long. "Is he still inside? Could you have missed him?"

"People, the meter is running!" said the cabbie.

"We'll pay," said the blind priest. "You just keep the motor running, OK?"

"There isn't another way out of that place, is there?" Joanna asked the priest.

"No," Father Peter answered. "Even if he uses the side door, he has to pass directly by here."

Just when they were beginning to despair, another cab arrived. Al walked out of the mosque and climbed into the waiting car.

Joanna spoke to the cabbie. "Follow that cab, but not too close, all right? I don't want them to know we're back here."

The driver had obviously been through some such exercises before. He was very good at following Al's cab . . . directly to the Spratton building.

"You were right," Joanna whispered. "We're stopping at Spratton."

Al stepped out of the cab, paid the fare, and walked inside.

Father Peter paid their fare and the threesome left the cab. "Now, Joanna," he said, "here's the tricky part." He pulled out a corporate badge with his picture on it. *Spratton Technologies of Yemen*, it read, with some Arabic letters underneath it.

Joanna was amazed. "Where did you get this?"

"I have a clever friend in computer design and laminating," he replied.

"What does the Arabic script say?" she asked.

"I don't know. I'm only hoping it gives me clearance or some such thing. The worst part is that I don't have one for you. I've seen both of those guys at the studies, and I think they'll recognize me and let us in. But it is most important that you act obedient. Muslims put a high priority on submissive women. Especially those dressed in burkas. A sassy woman is not readily accepted; plus, she'd be easily spotted as a phony. So be as Muslim as you can be, and pray they'll let you in."

Then he turned to Kinta and simply said, "Sit!"

The wolf obeyed.

"You must stay, Kinta. Stay until I come back for you." Father Peter was quiet before he turned again toward Joanna. "From now on, Joanna, I have to rely on you. You've got to guide me. You are my Kinta-in-a-burka."

"Great. Wait, Father, what am I doing here in the middle of the night with a wolf and a priest dressed like Zorro-ella, anyway?" she asked. "Do you realize how awkward this is?"

The old man said nothing. Taking her elbow, he walked with her to the huge glass doors. Once they reached the guards, one of them looked at Father Peter's badge. "You may go in"—the guard motioned—"but what about your wife?"

"Oh, she's not my wife," he replied, then leaned in the direction of the guard's voice and said, "Please don't think I have such taste as to marry a heavy person."

"I heard that," whispered Joanna.

"This is Jasmine, a friend," Father Peter explained to the guard.

"A fairly big friend," the guard replied.

The priest could feel Joanna's arm muscle flex underneath the burka.

"Yes, indeed. She's from Libya. Is it OK for her to enter? I can't see without her, and I'm here without my animal tonight."

"Well . . . we're not supposed to let anyone enter without a pass, but I guess I could make an exception for you, Father Peter. Go ahead." Even though he was a Christian priest, the guards had confidence in him.

Joanna nudged Father Peter past the guards and into the building.

Joanna read the corporate register and saw that Al's office was on the fifth floor. They were about to get on the elevator when Father Peter said, "If you can find the stairs, let's climb. Elevators like these often have cameras in them, and they always make noise when they stop at a floor."

They climbed to the fifth floor and located Al's office. He was seated behind a large glass panel amid a mass of empty desks that formed a huge steno pool. When he stood up to get a drink from the corporate water cooler, the two of them slipped in and concealed themselves behind a large, felted cubicle panel—close enough for Joanna to see Al's activities and for Father Peter to hear them.

Al returned and picked up his phone, dialing. He reached out and tore off the Saturday and Sunday sheets from his desk calendar, uncovering Monday, July 23.

"Hello." Father Peter could clearly hear a man's voice on the receiver.

"Zalton?" said Al. "Al here. Listen, Zalton, I'm sorry but I've misplaced one of the RLD devices."

There was a long pause.

"I don't know where!" Al protested.

There was an even longer pause while Al listened intently. "I was in the Market today and there was a skirmish in the streets around that priest I've been working so hard to convert." More silence while the other end of the receiver issued muffled rumblings.

"Yes, Carol was with me, and no, I wasn't rattled. I think she's coming around. She seems to regard me so highly. She would be a good—"

Zalton interrupted with angry rumblings.

"No, I tell you, I find her attractive, but I'm not at all rattled. I promise I won't let anything else deter me. Can you give me the combination to the titanium vault? I'm afraid I've misplaced that as well. Well, if you can't remember, we can go over all this tomorrow when we're both in . . . yes, I know what those RLD units cost. Yes, $17,000 is a lot of money, but don't despair. I may yet find the one I misplaced. We've still got plenty more of them in the TV. That's more than enough for the stadium job . . . OK . . . yes, we'll work on that tomorrow." Al hung up then got up to leave. He put on his Windbreaker and walked out of the office.

No sooner was he gone than Joanna said, "So that's what *TV* means: *titanium vault*."

The priest said nothing for a moment then blurted, "Wait! That must be Zalton's office. It would be the best place to look for a TV."

Taking Joanna's arm, he pushed her to go find Zalton's office, which they quickly did. Behind his huge glass desk was an enormous silver door with a combination wheel in its center.

"I think this is the vault; it looks like titanium," she said.

"OK, Joanna, I've got the combo memorized: 14 R, 37 L, 52 R, 19 L."

Joanna's fingers twisted the black wheel, following the priest's instructions this way and that, until the door swung open. Suddenly, a piercing alarm sounded and a red light began flashing. But Joanna stayed on her mission and had no trouble locating the RLD devices. They were in a gold box on the very first shelf of the vault. "You want all of them?" she yelled over the alarm.

"All!" shouted the priest.

Joanna scooped them up. "Let's get out of here."

She took off, yanking the priest with her free hand. She guided him back down the stairs, avoiding the two guards who were already in the elevator moving up to the fifth floor. No one was covering the main gate, and Father Peter and Joanna walked out hurriedly into the shadows where Kinta still waited obediently.

They moved quickly away from the building just as they heard the throb of police sirens heading in their direction. Only when they had covered more than a mile did Joanna use her cell phone to call a cab. She handed the devices to Father Peter while she discarded her burka, throwing it in a ditch, and got inside the car. "Come on, Peter and Kinta," she said. "Hurry."

"We're not going," said Father Peter, "at least not with you. My face will be all over the corporate security cameras inside Spratton. You, on the other hand, will not be recognizable. You will be safe, but Kinta and I will have to lay low for a while. I'm taking the RLD devices and stashing them out of sight. I don't want you to know where I am going. That way you won't have to lie when they ask you if you know where I am. 'Bye for now, Joanna. And thanks so much for your help. And by the way, I don't think you look all that ample in your burka. But then again, I'm blind."

The priest and his wolf walked off into the night and were swallowed up in the misty darkness.

"Where to?" asked the driver.

"Downtown," said Joanna.

CHAPTER 10

The al-Jabar worship center was proof that minarets are not necessary to make a mosque. But that mosque did own an adjacent storefront building that had been newly decorated and had a clean, unsophisticated air about itself. It was in this storefront mosque that al-Haj Sistani often conducted his Monday night Qur'an studies. Al hoped in the months before Ramadan to bring many of his students to embrace Islam. A good number of Arabs always attended night class along with a few Anglos.

Overall, this evening's crowd didn't have any professors or professionals; instead, there were many homeless people, whose attendance was in part paid for by Al's generosity. The word was now out on the streets that all who attended the studies would receive a McDonald's gift card. In spite of Al's continued insistence that they bathe (in the tradition of Islamic hygiene), they usually reeked in the summer heat.

Al always began his lectures with two phrases: one was religious and one a bargaining chip. First, Al would sing, "Greetings in the name of Allah and the Prophet." To which those gathered always replied with the *shahadah*, "There is no God but Allah, and Mohammed is his prophet." It was only then that Al offered the second part of his litany: "The Mac cards will be distributed at the end of the lecture." To which those gathered always sighed.

One bedraggled attendee mumbled, "That's one way Christians and Muslims are alike—you gotta go to preaching or you don't get the grub." Nobody laughed, and many of the street people nodded. One even boldly asked, "Did Jesus feed the 5,000 after they listened to his sermon or before?"

"I don't want to talk about Isa tonight," said Al.

"But you said all Muslims believe in Jesus," said another man.

"We do," said Al, "but tonight our lecture is on *rakats*, the importance of keeping your daily prayers. We keep prayers to approve ourselves to Allah, not just to ask Allah for things as Christians do. All prayer begins in our devotion to Allah and the book. In our prayers we begin by repeating the first Surah, or chapter, of the Qur'an.

"But," continued Al, "only the martyrs pray the most fervent of prayers. I have many friends who paid with their lives to show their love for Allah. For them, their sacrifice was a prayer that began in this world and ended in the presence of the Prophet himself. This is the last stage of prayer—when the disciple no longer offers his words to Allah but offers himself to Allah."

At this point in his talk, Al was aglow. He seemed to extol the prayerful martyrs with such reverence that Carol was struck with admiration for him.

Was she in love with his commitments or him? Did she admire his faith, or was she drawn toward him personally? Her feelings toward al-Haj Sistani were so immense and tangled. Still, he was warm and personable, insisting that all present call him Al. He was easy to admire and impossible to suspect of anything evil.

In the middle of his lecture, Al bid his listeners follow Mohammed and his teachings and learn his way of prayer. There was a mesmerizing response from his eager listeners. The men present dutifully followed him as he demonstrated the extreme posture of their prostrate praying toward Mecca.

Mary Muebles and Carol were not invited to join this particular activity, so they just kept their seats and watched as the group bent themselves toward Mecca. Carol wondered that anyone in the room could really know in which direction Mecca was from Seattle. But

Al had so much faith, he must surely have a built-in compass for his prayers, she thought.

Carol was entranced by the handsome young Yemeni's declarations of devotion and faith. But she was also inspired by the sparkle in his dark eyes, his glistening black hair, and his charm.

Carol suddenly felt ashamed for not focusing on spiritual matters but on Al's resemblance to Lawrence of Arabia, or what she assumed he looked like. He was handsome and magnetic. Still, for all his charisma, Al seemed to be less involved with the Qur'an than he usually was.

But neither Carol nor the sixteen other people gathered to meet with Al could have guessed at the agony that ripped through his soul that night.

His cell phone rang. Al stopped abruptly, apologizing, "Excuse me, men, but I must take this call."

It bothered Carol that he did not say "men and women." It also bugged her that he never seemed to have much to do with feminine names or pronouns. Some of his romantic charm momentarily faded. Al passed her by, stepping outside to take the call. He left the door ajar and Carol, who was sitting by the door, couldn't help but hear a bit of the conversation.

"I know, Zalton. I know how serious this is. I don't know how anyone could have gotten into the safe, and I have no idea where they have gone."

There was a long pause. "But where would I start looking for them?"

Another pause. "No, the priest I've become friends with isn't here tonight. I have no idea why or where he is . . . What! Are you sure? He was on the security camera tape . . . But it would be impossible for him to crack a safe, even if he had the combination. The man is blind, he couldn't . . . A woman! There was a woman with him? A Talabani woman . . . in a burka?" There was another long pause. "No, it's just that I've never known an American Muslim woman to have anything to do with burkas. I thought all that ended with the overthrow of the Talabani in Afghanistan . . ."

Carol moved away from the doorway to stop eavesdropping. Whatever the conversation was about didn't concern her. Still, it exposed Al as being less self-controlled and spiritually calm than she'd thought he was. He actually sounded panicked.

When he reentered the room, her impressions were confirmed. He was ashen and visibly shaken. He apologized to the group and left the room abruptly. Carol excused herself to Mary Muebles and hurried to catch up to him outside. When finally she caught him, she took his elbow, but he tried to shrug her off.

"Please," she said, "let me help, Al. Whatever it is that's gone wrong, let me at least inside the loop. I'm a good listener, and you know I'm on your side no matter the difficulties."

Al was trembling, and for the first time since Carol had met him, he was no longer the handsome, run-your-own-show kind of man. They walked together in silence for a while. Just ahead of them was a small diner. They stepped in and ordered two cups of coffee and two glasses of water. They drank slowly.

"Al," said Carol at length, "when we first met, you told me how Khadijah had once helped Mohammed through a despondent time in which the prophet seemed about to kill himself. Maybe I could be that for you."

Though the words were barely out of her mouth, she wished she hadn't said them. Who was she to compare herself to Khadijah? First, Khadijah wasn't a Methodist. Second, she was a very important historical figure. But Al knew that her effort was sincere.

All at once he broke forth in tears. "Carol," he said, "a great deal of very expensive merchandise was stolen from the corporate vault—hundreds of thousands of dollars worth. They think I was part of it. They're going to come after me."

"But why would they think that?"

"Because only Zalton al-Zhabahni, head of Spratton Laser Technologies, and I knew the combination. I didn't exactly know it, but I had written it down on a piece of paper, and during the riot at the Market yesterday afternoon, I must have lost it. I can only guess that the priest found it."

"Father Peter? Why would you guess him?" Carol shook her head dubiously. "He wouldn't and couldn't steal anything. He wouldn't because he's too moral to do it. He couldn't because he's blind! He would have no idea what he was stealing."

"Well, he and an accomplice broke into the vault at Spratton last night and took the merchandise."

"Don't say 'accomplice.' It makes him sound like some kind of practicing gangster."

"Well, somebody was with him who obviously could see well enough to work the dial on the safe."

"What sort of merchandise?"

"I'm not at liberty to say, but unless I can get it back—"

"What? What happens if you can't get it back?"

"Carol," Al paused, "I work for some very ruthless people. This will not be overlooked. I've got to find Father Peter and find out why he, of all people, should break into Spratton and steal."

"But he's blind . . . and he's religious," Carol knew she was repeating herself but she continued. "Father Peter simply couldn't break into any place anywhere to steal anything."

"Zalton said it was him, all right; they caught him red-handed. They got the whole thing on the security video cams."

"Well, if they have the whole thing on tape, they must have got a good shot of his accomplice."

"A woman, apparently. At least the person was wearing a burka."

"A Talabani? There's nobody of that Muslim persuasion in the U.S., is there?"

"I met the woman at the Qur'an study. Father Peter told me that she was the widow of one of the few Talabani that exist anywhere in the U.S. There's a small radical mosque in L.A.—mostly black Muslim radicals."

Carol said nothing for a full minute. Neither did Al. Then Al said despairingly, "The only hope I've got is that Father Peter is found. If they can locate him, they'll torture the truth out of him."

"Torture! Who would do that?"

"You apparently don't watch the news much. It's a way of getting information when the terrorists want it."

"Terrorists? Are you saying there are terrorists working— or even in charge of things—at Spratton?" *Then that would mean that Al worked with . . . So was Al . . . ?* Carol looked at him.

Al shifted uncomfortably, having said more than he wished he had. "Carol, I can't go home—not to my home tonight. If I do that, I won't be alive come morning. They'll make me talk, and I won't be able to supply them a single bit of information. So I've got to hide somewhere until morning. Then maybe I can see about finding Father Peter . . . Any ideas as to where the old blind priest holes up?"

Carol shook her head. "Tonight you must rest, Al," she said. "If it's not safe at your place, why not come on over to mine? You can sleep on the couch. Maybe by morning something will come to mind . . . someplace to begin. But please don't point the bloodhounds in Father Peter's direction. We must protect him as best we can."

Al was tired. He had not many options. As far as he knew, no one at Spratton knew where Carol lived. He didn't even know where she lived, and not knowing made him feel all the more secure for the night ahead. Whether Zalton would get to Father Peter or him first, he knew not. He only knew that one of them, if not both, was bound to pay for the loss of all those RLDs—and pay dearly.

■ ■ ■

Snoqualmie Road was safe—suburban safe—for it was miles away from the al-Jabar mosque. But the world was falling apart, and when it shattered, there would be no safe zones. Still, the Shapiros on Snoqualmie Road slept on with no idea of what the dark night held in store.

CHAPTER 11

The phone startled the Shapiros out of a deep sleep. Paul looked at the huge digital face of his bedside clock: 1:59 a.m., Tuesday, July 24. Groggily he grabbed for the phone, knocking over a glass of water and the psychiatric journal he had been reading at bedtime.

Finally he grasped the receiver. "Yes, hello!" he grumbled. Nothing. Then he realized he had the phone upside down. He turned it around and pressed it to his ear in time to hear his assistant say, "Dr. Shapiro!"

"Yes, Carol . . . what in the world . . . it's two a.m. What's wrong?"

"I'm fine. It's Al. His life could be in danger."

"Al's life!" Paul sat upright and turned on the bedside light. "What's going on?"

"Well, you remember Clarisse al-Zhabahni? She's one of your clients."

"Yes, of course I remember her, but what's she got to do with Al?"

"It isn't her; it's her husband, Zalton al-Zhabahni, head of Spratton Laser Technologies. He's Al's boss. He's accusing Al of stealing something from the company vault. Al says the man is absolutely ruthless and . . ."

Paul Shapiro was quiet for a moment, thinking of how Clarisse showed up bruised for her appointment. "But what could Al have taken from the company that has Zalton so upset?" asked Paul, wriggling out of the sheets to stand and pace the floor—a stride that was limited by the tether of a coiled telephone cord.

"He won't tell me, other than to say that what was taken was worth several hundred thousand dollars. He says that Father Peter may have actually robbed the firm and have the merchandise in his possession."

"Carol, that's preposterous! Father Peter could never do such a thing."

"I don't know whether he could or couldn't, but Al says they have the break-in on tapes from their security video and it's definitely Father Peter."

"But how could he have done it? The man is blind!"

"He had an accomplice, a large Islamic woman who was wearing a burka."

"Here in Seattle? Not a chance."

"But she must have led Father Peter to the crime scene and guided him through the cracking of the titanium vault."

"Carol, this sounds ridiculous!"

"I know how it sounds, but I know all too well how true it all is. And unless we can somehow help Al or Father Peter, they may both be in mortal trouble." Carol broke into tears.

"Carol," said Paul, suddenly intent on meeting the parties involved, "I'll meet you and Al at the clinic at five o'clock this morning. He will surely be safe until then. We'll work on some kind of plan or something. In the meantime, try to get some sleep. By the way, where is Al now?"

"He's here—at my apartment—lying on my couch."

"Why hasn't he just called the police?"

"I don't know. I'm guessing it's because he and his boss are involved in something so terrible that the police are the last people either of them would go to. I'm worried that—" her voice quivered—"that whatever this is could have a monstrous impact on our entire community—all of Seattle. I just . . ." She heaved a sob.

"Carol, take it easy. We'll think of something. I'll see you in a couple of hours."

"Al too?"

"Of course. Now try to get a little sleep."

He hung up, wary and anxious. Clarisse's bruised face was foremost in his thoughts. Clearly her husband was a bad man. A chill ran down Paul's spine. He felt the entanglements of darkness. The Zhabahnis were in league with that darkness, and when their foul plans had run their course, the city . . . no, the nation . . . would bleed.

"Honey, are you all right?" asked Rhonda quietly to avoid waking Barney. Carol's call had also wakened her. She had been listening to one end of a clearly disturbing conversation that had frightened her husband.

He stood in the darkness for a long time then snuggled back into bed beside his wife. She was warm and somehow made him feel more secure than he had just moments earlier.

"Honey," she said, snuggling back, "I have no idea what's going on, but let me help in any way I can. It's Al, isn't it? He isn't all we thought he was, is he? It's all of these Yemeni citizens—that's who it is, isn't it?"

"Ronnie, please try to go back to sleep. Maybe if you do, I will too."

But neither did. At four o'clock, Paul shut off the alarm and took a hot shower, followed by a very cold shower. The contrast in the water temperature woke him up. He managed to get dressed, and with a cup of yesterday evening's microwaved coffee, he even began to feel that life might be managed.

■ ■ ■

He pulled up to his clinic door at 4:55 a.m. Carol's little tan Mustang was already there. So was Al. The doors of the little car flew open as Paul pulled up, and Carol and Al emerged. The July sky was already paling in the east, though the sun was clearly sleeping late. Paul hugged Carol and went to shake Al's hand. But Al embraced Paul with a triple kiss in the Muslim fashion. Paul could tell by the ardent greeting that the man was in emotional turmoil.

Soon they were seated in Paul's very comfortable study.

Carol spoke first: "Dr. Shapiro, I'm so very sorry to have inconvenienced you at this horrible hour."

"I have found," said the psychiatrist, "that trouble doesn't always wait till office hours. You were right to come. Please don't trouble yourself about inconvenience. Instead, let's get as much of this out on the table as you're comfortable with. The more you tell me, the better I may be able to help."

Al cleared his throat, fidgeted uneasily in his chair, and began, "It's like this, Dr. Shapiro. I'm a Muslim and grateful to be so, but I belong to a highly dedicated team of disciples that are out to change the world for the sake of Allah."

Paul could tell that Al was picking his words very carefully— so carefully that it slowed his conversation to a measured walk. He wanted help but didn't want to betray anything that needed to be kept private.

"Remember Sunday afternoon, when we were all at the Market and that riot broke out?"

Paul nodded.

"A lot of pushing and shoving was going on. And I positioned myself in front of that van where they were trying to put Father Peter's guide dog."

Paul nodded again.

"Well," Al continued, "it must have been then that Father Peter somehow took a very technical piece of equipment out of my backpack and carried it away."

"But that's . . . what makes you think it was him?" Paul demanded.

"Hear me out," said Al. "At that moment he also took a piece of paper that contained some highly privileged information from my backpack."

"How privileged?"

"It was the combination to the Spratton titanium vault. Late Sunday night—very late—he and an accomplice broke into the company vault and stole more than $400,000 worth of specialized equipment. We know it was Father Peter because we have the whole thing on security video. Everybody at Spratton knows he did it, and if they find him and recover the equipment, Zalton is likely to let the whole thing pass. The corporation will likely just forgive or at least ignore the theft. To press it would declare it! And all must be held in secrecy."

"Why would they do that?" asked Paul.

"Because the nature of what he stole is so vital to national security, they would rather just drop the issue to keep it out of the press than prosecute the man publicly. But if he can't be located and all that is stolen can't be recovered, they'll be coming after me. They see the loss as my fault."

"Why would they blame you?"

"Because they know I had one of the items checked out to test it under pressure . . . it's complicated," said Al, checking his confession, knowing that he had already said too much. "They also know that only two people had the combination to the vault: my boss and me. I was working on memorizing it when Father Peter stole the paper where I had it written down."

Suddenly Al became angry. "I can't believe I actually helped protect the man and his wolf from being hauled off by the animal cruelty people, and that's what he did to me."

He paused again and wrung his hands. "If I don't get that back, they'll torture me till I tell them where it is. I'll die because I have no idea where the old priest is. Doctor, do you know?"

"Torture you?" Paul asked, alarmed.

"This was a pretty big theft!"

"Yes, but torture?"

"Dr. Shapiro, this is a Yemeni corporation. We don't play by the same kind of rules you namby-pamby Christians use." He grew increasingly agitated. "I need to know where Father Peter is. Do you know or not?"

Paul shook his head.

Carol pressed Paul for information. "Doctor, I know you're my boss, but you and Rhonda were very thick with the old man. You must have some idea where he is staying. We need to find him before Zalton does. We can get the merchandise back and hand it over to Zalton."

"I have no idea. Even when Father Peter was hospitalized at the clinic with paranoid schizophrenia, he had no address, no circle of contacts, no moorings in this world. It is only because of Washington law that we kept him: you can't turn a sick man out on the streets in Washington whether he has any insurance or not. We had to keep him and we did.

"We never knew where he went or where he stayed. Once he stayed in our old RV trailer for a week or so, but no longer. After that we never knew. We were as surprised to see him at Joanna's soup kitchen as you were. We last saw him when we were in our cabin near Carnation, Washington. Then he dropped out of sight for more than a year. We thought we'd never see him again. But when we did see him, we were glad, because so many wonderful things happen whenever he is around."

"Well, this isn't one of them," said Al. "Would you have any objection to our visiting your cabin up by Carnation?"

"Of course not. I'll draw you a map."

"I'm hoping it's still early enough in the day that Zalton will not have come looking for me. Carol, maybe we could take your Mustang over to my condo and pick up my Honda before anyone is the wiser. We'll have to think of a place to hide my car." Al paused. "I forgot to start with the first question: Carol, would you be open to driving your car up to Carnation with me and checking this out?"

"Well, Al, I don't mind you taking my car, but I can't go. I have to work today. I can't just up and—"

"Yes, you can, Carol. Take the day off," said Paul. "I'll see if Rhonda can cover for you here at the clinic. I'm pretty sure Joanna and some of her helpers at the church will watch Barney. All I ask Al is that if you find Father Peter, you don't rough him up or hurt him in any way. If he did indeed steal the stuff you're looking for, he'll be open in telling you so. You mustn't hurt him, OK?"

"That's a deal!" said Al, rather hastily.

"Do you promise?" asked Paul.

"Yes, I promise," said Al, but his tone was less than convincing.

CHAPTER 12

The soft rhythmic thump of the tires over the cracks in the roadway produced a hypnotic effect on Carol as she sat in the passenger seat of her Mustang. She thought of how sleepy her adolescence had been. Now she was in an uncertain world where almost anything could happen—brutally and all at once. Her new world kept its peace as it skimmed the foot of Mount Rainier. Everyone she knew seemed to have some sort of cosmic role to play in this drama of tragedy, whose end was in the hands of an unwitting audience called Seattle.

Carol's love for Al was becoming a huge problem. If he were involved in any kind of plot to harm the city, her obligations to all of life would overrule her romance. If she were participating, even unwillingly, in any plan that in any way harmed anyone, she would never be able to forget or forgive it. When her spinning thoughts had stilled somewhat, she asked Al, "How far is it to the Shapiro cabin?"

Al was in a funk all his own, so it was a moment before he answered her. "Sixty miles," he said. "Maybe more . . . I don't know." The question was unimportant to either of them.

There was another long silence.

"Al, I've had misgivings about our love . . . or rather . . . our interest in each other." Carol was choosing her words very carefully now. "Our worlds are so different. I'm not much of a Christian. But I believe that I could never be a Muslim and feel as ardently as you feel about the faith. But I don't see how even you could be so wrapped up in the whole thing as to be willing to be tortured by people who are of the same faith as you. I mean, how can Zalton be this boss you're so fond of and even think of torturing you or Father Peter? I don't see what good it does to believe in Allah if you can even consider doing such things."

Al said nothing.

"When you and your Muslim friends get together, you seem so loving and kind and devout. I would notice this on CNN during the Iraqi conflict. There would be shots of Iraqi men—and there's another thing, aren't there ever any Iraqi women in mosques? Why don't they ever get in the mosque pictures? Anyway, on TV specials, there are pictures of Iraqi men praying. But there are a lot of shots of Iraqi men beheading people or blowing others up. Help me understand why they behave the way they do. They pray and bomb. And all those Hamas people in Palestine—they wear hoods and carry jambias and automatic rifles and Qur'ans. I tell you, Al, it is all most bewildering for Westerners."

"Carol, do we have to talk about this right now!" Carol was getting on his nerves.

"No, we don't have to talk about this right now. But we do have to talk about it sometime. I know you are under a great deal of pressure, but we do have to talk about it."

"Do you understand that I may not have a long time to live?"

"Al, you're scaring me again. Why don't you have a long time to live? Do you have an incurable disease or something?" Carol knew that wasn't the case, but she wanted him to open up. She wanted him to say anything definite she could count on. "Al, help me help you. You come to us—us Christians: Paul Shapiro and me—when your world is coming apart at the seams. Why couldn't you go to some of your Muslim friends? Could it be that you really don't have any Muslim friends? All your Muslim friends love you so much that they'll cut your throat if you foul up their plans some way. What plans? What exactly are you planning on doing with those things Father Peter stole out of the safe? What are those things for?"

"Carol, I think we're being followed."

Carol whipped her face first to the outside rearview mirror and then to the back windshield. A silver Jaguar was following them, hanging back far enough to avoid looking suspicious but close enough to keep Al's car clearly in sight.

"It's Akbar's company car, but it looks like Ishaq is the driver for today. He sits a bit taller in the driver's seat. But whoever it is, either Akbar or Ishaq, he's definitely on to us."

"Will he try to stop us?"

"Not till he has some idea of where we're going."

"What if we happen to get to the Shapiro cabin and Father Peter is there?"

"I can promise you it will be bad for Father Peter."

Without signaling Al turned onto the exit ramp from the state highway. "In six miles we're going to get off this and go to Cedar Falls. And we're going to make it look like we're having a picnic. You got anything to eat that would make it look like we were planning a picnic?"

"No, Al, no."

Al slowed as they approached a glitzy neon truck stop.

"Look," he said, "there's sub shop in that BP." He turned into the service station. The Jaguar pulled to a stop along the road several hundred yards behind.

Carol and Al got out of their car and walked casually toward the sandwich shop. Carol's heart was racing a million miles per hour, but she reserved the calmest of demeanors. She talked to Al and then took his arm, laughing. "This laugh is for the people in the Jaguar," she said.

"So is this," said Al as he pulled her close and caressed her and then laughed and released her. Then they took each other's hands and walked into the shop. They soon emerged from the sandwich shop and got back into Carol's car, carrying big plastic bags of sandwiches, chips, and super-sized drinks.

They drove to the Cedar Falls exit with the Jaguar still in pursuit, finally locating a picnic area and setting out their lunch. They couldn't see the Jaguar but knew that somewhere Ishaq was watching from the trees.

They ate a very slow lunch, hoping it appeared to be a date. It was still fairly early in the morning for a picnic lunch, but neither of them thought Ishaq would notice their timing. Finally, their slow manner of eating prompted further conversation.

"Al, one thing continually puzzles me about your view of heaven. Christians generally want to go to heaven to see Jesus or their departed loved ones. But it seems like Muslim men want to go to heaven merely to have a sexual orgy. Is it true that Muslim martyrs get a harem of seventy-two virgins just for dying for the Prophet?"

Al nearly choked on his sandwich. "Well, yes. You know Mohammed had at least thirteen wives at various times in his harem. Maybe he felt that men just need sex so badly down here that it has to be a part of things up there."

"Yes, but such an obvious part? Is the sex drive stronger among Muslim men than Christian men? Yet none of the Christian saints ever listed women among their postmortem blessings. Jesus even said that 'in heaven there is no marriage or giving in marriage.'"

"What a dull place is Jesus' heaven!" said Al.

"And what a brothel Mohammed would have it be!"

"I don't like to hear anyone criticize the Prophet!" said Al.

"Oh, but it's all right if Muslims criticize the teachings of Jesus?"

Suddenly Al grew quiet . . . very quiet. Carol felt ashamed for criticizing anyone's religion. She hadn't gone to church regularly in years. What right did she have to criticize anyone else? "Look Al, I'm so sorry. Forgive me."

Al drew her close. "I'm the one who ought to feel sorry. But when you are a Muslim male, it's hard to think in any other way. I've been brought up that way. We study the Qur'an and honor the Prophet from the time we are knee-high to a camel. And the women never correct us. Most of them can't read. Most all Muslims from the Middle East are illiterate, and illiteracy is particularly high among women. So that's how men come to think of themselves as superior to women. And a Muslim woman would never think of interrupting her husband. It's men who know. We men are the active, thinking

Muslim faith. You think the way you do because you were brought up a *Medothist*."

Carol laughed. "The word is *Methodist*."

"Oh, sorry." Al laughed too. "I know you Christians don't talk much about sex, but we Muslim men do. I don't understand how all Christian men can be so dispassionate on the subject. Maybe Muslims aren't so driven about it. Maybe Christians are just passive on the subject."

"Do you remember all those 9/11 terrorists?" asked Carol. "The Feds found pornographic magazines in their apartments when they searched them later. It must be the kind of mentality that goes with believing in an orgy-driven view of heaven. But I just don't get it. Why do Muslim men enter heaven and begin having a long span of sexual indulgence as soon as they enter eternity? Why don't they even stop and talk a bit with Mohammed or the saints or say hello to their mothers first? Why? Why the Muslims? Why is it just so instant with all Muslim men? How is this a spiritual incentive of some sort? Why seventy-two virgins? Is it just for the martyrs or do all men get seventy-two? "

"For my part, thirty-five or so would be enough." Al laughed. Carol didn't.

"Carol," he said, sobering, "I think most Muslim men have a higher reason that motivates them than this. I know I do. I just believe that whatever we long for on earth is somehow what people long for in any heaven. When I told you I wasn't sure I would live much longer, you asked me if I had an incurable disease. In a way I think I do, and my terminal disease is an incurable love for Allah. When I die, I long to live in the bright light of Allah's preeminent presence. To me, this is the reward for all devotion—to spend eternity in the presence of Allah."

"Al, is it possible to become a Muslim—a real Muslim—if you're a woman? I don't see how any woman could stand being viewed as some kind of appendage to her husband's agenda. And Mrs. Zhabahni came into counseling so beat up and broken that Paul and I actually fear for her life. Can any man love a woman and treat her in that manner? I could never be a convert and be seen as he seems to see his wife."

Al seemed excited that she even used the word *convert*. Still, he just could not get Carol to see that she was overreacting to the dominance of men within Islam. Their discussion continued, never finding a course that pleased Carol. Al's insistence on the submission of women in the Islamic faith had no appeal to her at all.

All of this chitchat was occasionally interrupted by their awareness of Ishaq. They both tried to remember that they needed to look like they were on a picnic. At one point as they laughed, their faces almost touched, and Carol felt a great desire to kiss him. But Al turned his head. "We've gone far enough. Even if I were permissive enough to enjoy the moment, Ishaq is old-school Muslim. He believes that kissing is only for married people. Such trivial romancing can lead to other liberties that injure one's relationship with Allah."

"Why all this squeamishness over a kiss from the man who helped bomb the *U.S.S. Cole* and is looking forward to getting all his virgins in eternity?" said Carol. "How do Muslim men get so involved with the little stuff when they completely ignore the bigger stuff?"

Al looked alarmed.

Carol realized there was no way she could have known about the *U.S.S. Cole* except for her acquaintance with Shapiro's client, Clarisse. She hated herself for breaking doctor-client confidentiality.

"How did you know that?" Al demanded then paused. "There's only one way you could have known that, Carol. Zalton was wise to have Clarisse tailed. He needs to deal with that woman before she ruins everything."

It was Carol's turn to be alarmed. "Ruins everything? What's everything, Al?"

Al realized he too had said too much.

"A loud-mouthed woman—that's what Clarisse is. That's what's wrong with women getting messed up in the heavier stuff that men ought to be handling."

Carol clammed up. So did Al. Both saw sides of the other they didn't like. The picnic was over, whether Ishaq was still stalking them or not.

"If Ishaq is still watching," said Al, "we're going to have to give up on looking for the Shapiro cabin for the moment. I must put my hopes of finding Father Peter and the RLDs on hold."

They walked to the car and headed back to the interstate. They saw the silver Jaguar take its ominous place in their rear-view mirror.

CHAPTER 13

The picnic with Al troubled Carol. It wasn't just being pursued by Ishaq; it was the horrible conversation during their pretend picnic that had ended in a kind of Muslim-Christian stalemate. Carol wished so many obstacles weren't in the way of their relationship.

The next morning, she arrived at her desk, still consumed with concerns from Tuesday's picnic trip. She was getting involved in a web of danger from which she was powerless to extricate herself. She was involved with a man who sometimes seemed the hunted and sometimes the hunter. Whatever Al was involved in was bigger than both of them. It was certainly bigger than her hoped-for romance—a romance that seemed to be going nowhere and was likely to get there right on time.

As Carol began to tidy her desk, she saw a note from Rhonda Shapiro, who had filled in for her the previous day.

> *Hope your day was good. I know these must be tough times for you and Al, and while I have no idea what is going on, I sense that both of you are under a great deal of stress. Don't forget to say a little prayer for yourselves. God is always more interested in our troubles than we think he is, and to fail to give him a place in our frenzy is the most serious of mistakes.*
>
> *Love, Rhonda*

Carol put the note aside and for a moment returned to her personal reverie.

Then Clarisse walked into the office.

Her appearance was shocking. Her lip was split and her cheekbone sported a deep cut. Her left eye was swollen shut and her forehead was bruised and cut. Zalton's violence had gotten out of control once again. Carol thought that a man who could do this kind of thing to a woman would be capable of any kind of brutality anywhere in the world. She couldn't help thinking of Al and wondering if he were capable of such a thing.

"Have a seat, Clarisse," said Carol, no longer looking directly at her. "Dr. Shapiro, Clarisse al-Zhabahni is here," she announced on his office line. "Shall I send her in now?"

"Yes," the psychiatrist replied.

Carol stood and opened the doctor's door, and Paul rose to greet them both.

"Coffee for either of you?" asked Carol, starting to close the door behind Clarisse.

Both of them shook their heads, and Carol shut the door.

An intense urge to put a glass to the door and listen to Clarisse's information overcame Carol. She wanted to know about the Arab masculine mystique. She must not hide her love for Al so deeply in her psyche that she closed her eyes to the truth. She must not grow comfortable not knowing what to do and how to deal with the macho Muslim who would treat a woman—a wife—like this.

Inside the psychiatrist's office, Paul Shapiro forced himself to look directly into Clarisse's eyes. Obviously, the head of Spratton Laser Technologies was a violent man, but Paul focused on accepting and showing respect for this battered woman.

At one point in their long, pause-filled conversation, Clarisse became distraught. "Doctor, I can't go back home. Can you help me find a place to live? I hate to ask for help. My husband is a desperate man, and if he knew that you were in any way involved in my disappearance into a safe house, he would come after you with a vengeance. I wouldn't implicate you in all this if I knew any other way to go. But I don't." Clarisse was overcome by sobs.

He handed her a box of tissues and stayed silent while she attempted to control her emotions.

When Clarisse was calmer, she said, "You remember the microfiche, Doctor?"

"I do," he said.

"I believe Zalton is deeply involved—perhaps a part of a terrorist cell that is going to try to bring down this city. It will be like a West Coast 9/11. I have never discussed any of Zalton's plans with him, and I don't know what those plans are, but I do know that something major is up. Someone recently stole some technical detonators from Zalton's corporate safe, and he is fuming to get them back. I know he is stocking up enough plastic explosives to level the Space Needle and several other Seattle landmarks as well. And I believe the whole plot will be launched soon, maybe even opening day of football season. It really doesn't matter what happens to me, but that has to be stopped. Somebody's got to know. I think I should go straight to the police. Is this foolish thinking?"

"Not foolish—maybe noble," said the psychiatrist. "But maybe there's a way to handle this whole thing so that nobody has to die." He paused for a moment. "Clarisse, I'll make a deal with you. You go to the shelter for battered women, and I'll go to the police. Do you have any money with you? You'll need it when you get to the shelter. You don't dare write a check or use a credit card."

"I do have six or eight hundred with me. I could even pick up some more at the ATM if my husband hasn't restricted that part of my life since my last withdrawal."

"Good. Now, there's no time to waste. Leave here and go directly to an ATM and pick up all the cash you can. Then just leave your car on a side street—somewhere, anywhere—and don't let me know where it is. That way, I'll be honestly ignorant in case the police or some of Zalton's goons come around to question me. Take the car keys with you and put them in an envelope. Rhonda can mail them back to your house from any mailbox she passes. Then when Zalton gets them, he can send one of his goons over to pick the car up. I'll call Rhonda and Sister Joanna from the Pathway of Light Cathedral to drive you over to the shelter for battered women that I spoke of."

Clarisse got very quiet.

"Clarisse, I grew up Jewish. But Sister Joanna helped me see that Jesus was also a Jew and that wonderful things happen when our lives come into contact with his. Believe me, he's the person who lifted my needy life out of despair, and I began to live again. Who knows, maybe he's worth a shot for you as well. I want to give you a little book that Rhonda bought me at an antique store."

"But—"

"Believe me, Rhonda won't mind when she knows why I gave it to you. Besides Ronnie is always out antiquing. She'll find me another."

Clarisse opened the book. It was a very small volume: *The Greatest Thing in the World* by Henry Drummond.

"What is the greatest thing in the world?"

"Read, Clarisse, read. There's more light in the world than you would believe possible, especially when you're trapped in the darkness of any really dismal moment."

Clarisse put the volume in her purse. "Thank you, doctor," she said.

"You are most welcome. Now, here's a little envelope. Make it out for mailing the keys and then go to that ATM, get as much as you can, park your car, and mark the location. Do you have a cell phone?"

"Yes, I do."

"Good! Here's my home phone and Ronnie's cell phone. I'll call her right now and tell her to pick up Joanna. They'll both be in Ronnie's car, waiting till you call. Ronnie has one of those electronic guidance systems in her car and will be able to find you wherever you are. Can you handle all of this?"

"Of course, and thank you so very much. But I don't even know your wife. Why would she or Sister Joanna do anything to help me?"

"Well, Ronnie's always ready to help those in need. And Sister Joanna—she talks to Jesus a lot more than the rest of us do and always seems to have the answer to this sort of thing. Do you remember those funny little WWJD bracelets that everybody was wearing for a while—those what-would-Jesus-do bracelets? I think Sister Joanna must have invented those things. She just always seems to know what Jesus would do—at least she has the rest of us believing that she does. We've found that when anyone spends as much time talking to Jesus as Sister Joanna, it's probably wise to listen, so we do. Once you meet her, you'll probably feel the same way. Anyway I'm getting preachy when I need to shut up so you can get on your way."

Clarisse stood. "I don't know how to thank you," she said.

"Just go. And hurry."

She left.

Paul called Joanna and Rhonda.

■ ■ ■

Rhonda had just picked up Joanna when her cell phone rang. "Hello, Rhonda Shapiro here." Her pleasant voice put Clarisse at ease. And she needed to feel at ease. She was talking to a complete stranger upon whom she was very dependent.

"Mrs. Shapiro, I . . ."

"None of that Mrs. Shapiro stuff. My name is Rhonda. I assume you are Mrs. al-Zhabahni. May I call you Clarisse?"

"Yes, please. Thank you for taking the time to help me. I can't tell you what it means."

"Well, it means a lot to me too."

"Is Sister Joanna with you?"

"Yes, she is with me," said Rhonda. "And we're both looking forward to meeting you."

"Thank you so much, Mrs. Shap—, I mean Rhonda. I hope you won't mind that I look a little beat-up. But if it won't be too hard on you to see me, I can tell you I am very much looking forward to seeing you. May I give you my location?"

"Yes, go ahead."

She told Rhonda her location and they hung up. "We'll drop Barney off at the sitter's," Rhonda told Sister Joanna, "then head to the Market District."

Soon Barney was in the sitter's hands, and Rhonda and Joanna were driving toward Clarisse's car on an unmetered street close to the Market District.

When Clarisse appeared behind the car, Rhonda sucked in her breath at Clarisse's beaten face.

"Have mercy," exclaimed Joanna.

Rhonda parked her car, and both of the women got out to greet their new friend.

"Hi, Clarisse, I'm Rhonda. Is it all right if I call you Clarisse?"

"We just went through all that on the phone. Believe me, I'm so grateful to see you, you can call me whatever you'd like." Clarisse couldn't smile, nor could Rhonda and Joanna.

"And I'm Joanna Nickerson."

"It's nice to meet you, Sister Joanna."

"I see Dr. Shapiro has already told you about me."

"Is it OK if I call you Sister Joanna?"

"Sure. Everybody pretty much does. I've been called Sister longer than the oldest nun on the globe."

Finally, they all smiled. Clarisse even laughed a bit but then dissolved into tears. "How can I thank you two? There are angels, I do believe, and sometimes they keep their habitation on Queen Anne Hill."

There was a moment of silence before Joanna spoke again. "Honey, it's gonna take a pound of steak to get the purple shine out of that black eye."

Sister Joanna could tell that she had reminded Clarisse of something she was trying to forget.

"Well, friends," Rhonda said, motioning toward her car, "we'd better get back in the car and drive over to Esther's Refuge. It's an hour past Bellevue and there's always a lot to do to get people signed into the place. Do you have all the clothes you'll need? We can talk on the way. And maybe after we get there too."

"Well," said Joanna, "let's go. I've found that going is the only way to get places." She smiled, patted Clarisse on the arm, and opened the car door for her.

Soon they were driving toward Esther's Refuge. To Clarisse the day seemed to unfold with a kind of hope she hadn't savored in a long time. She kept repeating the words "Esther's Refuge."

Joanna overheard her. "You know," she began, "Esther was a woman of the Bible. She lived in the land of Iran—at least that's what we call it now. Want to know about her?"

"Was she married to a Muslim?" asked Clarisse.

"She lived in Iran a long time before there were Muslims," said Sister Joanna. "But she took a very dangerous stand in a male-dominated world and actually lived to tell about it."

"Well, if she could live through it, maybe I will too." Clarisse was thoughtful. "Did she have a psychiatrist's wife and a preacher to help her through the tough times?" She smiled.

"That's where the stories differ," said Joanna.

"Clarisse," Rhonda broke in, "before you get Joanna into a long and involved Bible story, I would like to tell you a much briefer tale and give you a little present, if you will accept it."

Clarisse found herself gradually warming up to Rhonda. "I can't imagine not accepting any story or gift you would want to give me," she said.

Rhonda could tell Clarisse was open to hearing her story. "Before I ever knew Joanna, our marriage—mine and Paul's—was on the rocks, and I felt like I lived entirely alone. I will never know what it was that actually kept Paul and me together. Both of us had more than once contemplated being unfaithful, and divorce was our constant preoccupation. I still don't know what it was that kept us out of the civil courts. I remember that I was so lonely I thought I would die. Sometimes I even wanted to.

"Then I met an old priest—one of my husband's wacky patients, I thought, and later I met Sister Joanna as well. And this old man of God and this dynamic woman of God seemed to lay aside their differences and speak to us so clearly and truthfully about their faith that I became a Christian. So did Paul. Once Paul and I saw the Lord, we suddenly saw straight. Our marriage was saved, but more than that, we found a way to make a difference in our world. There were plenty of needy people all around us, but we never would have seen them if it hadn't been for the wacky old priest and Sister Joanna."

"It may have been me that was wacky, Rhonda," said Joanna, "but I do know that God can use the craziest people to get some fairly sensible things done."

"True, Joanna, but I wanted Clarisse to see that what happened to me could happen to anybody. Anyway, Clarisse, I want to give you a little book that has meant so much to me."

"You too?'" gasped Clarisse. "I declare, all you and your husband do is to give out books and talk a lot about God." Clarisse pulled the little book out of her purse and handed it to Rhonda.

"*The Greatest Thing in the World*," read Joanna. "Well, that is a good book. I don't wanna give away the plot or anything, but the whole book is about the love of God."

"My book," said Rhonda, "is just a little psalter."

"Does a little pepper mill come with it?" Joanna nudged.

Both of the women laughed, puzzling Clarisse.

"A psalter is a book of psalms," Rhonda explained. "You know, like the Twenty-third Psalm. Read these; I think they might help you find a bit of peace."

"Oh, I could never become a real Christian. Zalton already hates me as just a disinterested secularist. If I actually believed seriously in Jesus, I wouldn't live through the night."

Rhonda gave her the little book of psalms and said, "Well, if you change your mind, give it a read—maybe just two or three psalms a day. It could change your life. It was things like this that changed mine."

"Well," said Clarisse, "if ever a life needed changing, it must be mine."

CHAPTER 14

Gary Jarvis, garbed in his homeless disguise, was searching for more clues to his case. This Saturday morning, July 28, he was approaching Mary Muebles in a Queen Anne park while she was painting a watercolor. For some reason, Gary didn't feel very convincing in his rag-tag costume. He approached Mary, trying to look as slovenly as possible while pushing his shopping cart at a dawdling pace. He noticed her work—it was surprisingly good.

His artistic appreciation came to a sudden halt at her greeting: "Inspector Jarvis, why do you insist on wearing this ridiculous costume?" she said without looking up from her painting. "Everybody on the street knows you're a policeman. There's a string of prostitutes who keep us all informed about who is legit and who isn't."

Mary's frank words knifed into Gary. How long had his cover been blown?

"Well, then," said Gary, momentarily stumped, then switching into his authoritative interrogator's voice, "there is a question I would like to ask you. Why would your name be listed among so many of these new Muslim immigrants in the Scarlet Jihad's directory? This list was open knowledge among those who attended the mosque!"

"If you mean why did Akbar have my number, I'll tell you why! The man is a raving maniac. He wanted to sleep with me. He wants to sleep with anyone wearing a skirt—and I'm not even sure that matters. Tell me this, Inspector Jarvis, did you find the names of any other women besides me? Were any of them ladies of the evening?"

"All of them," Gary admitted.

"Well, there you have it. Yes, he has not called me once but several times."

"How did he call you? You're a street person, aren't you?"

"What's that supposed to mean?"

"Do street people have phones?"

"You'd be surprised how many do. I do. My dad gave me a cell phone and pays the bills on my phone every month."

"Your dad?" asked Gary. "Where does he live?"

"In Santa Barbara. He's a very successful businessman."

"Well, back to how Akbar got your phone number."

"I'm not squeamish, Inspector. I've given my number out freely. Incoming calls give me a little conversation in life. So a lot of people have my number. I don't mind. I'll give it to you, if you want to explain to Melody what I'm doing in your little black book."

"I don't have a little black book!"

"Smart man. Where is Akbar, by the way?"

"I'm not sure. I tried to tail him and find out where he parks that silver Jaguar at night. I can't find him. The man must be holed up somewhere in the city, hid so deep you'd have to pipe air into him to keep him alive."

"An odd statement, Mr. Jarvis. He's a very common Arab— nothing special about Akbar. But that Jaguar of his *is*. The dashboard of that machine looks like the controls of Captain Kirk's *Enterprise*."

"Oh, so you've been in it?"

"Once. He took me to dinner at Ivars. We ate on the nice side of the restaurant—you know, the fifty-dollar side?"

"Never been there. It's too expensive for me. You gotta be a rich street person with a cell phone and maybe even a rich Arab consort to eat in those kinds of places."

Mary Muebles was not amused. "I resent that, Mr. Jarvis. Do you look down on my kind because you think we're poor and can't afford to live in the 'burbs like you and Melody?"

"Well, Mary, you gotta admit you're a step up from the average street person. Do you have to sleep under interstate bridges or ever spend the night at the Salvation Army shelter?"

"No, Mr. Suburbs, my father has bought me one of those month-by-month units in the Comfort 8 Suites. I suppose you don't feel like I oughta be living in such class. I've seen it in the eyes of nearly every Anglo that knows my story. 'You people'—that's what they always call us, 'you people'—ought to keep your place on the streets. It just isn't right for the down-and-out to have it as good as we who live in the 'burbs!'"

Gary was confused. Contrary to how Mary thought he felt, he really didn't mind her being an entrepreneurial, high-living street person, it was just . . . well . . . what was it? She just didn't fit the mode. He couldn't help noticing that it was more than the cell phone and her Comfort 8 Suite. She seemed high-class. Maybe she was trying to cast a spell over any who would receive her in any lesser light. He studied her from head to toe, trying to appear casual as he did so.

"Nice shoes, Mary," he said.

"Gucci's. Anything wrong with that?"

"No, but . . . your father?"

"No, the thrift store."

Gary laughed. She did too. "Look, Inspector, I know you may think I'm extravagant, but if I got a job and settled down, nobody would feel sorry for me and nobody would help me. This way, my dad doesn't get to brag about how well I'm getting on in the corporate world, but he feels responsible for me, so I get a cell phone and a suite. Life is good!"

"Sounds devious, if not dishonest."

"Let him who is without sin cast the first stone. It must be nice being a policeman. They're always out to catch the rest of us in the middle of some sin, with no sins of their own to confess."

"How about if we get off the sin lives of the Seattle Police Department? Would you mind if I take a picture of you and your watercolor?"

"With what? You got a camera on your cell phone?"

"Yes, as a matter of fact, I do. Standard police issue." Gary pulled out his phone and before she could object, he took her picture.

But she did object. "Did you want a picture of my picture or a picture of me? C'mon, Inspector, I wasn't born yesterday. Are you building some kind of file on everybody who's ever ridden in Akbar's Jaguar?"

Gary just smiled and didn't say anything.

Mary Muebles went on, "I'm going to trust that the picture you just took doesn't end up in someone's police file. I'd be upset if I thought for any reason you suspected me of being in business with these guys from Yemen."

"Why would I think that, Mary?"

"I dunno. I think policemen just go around suspecting people way before they work at making friends with them. They first take their pictures, and later they try to work up a relationship with them."

"Now, now, Mary. Don't tell me that, like all beautiful women, you don't enjoy being photographed!" Gary could tell that his obvious attempt at flattery wasn't getting him anywhere, so he set the conversation off in a different direction. "Mary, you must be aware that Akbar and his friends are up to no good. I don't know the exact nature of all they have in mind, but I know they're out to hurt and terrify as many people as they can. And I intend to do everything in my power to stop them. I believe that they are planning to hurt a great many people. In fact, *hurt* is a weak word to describe the monstrosity of their plans."

Mary dipped her watercolor brush into a muddy pigment and then turned away from Gary as if to say his investigative work was of little interest to her.

Gary, feeling himself dismissed, turned to walk away. But Mary laid down her brush and said, "You know, Inspector, you're worrying too much about Akbar and Jibril. I think they're becoming model Christians. They both told me they're going to the Promise Keepers rally in August."

"They're what?"

"They're going to the Promise Keepers rally in August."

"Is this rally going to be held at a local Seattle church?"

"No, of course not. This is a big deal attended by thousands of Christian men from all over America."

"But where would such an event be held?"

"I dunno. Ask Joanna. But I'm pretty sure it's going to be at Qwest Field."

Gary remained silent, digesting this bit of information.

"Still," she went on, "I don't understand why they won't be sitting together."

Gary was puzzled. "Who won't be sitting together?"

"Akbar and Jibril."

"What do you mean?"

"I mean Jibril and Akbar are going to be sitting in two separate seats. Both of them will be sitting forty rows up, but one will be sitting on aisle M and the other on aisle N. It's open seating, but they said that's where they each preferred to sit."

"From what Joanna tells me," she continued, "these Promise Keepers rallies are not all that well attended anymore, but this is a special attempt by the national leadership to reinstate the lost glory that the movement enjoyed in its heyday. She thinks there will be so few there, they will rattle around in the stadium. Still, it's good that Akbar and Jibril have taken an interest in Christianity."

Mary was rattling away. But what she was saying was of momentous interest to Gary. Suddenly Mary stopped, as if aware that her free-flowing chatter was boring Inspector Jarvis. She even seemed to blush a bit at the notion. After a long silence, she suddenly turned back toward her easel. "Excuse me, Mr. Jarvis, I must be boring you."

"Not at all, but thank you for taking the time to speak to me. I'm glad I rated even a few minutes of your time since my undercover garb failed to impress you."

Mary laughed slightly.

Gary smiled, thanked her, and pushing his shopping cart ahead of him, walked away. He walked too fast for a street person. Mary had forced him into a new honesty. He walked like the civil servant he was. If Mary had caught on to his undercover persona, his secret was out. He would have to find another way to tap the homeless for information.

His mind was whirling. Why had Jibril and Akbar suddenly taken such an interest in Christianity? Most of all, why would they want to sit separately in the stadium on aisles M and N and so far up? Odd. They had never been attracted to Christianity at all. And they were more likely to get a nosebleed at that height than they were to get converted.

Once, on Policeman's Appreciation Day, he and Melody had been given free tickets to a Seahawks game, and they had sat in section M, fifty rows up in the stands. They were so far from the action, right underneath the . . . VIP boxes and press cages!

The lights blazed on in Gary's darkened mind. The press boxes and VIP rooms were directly above sections M and N. It was the very place where a well-placed explosive device would bring down the most strategic part of the stadium. It might even bring down the entire western half of the stadium, killing thousands. And all of those would be what the Muslim terrorists would call infidel Christians.

Gary had stumbled on a rationale for what the terrorists were planning. This was jihad carried to the nth degree. Every Muslim grudge would be answered before the gawking eyes of the unbelieving world.

But why did Mary know so much? And how long had she known it? More important, who would be the Promise Keepers' key speakers? The nation's megachurch personalities, the television evangelists, the Christian athletes. Yes. All of the above. And they would all likely be in those VIP areas of the stadium that would be the first to fall. And there would probably be some major political players there . . . like the president of the National Association of Evangelicals. Wait a minute. The president. The president of the United States! He had always considered himself an evangelical. Is it possible that he was going to be there? Had Scarlet Jihad known this all along?

This would be the coup above all coups for the Yemeni desperados. When was this event to take place? He had seen an ad for it on a billboard . . . ah, yes, August 8. Gary felt the desperate frenzy of a trapped mind. His desire to act on this inadvertent hunch given by a homeless woman would be hard for anyone to take seriously. Still Gary took it seriously. He was caught in an ancient struggle between the demon Esau and Jacob, the child of promise. He was a soldier on a battlefield of cosmic struggle, and he was alone. Completely exposed, no armor, no sword. Naked on the day of battle.

"Lord," he suddenly blurted out, "make me strong enough for the struggle ahead. Teach me the faith of David, the way of courage. Give me an outline for the rest of my life. Keep my weaknesses from retreating into cowardice. Shield me from the ego of pretension, for this is not a time to be pretentious, but it is a time to step forward in strength."

His prayer ended without an amen. But then, the best of prayers don't end. They are ongoing conversations with God. Such prayers weave the fabric of the robes of priests and angels. In moments of such desperation, prayers dare not end, for saving the world is a mighty calling that demands constant contact with God. And saving the world raises the oddest crosses in the oddest places—on ancient Easter hilltops or in the stadiums of August.

CHAPTER 15

Al-Haj Sistani also had been sleeping in the back apartment of the Spratton East facility. He was a man whose devotion to Allah had allowed him occasional flights of pain or fear. As of late, he found himself being stalked by both. He couldn't sleep. His strength and self-confidence seemed to be out the window. So he struggled with insomnia when he tried to sleep and terror when he couldn't. His boss sought him to answer questions that he had no reply for. Without those answers, neither he nor his boss would probably live very long.

He had called Carol from time to time but always from phones that could not be traced. He didn't want Carol to know where he was, lest Zalton's goons pump her for information. Still, he had to see her and had asked her to meet him for dinner on Saturday at Jonathan's Catch, a seafood restaurant only a block or so off Puget Sound.

Al arrived first and found a table and was seated where he could keep an eye on the door. He had taken to watching every door in his life. He wasn't sure whether the next person framed in it would be his love or his executioner.

Al had not met Carol since their picnic. Since then, Al had drastically changed his appearance. He had shaved off his thick head of black hair and dense beard and was now completely bald. He had an oversized earring in his left ear. A short-sleeve T-shirt exposed a

Harley Davidson tattoo—all in henna, of course—on one arm. It was hopefully enough to make him appear the very kind of American "beach freak" that Muslim men despised.

Eventually Carol arrived, but not alone. Joanna Nickerson was with her, Al was upset to see. Carol was aware that antipathy existed between the two of them, but Al knew almost instinctively that she had brought Joanna along just to not be alone. Jonathan's Catch was in a shady part of town; still, none of his friends from Yemen had ever been there.

Carol looked around the room for Al, her eyes finally stopping in his corner. He gave a small wave and she rushed over. "Oh, Al," she blurted out on seeing him in his new disguise. "What in the world have you done with the old Al?"

"I'm sorry, Carol, but I had to lose him to stay alive. I've traded him in on a Southern California model just to keep the Arabic Al safely hidden."

They hugged. Joanna simply smiled and nodded a brief hello to the new Al.

"Hello," he replied, feeling a bit strained in her presence. "Let's order up. I'm starved."

"Me too," agreed Carol.

Joanna said nothing for a moment or two as she picked up the menu and thumbed the parchment pages. "Whew!" she said. "This is expensive!"

"Ah, but good," said Al. "I like to come here because there isn't anything with pork on the menu. That's what I like about fish . . . those with scales, that is. You know we Muslims don't eat much catfish or any of those slimier fish. The faith is against it."

"Oooh," said Joanna, "I don't know if I could ever be a good Muslim if you can't have cornbread, hush puppies, and a nice catfish filet sometimes."

"Well, Joanna, you must know Jesus was a Jew and probably wouldn't eat catfish, as Jews don't eat slimy fish either. Wouldn't you want to eat only what Jesus ate?"

Joanna was silent for a moment. "Well, you may be right, but somehow I know Jesus ate a lot of fish and ran around with fishermen all the time. He surely must have had a little hush puppy and catfish once in a while. But then, what do I know? I don't eat with Mohammedans very much. I haven't eaten with you, Mr. al-Haj, since the Sunday we got into a street brawl and you lost the RLDs."

Al stared at her. "How did you know I lost them? Who told you?"

Joanna clammed up, but the silence seemed to roar like a lion even as she shifted in her chair. It had happened just that fast. She had given away too much—maybe even the secret as to who Father Peter's accomplice was on the night of the titanium vault theft.

"Just why don't Mohammedans eat catfish?" Joanna grasped for something to draw their thoughts back to the food. She paused for a moment then said, "And there's something else I want to know: why do you Mohammedans always blow up things?"

"Why do you insist on calling us Mohammedans; we're Muslims. To call a Muslim a Mohammedan is like calling a black person by the *n* word. You wouldn't like it if I called you by the *n* word, would you?"

"No, but I wouldn't go out and blow up a bus if you did it."

"Joanna, please," cautioned Carol. "Look, you two, surely for one meal we can all be pleasant. It was a lovely afternoon, wasn't it?"

"It was," agreed Joanna. "I worked in my flower boxes all afternoon. Did I mention that I was famished?"

"Me too," said Al, managing a smile.

Soon Joanna was enjoying her coconut shrimp and Carol her crab almandine, while Al was eating his grilled mahi-mahi with gusto. Once the edge was off his hunger, he became civil. "Joanna," he said, "I feel bad for losing my temper so often when I'm around you. But there is one thing I gotta confess to you. I do admire the way you lose yourself in little acts of kindness. It seems like we Yemenis want to do dramatic big things. Force governments to their knees. Get even with people with the worst kind of vengeance. And when we can't find some cause to vindicate, some great statement to make, we'll level our rifle barrels at each other. Look at me. I'm having a wonderful meal with two Christian women who just want—it would seem—to enjoy the pleasure of my company.

"The people who I fear most right now are not Christian infidels, but my own people—Yemeni, whose stern inability to forgive the loss of the RLDs will make me pay in blood. If I can't elude them, I'll die. And for what? Not because Allah doesn't like me, but because some guys who say they love Allah have got it in for me. Joanna, I gotta hand it to you. There are a million little acts of love that I have never shown anyone, and yet you go on doing it time after time. You don't want to kill anybody. Sure, you're kind of narrow-minded occasionally, but you don't want to hurt anyone just because they don't think like you."

"Who's narrow-minded? I don't want to blow up people who disagree with me. It's you Mohammedans . . . Muslims . . . who do that. I want everyone to live and be happy." She paused in thought. "Maybe there is a fundamental—no pun intended—difference between Jesus and Mohammed," she said.

"Maybe, but what is that difference?" asked Al.

"Well, Jesus said one thing that Muhammad never said."

"What's that?"

"Love your enemies and pray for them that despitefully use you."

Al sat stunned. Joanna took advantage of his momentary silence.

"You see, Al, there never would have been a 9/11 if eighteen men had been able to love their enemies."

Al remained quiet.

"I most admire Jesus for what he did on the cross, Al, for he prayed, even as he died, 'Father forgive them, for they know not what they do!' Don't you see that even as he died, Jesus did not want to wipe his enemies off the face of the earth? He even told Pontius Pilate that he could call twelve legions of angels to hack his executioners to pieces, but he didn't do it.

"Now, I know you Muslims respect the Crescent of Ramadan, but I'm stuck on the Christian symbol of the cross. Every time I see one, I am reminded that Jesus would rather die than hurt anyone else. He never carried a weapon, and he talked incessantly of the power of love.

"That cross and what it says are why I have lost myself in little acts of kindness. I won't change any political systems in any big acts that get printed in the newspapers. But this I guarantee you: I will die committed to loving God and everyone he loves, and I will never hurt another person for any reason. This is my code. It's ground into the wood and fiber of the cross."

Al had tears in his eyes. Something seemed clear to him. Something new. It was as though the world had suddenly changed.

"Joanna, tell me more about this Jesus."

"He can be your Savior too, Al, by power of sheer desire. All you have to do is to want Christ and you've got him. Come by the soup kitchen next Wednesday, and we will ladle broth into the bowls of those who are hungry. Serving soup is no grand act, unless you live among the hungry. But knowing Christ gets us involved in the simple acts by which the hungry come to understand that God has never enjoyed seeing people go hungry. God always blesses those who follow him into the simple places to keep a simple trust. It's Jesus who wants to feed people and the Prophet who appears to want to blow them up."

The moment Joanna made the last statement, she knew she had botched the conversation. "Listen, Al, I'm so sorry," she said. "One thing is for sure—Jesus isn't insensitive like I just was." She paused again. "Forgive me," she said, looking up at the ceiling of the restaurant, so that it wasn't immediately clear to her companions if she were talking to Jesus or Al. But she seemed so utterly sincere that Al, who at first bristled at her comment, was immediately able to overlook it.

"Joanna," he said, "insensitivity is a common fault. And I know it must appear to Americans that all Islamic people are terrorists. It is not so, I assure you."

"I'll take your word for it, Al," said Joanna. She thought for a moment before she changed the subject. "But, Al, you know that we Christians want to go to heaven—when the time comes, of course, and not a day before—but we're going there to see our Jesus and not to get to lollygag through the golden harem rooms of Allah where the men are lying goggle-eyed in the midst of their seventy-two virgins."

"Joanna, it's only the martyrs who get that many virgins." Al felt suddenly awkward.

"Well, even so, it sounds like the shallowest of reasons for wanting to go to heaven." Joanna wondered where the deep and mystical conversation they had just been enjoying had gone. "So ordinary Muslims don't get the virgins—just the martyrs?" she continued.

"Joanna, please . . . ," begged Carol, anxious to see the conversation head in a friendlier direction.

"It's all right, Carol. She just wants to know."

Joanna nodded.

"I was almost a martyr once—not because I wanted the virgins, but because I believed so much in the Muslim cause. I was once part of a jihad against the French and tried to help blow up the French embassy in Sanaa."

"Was anyone killed?"

"No one of any importance," said Al.

"All people are important," insisted Joanna. "This is my problem with radical Islam. Why do they divide the world into people of importance and people of no importance? For Christians, there are no people who are unimportant. We are bound by the love of Christ to love all people, just like Jesus did."

"What about your enemies?" asked Al.

"Al, we just went through all of that. Jesus said we gotta love them too. The whole point of the Christian faith is that we gotta love everybody God loves, and since he loves the whole world, the boundaries of our love have to reach out to all the people of the earth."

"Now that is radical!" said Al.

"We're supposed to be radical in our love, but not in our politics."

"Well, Joanna, you don't always seem to love me."

Joanna ducked her head. "When I don't act in a loving manner toward you, Al, God isn't pleased with me. I should love you too."

"Even when I blow up things? Not that I have blown up things . . . at least, very many things."

"Even then. Not that I understand your need to blow up things."

"I don't exactly know why we Muslims do it either. I think it's because we feel so oppressed and put down by the West. The West is the mother of all demons to us. Maybe it's because you have demonized us that we reciprocate in kind and demonize you."

"Maybe," she replied.

"Well, maybe I ought to be going," said Al, standing.

"Wait, Al," said Carol. "Could you sit down a moment? There's something I need to ask you."

Al sat.

Carol trembled as she spoke. "Al, I am terrified. I believe I am being followed not by Ishaq but someone else. This person doesn't drive a silver Jaguar but a gold Lexus sedan."

Al looked like he had been punched in the stomach. "Carol, that's what Ishaq drives. That's his car. He had only borrowed Akbar's Jaguar the day he was following us. And you have a right to be afraid. Ishaq's style of terrorism makes Rasul look like a Peace Corps worker."

Carol grew very quiet. So did Joanna.

Al fidgeted in his chair. "Carol, you've got to find somewhere else to stay. Believe me, these guys won't make the same mistake twice." He paused for a moment. "I still have to find the old priest. I've got to get those RLDs back. They blame me because they believe it was my relationship with all of you that led to the break-in at Spratton. It's only a matter of time till they catch me. And when they do, I'll be dead. They already suspect me of being an infidel sympathizer. If they knew I was with two Christians tonight, none of our lives would be worth anything. I'm just grateful they don't know where to find us."

"Al," asked Carol, "just what part does Zalton's wife play in all of this? She comes into the clinic so battered and bruised that I am amazed she is breathing. Thank God, Rhonda Shapiro has befriended her and put her somewhere her husband will never be able to find her."

"Where's that?" asked Al.

"Rhonda put her in a place for battered women, run by the Salvation Army. It's called Esther's Refuge. She should be safe from her husband. Isn't that grotesque that we have to keep a woman safe from her husband?"

There was a brief pause. "Al?" Carol had more questions—and not just about others. "Where are we? You and I? Where is our relationship going?"

"Hey, you two," Joanna interrupted. "I'm still here. If you could save the mushy stuff till you're alone, I'd sure appreciate it."

Carol smiled weakly at Joanna then turned back to Al "I just . . . ," she began. "Our lives are so different, and I don't see how we can ever bring our very separate planets into a common orbit."

"Carol, I just don't see how we are all that different." Al stopped and cleared his throat and, remembering Joanna's presence, returned to the previous conversation. "Tell me more about Rhonda and Clarisse. What right did Rhonda have to befriend her? What business was it of Rhonda's to interfere in their marriage?"

"Al, the woman is being battered almost senseless. Where in this world can she go for any protection? She was doomed until Rhonda 'interfered,' as you put it."

Al-Haj Sistani seemed suddenly to turn the chit-chat in a more urgent direction and ignored her tone. "Just where is this Esther's Refuge?"

Suddenly Carol felt a chill. She had betrayed a confidence that might put Clarisse in jeopardy.

"Why do you want to know? No, I won't tell you. Rhonda did the right thing. Clarisse has got to be kept safe."

"Where is this place? Please tell me, Carol. I can help with this thing!"

"What thing?"

"This thing about keeping Clarisse safe. Why are you suddenly so afraid to trust me? Have I ever given you any reason to doubt me?"

Carol shifted in her chair. "I know you've risked your own life just being our friend, but Clarisse's safety is too important to let the truth be known on a wider basis. Anyway, I don't know exactly where Esther's Refuge is. It's somewhere out past Bellevue. Why?"

"Do you know the actual address?"

"I don't know the address. Why would that be important to you?"

"No reason," said Al. "It's just that . . . Esther's Refuge . . . it must be in the phone book."

"I don't think so, Al. Those places are never listed. Nobody in them would be safe if everyone knew where they were."

"Carol, could you find out where the place is?"

"I probably could; I'm sure Dr. Shapiro knows where it is. He might or might not tell me."

"Well, find out."

"Maybe I will and maybe I won't, but why should you have such an interest in where Clarisse is?"

"I might be able to protect her somehow." Al realized that even to him there was a glaring inconsistency in the statement. "No, Carol, with you I must be completely honest." He paused again to select his words. "Carol, I believe Rhonda might know where the old priest is. If these women are really good friends, she might have told Clarisse. Maybe if I would just hang around Esther's Refuge, I might get out of Clarisse where he is."

"Just how would you go about 'getting it out of her'? That's the oddest thing I've ever heard you say," said Carol.

"It's mighty odd, Al," said Joanna, who had sat quietly as long as she could.

"Look, you two, my life is at stake. Don't you get it? If I can't find those RLDs, I am not going to live very long. Clarisse has got to help me, if she possibly can. I've got to get it out of her."

"Well, Al," Carol stated, "I'm not going to help you. I know your life may be at stake, but what about Clarisse's life? What about Rhonda's life? What about Ishaq's following me the other night?"

Al stood up again. Both Carol and Joanna saw the blood rising in his face. "Who do you people think you are? Do you think that you can play with my life like this? Do you realize you're sentencing me to the firing squad? I want to know where the old man is. I'd prefer you tell me, but if you don't play ball, I'll be forced to pay a call on the good Dr. Shrink myself. He'll tell me where the priest is."

"He won't tell you!" Carol said defiantly.

"Oh, he'll tell me all right. He loves his wife, doesn't he?"

"He does . . . above all else," Carol faltered.

"He'll tell me where Esther's Refuge is, and he'll beg Rhonda to level with me. And if either of them refuse . . ."

Al turned on his heel and stomped out the door of the restaurant.

Carol and Joanna sat stunned.

Joanna said, "We've go to get word to Rhonda. She's in danger, Carol. We've got to help her."

"But I hate to betray Al's confidence."

"Carol! Listen to what you're saying! We're mixed up with some mean people here."

"Not Al!"

"Carol, Al hasn't convinced me that he's batting for our team. I think the man's a kind of double agent. He needs to make up his mind about who he is loyal to. I'm not sure he's as loyal to you as you may think. We both know for sure that he's tied in with all these terrorists who work for Spratton Laser Technologies, and as long as he won't break those ties, he's more a threat to you than a blessing."

Carol didn't like thinking about it. She stood up to go.

"Now, ain't that something?"

"What?"

"Looky there! He left us the check! Now ain't that just like a Muslim terrorist? He eats the most expensive thing on the menu and walks out, leaving us the check. Muslim men may not like infidels, but they don't mind taking advantage of their Christian generosity.

"Carol"—Joanna looked her friend in the face—"I beg you. Wake up and smell the coffee. I know you're carrying a torch for this guy, but he's up to no good. He doesn't love you; he's using you. To him, love and use are the same thing. When you're no longer any use to him, he's going to dump you and run."

Tears formed in Carol's eyes.

Joanna softened her tone a bit. "Mind you, I don't mind payin'," she said, her tone making it clear that she did. "But I think we just been soft-soaped. That's a man who pretends to have some interest in Jesus, but deep down, while he's sweet-talkin' you, he's countin' up those virgins he's gonna get in the great beyond. He'll be having a high Muslim time, while all the Christians who tried to be his friend are a-smoulderin' in the ashes of his treachery."

"Come on, Joanna, maybe he's just a man on the lam. Maybe it's just like he said. Maybe if he doesn't get the goods for his boss, his life is forfeit. Maybe he's just so scared, he'll grasp at any straw that will help him keep alive."

"And maybe he's just too scared to pick up the check. But I tell you, I don't believe a good man gets too scared to pick up the check!"

Irritated, Carol grew quiet. They paid and left the restaurant.

Carol drove Joanna back to her apartment and then headed toward her own condo. It was getting late. Too late to notice that a pair of headlights swung onto the road behind her as she pulled away from Joanna's.

CHAPTER 16

While Carol, Joanna, and Al were dining that night, Paul Shapiro was driving to his Snoqualmie River Road house. He was worn out from a long flight from Boston and a long drive to his home. He had called Rhonda on the way home, and she had promised him that dinner would be waiting for him the moment he walked through the door. She had said the meal would be a special surprise.

He was ready for anything special or surprising. The AMA convention had been more stressful than usual. At the Friday morning session, he had delivered a paper: *The Effects of Debilitating Post-Traumatic Stress on Patient Recovery.* Just the title wearied him. But the speech had gone over well. Two different medical journals were vying to publish his paper.

Still, he was bone tired. He swung his Town Car into his driveway, pushed the button of his garage-door opener, and drove into his parking slot. It felt good to be swallowed up in his private world with the woman he loved and the child he adored. He climbed out of the car, lugging his suitcase to the kitchen entrance.

"Pauly? Is that you?"

"Grr!" he said, dropping his suitcase as he took her in his arms. "What's that I smell coming from the kitchen?"

She didn't really have to tell him. He knew it was Steak Diane, the one dish he would choose if it were his last meal. He smiled and embraced her again, then dragged his suitcase into the kitchen.

Paul was sorry the baby was asleep, and yet grateful as well. He needed some down time to unwind.

They sat down to dinner. With Paul's first bite, he knew the meaning of Eden.

"Ronnie, this is more than wonderful!"

She smiled and they settled down to enjoy the feast and catch up with each other. He was glad that she had gotten Clarisse into Esther's Refuge. She was thrilled that his AMA paper had received so many accolades. They both agreed they were ready for church in the morning.

"It will be good to see Sister Joanna again," Paul said. "I don't know why this simple woman holds such power over me. She isn't educated like all those fancy preachers in downtown Seattle are, but she's so completely transparent that every spark of goodness or prejudice is right up front. All she is you can see at once. And best of all, she spends her entire life helping others. And who's it all for? Jesus. Rhonda, somehow I want to get to where she is. I want everything I do to be for something or someone bigger than I am.

"Joanna never has to practice her humility. She just stands herself up alongside Christ, and there she is, honestly humble with a true perception of herself. She never has to think lowly of herself; she just thinks so highly of Jesus, she always keeps a sense of balance about who she is. She has so much to teach me, I hope I have time to learn it. Anyway, I'm looking forward to hearing her in the morning."

"As am I," Rhonda said. "I called her this morning to report on Clarisse's progress, which—by the way—seems to be wonderful, Pauly. Esther's Refuge was exactly what she needs to make it back to mental and emotional health. In other news, guess what Joanna told me earlier today."

"What?" Paul asked.

Rhonda enjoyed some momentary suspense. "Joanna is having dinner with al-Haj Sistani! In fact, that's where they are right now."

"Well, what in the world could have prompted this? They've never been good friends. Why would she want to have dinner with him?"

"It was Carol's idea. She didn't want to meet Al by herself. It's like she's somehow afraid of him. I'm afraid of him too. I'm afraid of Zalton al-Zhabahni as well. These guys are not normal—they're sociopathic."

Paul nodded but his mind was somewhere else. He was quiet for a moment or so and then turned his attention back to their conversation. "But if Carol's so afraid of Al, why would she agree to see him in the first place? Why would she want to be anywhere near him?"

"I think there are two reasons," Rhonda said, holding up two fingers. "Number one, she's carrying a torch for this guy—worthy or not—and she just doesn't want to give up on him. Number two, while he appears not to care much for Sister Joanna, Carol says she is having quite an impact on him. She thinks if Al and Joanna could just get to know each other, Al might lean more in the direction of Christianity."

Rhonda sighed and continued. "Of course, Carol would like that a lot. But I don't think that's going to happen. More than that, I believe Al and his friends are planning some catastrophe that is going to shock all Seattle and maybe the entire nation. And I don't think Gary Jarvis has thought of a way to foil their plot. I wish he had, but I think he hasn't."

They both sat quietly for a moment.

"Pauly," said Rhonda, "Have you ever told Gary what Clarisse told you about the microfiche on her first visit to your office?"

"Of course not. How did you know about it?"

"Clarisse told me that she told you—just this past week when I drove her up to Esther's Refuge."

Paul looked concerned. "Keep that under your hat, Ronnie," he said sternly. "I don't know what Zalton and his goons have in mind, but if they suspected that you knew . . . ," he trailed off. "Clarisse shouldn't be blabbing that stuff."

"Pauly," Rhonda said firmly, "I think you're wrong. We must not forget that what these guys have in mind is horrendous. You need to square with Gary. Tell him what you know and put the ball in his court. He'll take care of it. But if he doesn't know the whole truth, he won't be able to act on it."

Paul was quiet. He didn't want to get mixed up in a possible terrorism plot. Still, he knew that keeping silent was a coward's way out of the dilemma.

Rhonda had faith in her husband, but not much patience for his desire to delay matters until they sorted themselves out. She believed that in the end, when things got desperate enough, Paul would act. But the time for him to act was sooner, not later. Still, the situation seemed to ask more than Paul could supply. It would take something pretty big to get him involved.

Both of them remained quiet with their thoughts. Then the buzzing of the security system jarred them back to the present.

"Who in the world could that be at this late hour?" asked Rhonda.

Paul ran to the hall and looked at the security display. The front gate had buzzed. The gate camera showed a tall, thin man and a . . .

"Rhonda, it's Father Peter and Kinta!"

The man and his animal companion were standing in the soft rain that had begun to fall. The drops splattered across the lens of the gate camera, slightly blurring their image.

Rhonda was overjoyed, but Paul was as troubled as he was exuberant. Father Peter never just stopped by to visit and pass the time. He always had some gigantic agenda, some unwieldy request that he wanted help with. Paul stood for a moment almost paralyzed, looking at the camera screen.

Rhonda finally sidled up to her husband and jabbed him in the ribs with her elbow. "For goodness' sake, Paul, push the buzzer and unlock the gate."

Paul at last broke his gaze at the small screen and pushed the release button, then watched again as the gate swung open to admit Father Peter and Kinta into their front yard.

Rhonda ran to the front door, opened it, and waved to their visitors, calling, "Father Peter! Kinta! Come on in and make yourselves at home."

She embraced Father Peter as he walked in the door, forgetting that he was not big on embraces, for his thin form was skeletal-hard underneath his warm demeanor.

But Kinta was another matter. He leaped to put his paws on Rhonda's shoulders, sniffing her as she hugged him. Then he dropped to twine around her legs, enjoying Rhonda's vigorous, affectionate petting. It was as though he retained those memories of the woman who had found him in the river and saved his life, even before he had saved hers.

Paul also greeted his guests and invited them in to sit down. Father Peter settled in a chair in the den and Kinta sat down by his side. Then, thinking better of it, Kinta left the old priest's chair and walked across the room to sit down by Rhonda.

Father Peter, sensing Kinta had shifted owners temporarily, took off his dark glasses and said, "Rhonda, would you mind loosening the harness on Kinta's shoulders? I know he gets so tired of the sham. He's a wolf, playing a sentry dog, and as uncomfortable in his "dramatic dog" role as I am being a . . . well, never mind. I am tired of playing a blind priest. But we all wear costumes when we do the work of God, don't we?"

Rhonda leaned down and unbuckled the leather straps of the harness and threw it aside. Kinta looked greatly relieved and gave her hand a sandpapery lick. Father Peter spoke quietly but with a distilled passion in his voice. "I don't have very good news for you two. Paul, the dramatic events you always seek to avoid have come your way once again. The world—as it has been since Adam ate the Macintosh—is falling apart, and you're the man our heavenly Father has to fix things up."

Paul groaned. "Please, Father, this time I want to be a bystander."

"Ah, Paul, how much you misunderstand the business of God. There are no bystanders when God gets involved. God is directing a great drama in a cosmic theater, and everybody's a part of the cast." He paused. "Last time was too small a drama for God. And as the world has gone downhill since then, this time God's into a truly epic pageant with more actors and a bigger finale."

Paul was not excited. "Last time, the production was called *Serial Homicide and Saving the Forest*. What's the bill of fare this time?"

"*Osama's Playmates Visit Seattle*," the priest replied.

Rhonda, who had been stroking Kinta's brown and silver fur, groaned and stopped petting the wolf.

"Please, Father," said Paul, "I don't think I can take anymore of your cosmic adventures. Ronnie and I are just two people who want to live and let live. We'll go to church every Sunday and help everybody we can, but I don't think we have the strength for this play. Can you help us get this across to God? He just asks us for more than we can deliver."

Father Peter grew serious. "Look, you two, nobody wants the huge effort it takes to do the will of God. That's because it is never easy to obey the Almighty. But the world is in peril. And as the angel once said to Mary of Nazareth, 'The power of the Almighty will overshadow you.' Someday you'll look back and say, 'The job ahead of us was never as great as the power behind us,' and 'We wouldn't take anything for our journey now.'"

"Did the angel really say all of that?" asked Paul.

"Just the first part," said Father Peter. "The second part was by Robert Schuller or Joel Osteen, and the last part came from Maya Angelou."

"I can't do this," said Paul. "Please, Father Peter, you know God so much better than the two of us. Please tell him we're on temporary leave from his will." Paul turned frantic. "We can't do it. We won't do it!"

Just as he finished his loud denial, the soft rain that had been falling earlier paused. There was an uncanny stillness. Then the silence was shattered by a clap of thunder. Both Paul and Rhonda shivered a bit.

"Maybe we will do it," said Paul.

"Maybe?" asked Father Peter.

There was another rumble of thunder as an aftershock of the first.

"OK, OK! What's the plan?"

Father Peter leaned toward their voices. "When I took the RLDs, I only postponed the city's ordeal, draining almost a half-million dollars out of the Scarlet Jihad's budget. But there's a new shipment arriving from Yemen through Japan tomorrow. It will be coming in at Sea-Tac on Northwest Airlines flight 101 from Tokyo. Paul, here's the mandate for shipping."

Father Peter pulled a double-folded manila envelope from an inside pocket of his coveralls. "You will go to the cargo deck at ten o'clock—"

"But tomorrow's Sunday, and Ronnie and I were going to go to church. Father, you know what the Good Book says: 'Remember the Sabbath day and keep it holy.'"

"And you haven't been going to church for so long that you've forgotten the Sabbath begins on Friday night and ends on Saturday night."

"Must you be such a legalist? Christians often refer to Sunday as their Sabbath, and I'm a Christian now."

"Could we go on?" said the old priest. "The plane will be at the airport by 10 a.m. You will be too. I'm sorry it's on Sunday. Sing a hymn on your way into the airport if you wish, but be there. When you get to the cargo office, just tell them you're with NSA security. Then give them the manifest in this envelope and tell them you want the package placed in a federal transport case. They will do this with no questions asked."

"But won't one of these terrorists beat me to the punch and ask for the package?" Paul asked hopefully.

"The two in charge of picking up the package are Akbar and the other one."

"What other one?" asked Paul.

"I can't think of his name, but he's one of the two who doesn't own a silver Jaguar. I'm not into fancy cars, but these guys do drive better cars than the average Seattle resident."

"Father Peter, I know this must be terribly important or you wouldn't ask me to do it, but I gotta level with you. These guys don't love only nice cars; they love killing infidels. And when you look up 'infidel' in a Muslim dictionary, there is my picture. I don't want this assignment. I've got back trouble."

"What's wrong with your back?" asked Rhonda, dumbfounded.

"It's got a yellow streak down it. I've always suffered from instant attacks of cowardice. I feel one coming on right now."

"There's nothing to fear," said Father Peter. "The Lord will be with you, and I will take care of Akbar and the other one—"

"Exactly how will you take care of them?"

"I have my ways," said the old priest. "But let's just say they will be temporarily detained. And you will have a few minutes before they are out of detention. Once you have the package, go to your car, which will be a gold Lexus parked on parking level D, zone three. The keys will be in it. The man who would've been driving it will be asleep in a motel room on Queen Anne Hill. Believe me, when he wakes up, he won't call in the theft. And even if he did, by that time you will be on your way to the monastery near Old Bellingham Road. It's a long drive. I want you to hurry and not stop."

"But what if there is more than one gold Lexus in the lot?" Paul protested.

"There won't be. Besides, your Lexus will be open with keys in the ignition and have a little lunch in the front seat. I'll leave a Subway turkey sandwich for you. Want some Lay's baked chips with it? Unsweetened tea or water?"

Paul was dumbfounded at how the old priest seemed to think through every act of his major larceny down to the last detail of a Subway sandwich. "If I'm caught, won't I be arrested?" he asked.

"Of course," said the priest, "so the trick is not to get caught. In this bag"—he pulled out a bulky sack from a large pocket in his coveralls—"is a security guard's costume, right down to the matching ball cap."

Father Peter handed Paul the sack. "Remember this, Dr. Shapiro: we're all actors. Do this job right and the Oscar is yours. The main thing to remember is as soon as you get the package, walk casually away and go directly to your car. Then drive like the dickens—once you're out of the airport, of course—toward Holy Faith Abbey, the Benedictine monastery just off the Old Bellingham Road. Do you know where it is? The brothers there will be expecting you. They'll take over the terrorist's car, and Rhonda can pick you up. Do you know where the monastery is, Rhonda?"

"I've been there," said Rhonda. "I'm not exactly sure about how to get there, but we have a GPS in our car."

Father Peter nodded and stood. "Well, Kinta, are you ready to go now?" He put on his dark glasses. "Rhonda, would you mind putting Kinta's harness back on?"

It was more an order than a question. Rhonda complied and in a moment the wolf was refitted with the harness. Without further ado, the old priest walked toward the door. "*Pax vobiscum,*" he said, exiting.

Once outside the house, he and Kinta seemed to evaporate.

Paul and Rhonda took hold of each other in fear.

"In the name of all the saints," Paul spluttered, "what are we doing obeying a priest in blue coveralls? I'm scared to death to do this, and I'm scared to death not to."

"It's like Joanna said last week in her sermon, Paul."

"What?"

"If a thing is so easy that you don't need God, God isn't behind many of the easy things of our lives. It's only those callings that drive us to the edge of ourselves that God sponsors."

Rhonda knew she was being glib, spouting proverbs from old sermons. Still, both Paul and she knew the importance of their criminal assignment. Father Peter had asked for it. It had to be done. It was for the best. They were sure of it.

CHAPTER 17

It was almost midnight on Saturday, July 28, when Joanna found herself looking over her sermon notes for the next day. She wanted to preach a sermon on grace called "Getting a Better Deal from God Than We Deserve." But she just couldn't make it come together. Her passage was on Naaman the leper from chapter 5 of 2 Kings. The sermon was pretty strong on sin. Joanna was pretty much against sin and felt sure that was God's viewpoint too. But she knew Mary Muebles wouldn't like it. She just liked for Joanna to talk about the love of God and how God created all of us and not to get too tough on anybody's particular sin. But Mary, in Joanna's opinion, was too fond of living in sin to enjoy hearing about it.

She was dozing in and out of consciousness when she thought she heard the door buzzer ring. In the mist that swirled around her, she got up and went to the intercom of her secured living quarters, pushed the button, and said, "Yes?"

"Joanna, it is I, Isaiah."

"Now come on, Ike. It's late!"

"Hast thou no time for the voice of Jehovah? Rememberest thou not what happened to the emissaries of Jehu on the road to Dar Saleem when they refused the prophet at midnight?"

"No, I don't. Is that in the Bible?"

Clearly Isaiah was using his King James voice, and he never used Old English but what he got stern with all he required. "Well, they perished in the Abyss of Achan . . . that's what!" said Isaiah, ignoring her question. "Please let me in or thou too mayest perish in the bottomless abyss of thine own refusals."

Reluctantly Joanna "buzzed him in."

When she opened the door, she groaned. Spotty the owl was on his shoulder. "Did you have to bring him?" asked Joanna. "I thought he was holed up in a pine tree in British Columbia. In my opinion, he only complicates your work. You should leave him where he belongs."

"Now tell me, thou sweet woman of God," Spotty began, "if you think I belong in a pine tree or on the endangered species list? I don't know why our good Lord ever called you to preach. Your lack of love for the likes of me says you're just not qualified. Can't you remember what the psalmist said—'The earth is the Lord's and the fullness thereof, and all that dwells therein'? And this is my planet as well as it is yours and I happen *to dwell therein*. So I'd appreciate it if you'd have a little more respect for me."

"I'll respect you when you learn to open your beak and speak like a . . . a . . . a true Christian spotted owl. Did you ever stop to think why your kind is on the endangered species list? Maybe it's because your kind is so obnoxious."

"Well, I like that! That's the very kind of logic that we owls call people-centrism. It's your infernal tendency to think that your type is superior just because you have bigger brains and opposable thumbs. You're always telling others to practice what they preach, Joanna. Why don't you try practicing what you preach? It would end all your ill feelings of hypocrisy."

Isaiah intervened. "Hey, hey, hey! You two, close thy traps, lest the good Lord come at midnight and blast thee with worm and mildew." He pinched Spotty's beak shut, and Joanna managed to get control of her "people-centrism."

"Now, listen up, Joanna, after your all-star role in the Mount Rainier exodus, it seems to the good Lord that you've been extra bossy. God wants you to know that he will no longer tolerate your glib and arrogant ways. So God wants you to know that he hath many things left for thee to do, and there is a great deal still on thy plate that thou must eat if thine obedience is approved in the high court of God. But thine obedience doth not yet seem complete in the high court of heaven."

"In other words," Spotty butted in, "thou art not yet complete before thy Maker, for thou wilt not do as thou art told. For if thou art self-willed and continuest in thine evil ways, then thou will soon be on the disobedient list and fall into the Abyss of Achan and perish in the fires of thine own self will—"

Once again Isaiah pinched Spotty's sassy little beak closed.

"Joanna, at midnight of this very evening, thou shalt have a visitor. Do all that he asks and thou shalt be blessed by seven legions of angels, but refuse to obey and thou shalt . . . well, there's no use going into all that right now, but it ain't gonna be pleasant!"

With that, Isaiah winked out of her sight. Spotty flew up over the top of her mantle and stuck his rigid little tongue out of his sassy beak. Then he, too, disappeared.

Joanna suddenly found herself fully awake, glad that all she ever had to do to get rid of her two intruders was to come to full consciousness. Still, she was undone by Isaiah's words—particularly the prophecy of being visited by a midnight messenger. She tried to shake it from her mind as she took a final sip of her tepid coffee. Just then, the intercom buzzer rang. But now that she was fully awake, this was the real thing. She walked to her intercom panel.

"Yes?" she said after depressing the button.

"Joanna?"

"Yes. Father Peter?"

"Yes. Who on earth were you expecting—Isaiah?"

"Father, what are you doing here so late on Saturday night?"

"I need to talk to you."

"Whatever for? Father, it's almost midnight. I've got a sermon to preach in the morning. What could you possibly want?"

"Joanna, I'm old and blind, and you're a minister who's supposed to help the old and blind. Could I possibly come in?"

"Have you got your dog with you?"

"If you mean Kinta, he's a wolf. And when you start showing him the respect that you ought to show him, he'll probably warm up to you a little better."

"Father Peter, when you get a dog, people will probably start seeing you as . . . well . . . as more normal. What kind of priest are you that runs around with a wolf and tries to get into women's houses at midnight?"

Suddenly Joanna felt a rush of shame. Why would she leave anyone standing outside? He was right. He was old and blind, and she was a minister. "Come in," she said, pushing the access button.

In a moment the priest and wolf were at her door. She let them in, and Father Peter released the harness on Kinta. The wolf looked at Joanna only an instant, as though seeking permission to be there.

Joanna managed a weak smile at the animal, and Kinta lay down on the carpet a short distance away from them.

"Now, what is it you want? I know you didn't come for tea and sympathy at midnight."

"Joanna, you really aren't working very hard at being civil. Let me get right to the point. I know your little Janie is at a Sunday school sleepover, so there's no real reason you can't help me since her needs are all cared for."

Joanna was quiet for a moment and then said, "Well, I'm sure there is a point to your visit, so it would help if you would get to it."

"Well then, I need your help. And remember this—to fail to help a prophet is to fall into the Abyss of Achan!"

"What made you say that?"

"What?"

"That thing about the Abyss of Achan?"

"I don't know. Why?"

"Oh, I don't know. It's nothing. It's just that I . . . oh, never mind. I'll get my appointment book out and we can talk about scheduling you in for an appointment."

"I don't want to be scheduled in. I need your help right now. Tonight. There's something I have to do and places I have to go, and I very much need your help. I don't drive, you know."

"Well, get a taxi."

"It's too complicated for this. I need you to help me. I need you to drive me."

"Where and why should I?"

"Which question do you want answered first?"

"The second."

"Because the safety of Rhonda and Paul Shapiro and little Barney depend upon whether or not you will help me."

"Why? What kind of trouble are they in?"

"Ah, ah! That's a new question. Let's work on the two that we've got on the table right now or we'll be here the rest of the night," said the old priest.

"Will this take long? I've got a sermon to preach in the morning, and I need a good night's sleep."

"This is yet another question, but the answer to your previous question is no. It will not take long. But you're always telling your congregation to trust God and he will see you through. Why not just practice what you preach?"

"Where did you hear that?"

"I dunno. I think from a spotted owl I used to know."

Joanna felt an immense discomfort in Spotty and Father Peter's shared clichés.

"Anyway, Joanna, since you're always telling others that they ought to trust God, maybe you ought to try doing a little of that yourself. Right now would be a good time to get started doing it."

"I trust God; it's just priests with wolves that I find so hard to obey. They always seem to ask so much more of me than God does."

"If it's easy, Joanna, God hasn't asked it of us. The things God asks of us stretch us to the very limits of our souls."

"So?"

"So, here's the deal: We're gonna call on a couple of Yemeni terrorists."

"Oh no, not that again!"

"We don't have to steal anything from a vault again, and no burkas are required. Deal?"

"Deal! When do we start? And what do you want me to do?"

"Now," Father Peter said simply. "We start now. Get your umbrella. It's starting to rain again."

"Wait a minute. What do you want me to do?"

"That will be revealed to you on a need-to-know basis, and right now you just don't need to know."

■ ■ ■

"Mary, I love you," said Jibril, "and someday when this whole Seattle assignment is over, I'm gonna get you out of this crummy motel and move you to a proper place out in the 'burbs."

Mary smirked. "Yeah, sure. It's a lovely plan, but you are committed to getting your name written up in the Martyrs' Brigade, remember? You better have all the fun you can before you're just too dead to move to the suburbs and have kids and join the PTA. Just pay me the money, Jibril. As long as I'm charging you for the good times, you won't have anything to feel bad about when you're blowing yourself to bits for the sake of Allah."

Mary undid the jeweled combs that held her hair back. It fell in full, dark curls that caressed her naked shoulders and framed her entire torso in an ebony halo.

"Mary, you are truly beautiful!"

"Yeah, yeah, yeah. You always say things like that till you've had your way with me. Then you lay your $500 on the table and kick your way back into your blue jeans, and the romance is over till you bring me another $500 and tell me how beautiful I am. This is, however, the first time you've brought up buying me a house in the suburbs."

Jibril walked over to her and took her in his arms and held her. Then he kissed her—at first tentatively and then recklessly. "I do love you," said Jibril.

When their passion had subsided, Jibril reached over to his shirt that was hanging on the back of a chair. "Here," he said. He handed her a small leather folder.

"What's this?" she asked, opening the folder.

"It's a passbook savings account."

"But it has my name on it."

"That's right."

"And it's for $100,000."

"That's right too."

"What are you saying?"

"Mary, I've probably got no more than two or three weeks to live. When the stadium blows, I'll be gone too. I want you to have this. I can't stand the thought of never seeing you again, but even worse is the thought of your not having a way to live when I'm gone. Mary, I don't know what love is, exactly, but I believe with all my heart that I love you. And each time I see you, I realize that one of the reasons I volunteered to be a martyr was that I had no real reason to live. Now I don't know. I want to live. I think I want to live as much as I used to want to die. Mary, maybe we could run away."

"But Ishaq and all his boys in scarlet head rags would hunt you down. They'd hunt both of us down. We have no place to run, no place to hide. Just let me be your hooker, if you really love me. As long as you're paying for love one night at a time, Ishaq will leave me alone at least."

"Maybe, but if I could get out of this trap, I would. And if I die, I want you to have all the money in the passbook account."

"We'll talk about it in the morning."

They kissed again, and Jibril, instead of leaving his money and running as he usually did, slept snuggled against Mary's warm body, feeling her hair flowing all around them on the pillow.

■ ■ ■

Joanna and Father Peter were in Joanna's car, headed south on the interstate toward the Comfort 8 Suites. Joanna began to get a glimpse of the priest's plan: they were obviously going to call on Mary Muebles.

Joanna turned her old car into the parking lot of the motel and switched off the headlights. At Father Peter's request, she stepped out and silently closed the car door. Kinta preceded them toward the hotel.

"Got any ideas as to how you're going to get past the night clerk with your wolf? They don't allow pets in these Comfort 8 Suites, you know."

"Just leave it to me."

As the three of them entered the motel lobby, the night clerk appeared not to see them. It was as if they didn't exist.

When they entered the hallway, Father Peter whispered, "It's room 117, Joanna. Here's the key card." He pulled the room card out of his pocket.

"Well, I'll be!"

"You'll be what?" asked Father Peter. "Shh! Stay focused. Here's a bag, complete with eye holes. Put it over your head."

"Put a bag over your own head!"

"I will. I've got one too," said Father Peter. "Only mine doesn't need eye holes. Still, it has to have them just the same, so everybody thinks I've got good working eyes. Here's something else you'll need. It's the new mace—instant paralysis in an aerosol can. Just be sure you have the nozzle pointing away from you."

Joanna pulled the bag over her head and slipped the key card quietly through the slot to 117. The door opened as far as the chain allowed.

"Here," said Father Peter, handing her a pair of steel cutters. Dutifully, she clipped the chain. When both of them were in the room, Father Peter slammed the door shut behind them and turned on the lights.

"What the—!" said Jibril, sitting straight up in the bed, trying to rub the bright light from his eyes. Mary Muebles also sat upright and issued a weak scream as Joanna approached her side of the bed.

Joanna forgot herself. "Mary, I'm so disappointed in you. But this is what you get for living in sin!" She pushed the nozzle and a quick fog of paralysis knocked Mary back on her pillow in silence.

Jibril reached for the gun beside his bed, but just as he caught it, Kinta sprang and clamped down on his wrist with a feral growl.

"Ow!" Jibril screamed, dropping the gun.

By this time Joanna had leaned across the inert body of Mary Muebles. She promptly shot a volley of the fog directly into Jibril's face. He, too, fell back in the bed, unconscious.

"That's for 9/11," Joanna announced. "It's about time the common folk got a chance to get back at you for your atrocities." She gave him a little extra squirt. "This is for all the friends who died." She gave him one more squirt. "And this is for United flight 93."

"Joanna, stop it! You're gonna run out of mace," said Father Peter. "Stay focused."

"And you, Mary," said Joanna to her comatose friend. "I can't believe you parade around as some kind of Christian seeker, and here you are sleeping with a terrorist. They used to stone folks like you. I wouldn't stone you 'cause I believe in grace, but I'd sure pelt you with handfuls of pebbles till you sat down and read the Bible for one solid month."

"Come on, Joanna. It doesn't do much good to put a bag over your head if you're going to preach them a sermon before you mace them—and they can't hear you after you mace them. Now stay focused. I assume these two are lying on their backs. Roll them over and handcuff them behind their backs." He handed her two sets of cuffs.

"Where do you get all this stuff?"

"I've got my places for getting stuff."

"Anything else?"

"Get Jibril's gun and car keys. That'll keep him from leaving the hotel and messing up the works at the airport in the morning."

"What works at the airport?"

"That's more than you need to know. Come on, we need to pick up his gold Lexus."

"A terrorist with a gold Lexus?"

Father Peter nodded.

"We're gonna steal it?"

"You're gonna steal it."

"Could we then go back by my place so I can pick up a few things for my extended stay in jail?"

"Well, you won't be stealing it exactly. You'll just be leaving it at the airport. And don't worry. Jibril won't report a thing. With the plans he has in mind, he wouldn't dare involve the police just to report a stolen car. C'mon, Kinta."

Kinta came to his hand, and all three of them left room 117.

They found Jibril's car and drove toward the airport. Joanna was amazed at how easy it was to get into grand theft auto.

Everything seemed to be going according to plan, until . . . "My wallet," blurted Joanna. "It's gone. I must have dropped it in Mary's hotel room."

"That's bad, Joanna, real bad," said Father Peter.

"We'd best go back and get it. They're probably still asleep now."

"Not likely. They're probably coming around. But they can't go anywhere, and they're probably not going to make much of a fuss until the hotel maids find them. And we for sure can't afford to stop this night's business. Paul Shapiro's life demands that we keep on track and not let ourselves get diverted. But when they find your wallet, you'll have the whole Yemeni goon squad after you. I guess I don't need to remind you that you're both a woman and an infidel. Do you want to know what they do to infidels in Yemen when they are caught in a crime?"

Joanna didn't want to know.

CHAPTER 18

R honda laughed as she drove up to the Sea-Tac airport. Barney was asleep in his infant seat in the back. Paul sat rigid in the passenger side of the front seat. "I don't want to discourage you by laughing at you," said Rhonda, "but I can't help it. It's mostly your costume, Paul. It's not really very believable. And the low-rider ball cap, the dark glasses, that paste-on beard—anyone could tell at a glance it's all fake! I just hope it's good enough to throw a kink into those security cameras."

Rhonda kissed Paul good-bye as she parked in front of the air-port cargo building. She had gone there a few times to pick up phar-maceutical samples Paul had ordered.

"Ronnie, I love you!" said Paul, still sitting in the front seat, para-lyzed by the fear.

"I love you too," she said.

"Am I doing the right thing? Are we?"

"Paul, it must be right. I hate missing church, though. Whatever will we tell Joanna? You know how she feels about Sunday absenteeism."

"Ronnie, I'm about to set off on a huge case of larceny. If I get caught, I'll be attending prison chapels for years to come. You can comfort her with that. Now I'm nothing but a common car thief."

"Wrong! You're an uncommon, very special car thief, and very much loved by an accomplice who's aiding and abetting your every crime. Really, when I think about you being all mixed up with dangerous terrorists, I'm so proud."

Paul laughed nervously. "I'm sure that's what Mother Capone said when little Al graduated from reform school."

Rhonda smiled. "I know this is eating you alive, but look at it this way. This is important. Someday when we know the whole story, we will know just how important it all was. Joanna will understand, at least later. When she knows the whole story some day, we'll all laugh about this. We'll probably brag about it every time we go to church."

"I don't want to talk about church right now."

"Oh, all right, honey. I'll meet you at the monastery. I'll be wearing dark glasses and reading *Fortune 500* magazine." Rhonda turned up her collar and attempted to look mysterious.

She could tell Paul felt the mood was too heavy for such a playful gesture. Still, as nervous as he was, Paul couldn't help but laugh at her odd antic.

Someone behind them in the parking lane began yelling out the window of his car. "Hey, buddy! Keep it moving. If you gotta talk, there's a Starbucks inside the terminal. You can jaw in there!" He honked a long, loud honk.

Paul kissed Rhonda and stepped out of the car. She drove off.

"About time, Romeo!" shouted the unhappy honker.

Paul stared down at his Rolex Chronometer—Sunday, July 29. He felt odd in his blue security outfit. His thick mop of red hair poked out from under his cap. His dark glasses, red moustache, and cap brim almost entirely hid the recognizable part of his face. But the watch was his one giveaway. He rebuked himself for wearing his Rolex. What security officer would be able to afford one? Yet to take it off was even more of a giveaway, for what security officer would go without a watch? He was all nerves under a very quiet and practiced exterior.

He walked up to the receiving window, surprised at being the only one in line. The woman behind the grating smiled at him, and he smiled back. "Good morning, madam!" said Paul too loudly and quickly, or so it seemed to him.

"Good morning, sir. What can I do to help you?"

"Is Northwest 101 in yet?

"It is. It was twenty minutes early. All the specialty orders have just now arrived."

"Good," said Paul, pushing the manila envelope through the slot at the bottom of the grating.

"Whoa!" she said. "Insured for a half-million. Must be South African gold you're picking up. Tokyo moves a lot of their West Coast metal right through this little window."

Paul didn't reply. He did manage another forced smile. His paste-on beard was too stiff to move as freely as his smile seemed to mandate.

"I'll be right back," said the chatty attendant. She left Paul standing alone at the window. He was happy to be alone. While he hated all racial profiling, he kept looking for anyone Arabic to butt into the cargo disbursement office. But to his great relief, no one came in.

In a moment, the attendant was back with a cubical package. "Heavy," she said. "But not heavy enough for gold. You must be a dealer in Cartier watches."

Paul took the package, smiled, and turned to leave.

"Hey, wait a minute. You gotta sign this manifest," said the woman. "No signee paper, no gettee box." She laughed.

Paul froze. How should he sign for the package?

He picked up the pen on the window ledge and scratched the name of Rev. Peter Galonka. He was thinking of Father Peter. He had no idea Father Peter even had a last name.

"Polish security man, huh?" said the woman as Paul pushed the manifest back through the slot in the window.

"Got any identification? On manifests of over $100,000, we have to see some identification."

Paul's mind flew in panic over the next step he would have to take. There was no way out. This was one contingency Father Peter forgot to mention. What in the world was he to do? He kept his calm exterior pretty well for an actor who had not anticipated the full extent of keeping his role and costume authentic. Still, he did have the box. And the clerk had the manifest. He took the only course open to him. He ignored her request for his identification. He rudely and briskly turned on his heel and literally sprinted from the office.

"Hey!" he heard the woman calling after him. "Hey! Get back here, or we're both in a world of trouble! Get back here right now, or I'm calling our own corporate security and you'll be in the slammer." Her hand reached for the phone, but Paul was gone.

Once in the narrow corridor to the parking garage, he broke into a full run. He tossed his jacket and oversized cap in a corridor trash can as he ran. He peeled off his dark glasses and fake beard and crammed them into his pocket. His red wig also came off and was jammed in his pocket as well. He felt like Clark Kent as he ripped off his coveralls and threw them to the floor.

Soon Paul was in the parking garage. "Oh, God," he prayed, "please let that gold Lexus be where it's supposed to be."

Still clinging to his box, Paul dashed up two flights of stairs and onto level D. He quickly found zone three. There were only three cars up there.

"Thank you, Jesus! Hallelujah!" said Paul, sounding like Sister Joanna at a sermon's high point. "There it is!"

The motor was even running.

Paul walked up to the beautiful car and opened the unlocked door. There on the front seat was a Subway sandwich with a package of Lay's baked chips and a tall cup in the beverage holder. Paul slid into the seat and took a drink of the beverage—unsweetened iced tea with lemon.

Paul inwardly exulted that Father Peter made car theft easy. Paul shifted into drive, picked up the parking voucher from the dash, and drove to the parking attendant's booth. The attendant took his $3 and set him free. There were no more stops. He hit the interstate for his trip toward the monastery.

He was barely on the interstate when he decided to listen to the radio. He turned almost immediately to a religious network station. Joel Osteen or one of his disciples was preaching a sermon called "God Intended You for Good." It made Paul feel bad listening to

Osteen tell him how character was essential for the Christian life. Fortunately Joel didn't even bring up sin like Sister Joanna usually did. Paul was glad. He felt bad enough just stealing a car—even from a terrorist. He turned off the radio and was glad to be free of radio preachers. He didn't know whether it was worse to steal cars or beg for money.

He was surprised when his cell phone rang. He heard Rhonda's voice. "Paul, darling, I'm going to church. Is that all right? It just struck me that if we're going into grand theft auto, I probably ought to go to church to look respectable. Besides, Joanna will be expecting us. Is that OK with you?"

"Sure, I'll just hang out with the monks till you get there. Hopefully they'll be all through with mass, and we can all hang out and laugh and make wine or cheese together."

"Pauly, if you're sure it's all right, I'll see you in a couple of hours—sooner if need be. I'll put my cell phone on vibrate so you can ring me even during the service if you need to."

"I love you just as much as I did before I quit asking, 'What Would Jesus Do?' and started asking, 'What Would Bonnie and Clyde Do?'"

"I love you, too, Pauly."

They both hung up and Paul continued driving.

His Subway sandwich was long gone when he finally reached Old Bellingham Road and headed directly for the Holy Faith Abbey. When he drove onto the grounds, he saw Father Peter and Kinta and a dark-haired, cheerful brother.

Paul pulled the Lexus to a stop, stepped out of the car, and called out, "Hello, Father!"

"Hello there, my good friend," said Father Peter. "I want you to meet Brother Lawrence, or Hermano Lorenzo, as he's most commonly known around here."

"Hello," said Brother Lawrence shyly. "I am glad to meet you. You can call me Ned Baker, if it's easier on you. That's my civilian name. We all have to take a saint's name when we enter the order, so I chose Lawrence as my Benedictine name. I am Hispanic, but many people tell me they think I'm from the Middle East. Peter tells

me you are a Jew, and I don't want to make you feel as though you
have to get into all our Benedictine ways and Catholic lore."

"No, Brother Lawrence is fine with me. I'm Paul."

"Is Brother Paul OK?"

"It's fine, but so is just plain Paul."

"Did you get the shipment of RLDs?" Brother Lawrence asked.

"I got the box, if that's what you mean," said Paul.

"Let me see," said the Benedictine.

Paul removed the airfreight box. Eagerly the Benedictine brother
took it from him and slit it open with his pocketknife. His face broke
into a broad smile.

"Ah," he said. "You pulled it off, Peter. The RLDs just keep stack-
ing up here at Holy Faith Abbey. I'll put these with the others."

"The others?" asked Paul.

"Yes, we've also got those that Father Peter stole earlier."

"I can't believe it!" Paul gasped. "Father Peter? You stole too?"

The old priest didn't reply.

"This old monastery may not look like much, but we've got a
million dollars worth of Yemeni detonators," said Brother Lawrence.
"I can only guess that when Jibril gets out of the cuffs and finds that
both his Lexus and the detonators are gone, there will be war within
the Arabian mafia. Paul, hopefully they won't find out you had a
part in all of this. Nonetheless, both you and Rhonda need to be
careful. Father Peter tells me that Rhonda has secreted Clarisse in a
refuge. Her husband isn't going to look with favor on the Shapiros
when he makes the connection, and he surely will."

Paul didn't like thinking about Zalton. He felt a strong pang of
concern for Rhonda in particular.

"I know you both are men of the cloth, and I've only lately come
to any sort of faith myself, but would you keep Ronnie and me in
your prayers? I don't believe that I could face another day of life
without her."

"Now, now," said Brother Lawrence. "If you find yourself in any
danger, you and Ronnie come on up to the abbey here. We've forty-
three monks and a pretty mean janitor, and while we are committed
to peace, we're a federation of fellow protectionists." He smiled. "Of

course, we've never had to stand up to Muslim terrorists, but we've had to put up with some unrepentant Catholics here and there, and we can do a lot of good without being really bad."

Paul wasn't sure exactly what Brother Lawrence meant but found solace in knowing there were forty-three monks who would pledge themselves to his safety. "Thank you, Brother Lawrence," he said. "If life should come to this extreme, it would be nice to know you're in the wings—no pun intended."

"Come in for a little lunch while you wait for your wife to come. The food here is tolerable on Sundays," said Brother Lawrence. "The men of the abbey all know about the terrorist plot centered in Spratton Laser Technologies. And we're determined to help Father Peter stop the bloodshed before it happens. He may be blind, but he sees so much farther than the rest of us."

"Is Father Peter a Benedictine, Brother Lawrence?" asked Paul.

Father Peter leaned in to hear how the monk would explain his identity.

"Well, Father Peter is the sole North American member of his own order. There is one on every continent, so there are seven in all. They are all called the Monks of Lobos Rey."

"Is this an accepted Catholic order?" asked Paul.

"These monks are not actually Catholic, but they're Catholic sympathizers," said Brother Lawrence.

"Why won't the church recognize his order?"

"Oh, the church would take them in; it's the priests themselves. They love the Catholic church, but they have a fondness for international matters that most of the other Catholic orders believe is *contra natura*."

"How are they against nature?" asked Paul, glad his rudimentary knowledge of Latin was good enough to serve.

"Well," said the monk, "each of the seven brothers keeps an animal. Brother Timothy in Africa keeps a lion. Brother John of India, a tiger. And so it goes. And of course, Father Peter keeps Kinta, the wolf, for whom the whole order is named."

"The ways of the wolf are strange and wonderful," added Father Peter. "He is the noble creature who, hunted to the edge of extinction, lives on as a kind of symbol that the world might be better served by believing that all life is sacred." The priest paused. "I do not believe that all animals will populate heaven, but I do believe that when God finished creating the universe on day six, he looked around and saw that it was good—just as he made it. And life was exactly what he intended it to be.

"And when Kinta walks through Seattle at noonday, people look at the priest and the wolf in wonder. They realize that the world was somehow made for both of us. And now Kinta serves his old blind master. Kinta is my eyes. He stands for all that ought to be right in the world. He is unafraid of the terror that preys by day nor the arrow that flies at night. A Muslim terrorist is for him only another soul in search of significance. And he travels with me to promote the greatest good that Christ, our unseen master, would lead us to— the epicenter of love. All who would kill any of those whom Christ loves need to be prevented, which is why we steal the detonators from Spratton. We are only pulling fangs from the serpents of Eden. That is all. We don't want to hurt anyone; we want only to be sure that no one anywhere willfully hurts anyone else."

"It is rather like the seven Monks of Lobos Rey are the continental guardians of our vast parishes," Brother Lawrence added. "It was a nightmare for Timothy of Africa during the purge of Darfur, I can tell you. But always the great lion, Kuwami, was by his side while his war for human redemption was being waged."

He looked at Father Peter, silent by his side. "Come," said Brother Lawrence to Paul. "Let us go join the brothers for black bread and broth."

Paul, while walking with the two men and the wolf, was lost in his thoughts. With an odd new understanding of the wideness of God's love over all creation, he had come at last to understand what he wished he had known when Father Peter had first appeared at his clinic: the world is bigger than he had imagined. This far-seeing blind man knew the world he guarded. He was incapable of theft. He merely "requisitioned" what God needed to keep the people that he loved safe. He would return the RLDs and the Lexus when the time was right. And if he could, he would requisition God's holy sun to drive the shadows of bloodshed from Seattle. That was the glorious calling of the Monks of Lobos Rey. They served the God of what needed to be done and reveled in the doing of it.

"Coming, Paul?" asked Brother Lawrence, noticing that Paul had stopped walking in his reverie.

Paul snapped out of his stupor. He felt renewed by the knowledge of the activities of a monk who served the Order of Lobos Rey.

■ ■ ■

Back in Seattle, the housekeeping maid discovered two handcuffed guests in room 117.

When the police arrived, Mary and Jibril were set free, as they had done no crime. Still, both of their names were written down in a police report that would be filed at headquarters.

Mary and Jibril had stuck with a manufactured story that some thugs had broken into their room and cuffed them to the bedposts. Their story seemed credible to the police, except that Jibril was carrying a great deal of money in U.S. hundred dollar bills, plus a large wad of Yemeni bills.

"How did they happen to miss all this money if they broke into your room to rob you?" asked one of the policemen.

"They missed it. I had stuck it between the box springs and the mattress, and they just plain missed it."

"Lucky you," said the policeman, eyeing him.

"Yeah, lucky me," said Jibril.

"We found this in the bed sheets," said the policeman, showing Joanna's wallet to Jibril. "Did you steal this or how did you come by it?"

"Steal?" Jibril scoffed. "No. This belongs to a close friend of ours. He was visiting us last night before the marauders broke into our room. He must have left it. If you don't mind, officer, I'd like to return it to him. I know he must be frantic, wondering where it went."

The investigating policeman, still looking at Jibril, opened the wallet. "Would you mind telling me the name on this driver's license?"

Jibril's dark skin reddened. He was silent.

"That's what I thought!" said the officer. "You have no idea whose wallet this is, but it clearly was dropped by someone who had an agenda for you—maybe both of you. By the way, your close friend is not a man. Strange your friend could be so close and yet never disclose their sex!"

Mary Muebles caught a glimpse of the photo on the driver's license. Joanna. She hated for Jibril to find out that the hooded person who had broken into the room was Joanna, but she was trapped between the policeman's interrogation and her desire to hide the truth from Jibril. Fear of the police won. "The woman's name is Joanna Nickerson," said Mary reluctantly. "She's the pastor at the Pathway of Light Cathedral in downtown Seattle. We've been friends for a long time. Jibril doesn't know her well because they really haven't known each other all that long. But Joanna and I are very close."

"Very well," said the investigator, "there isn't much money in it, so you can return the wallet to your friend."

Once the police were gone, Jibril discovered his gold Lexus wasn't where he left it. He knew it had been stolen by Joanna Nickerson and her accomplice, whoever he was. Still, he dare not report the theft. He had already come closer to the police than he should have, given all that he had in mind for Scarlet Jihad. But he knew instinctively that a close circle of infidel women was blocking his plans. Unless those women were stopped, Scarlet Jihad had no future, and Seattle might escape the judgment Allah longed to visit upon it.

His anger flared, and he determined he would get even with Joanna at the first light of dawn. But Joanna was spared his immediate revenge. For when morning came, Jibril woke up with the flu—and the fever and nausea drained the fire from his vengeance for a couple of days.

CHAPTER 19

On Wednesday night, August 1, Joanna Nickerson held a very special banquet at the church to recognize the kitchen crew who offered their time serving meals to the city's poor. Among the honorees at the happy occasion were Mary Muebles, Rhonda Shapiro, Carol Jones, and Wanda Williams.

Wanda, who had just returned from a few days of rehab at the Salvation Army's Adult Recovery Center, was still a little disoriented from her most recent bender.

"You know, I think the president of Iran, President Abu-Mack-Mah-Tinnies-Dad," announced Wanda, horribly mangling his name, "could be the next Antichrist. At our last coven, me and some other witches mixed some tannis root and oleo and smeared it on his picture and pronounced a curse on his life, but I noticed the next night he was still on television—he was quite alive! Maybe we should have used less tannis root and more oleo."

Mary Muebles knew Wanda was confused. "Don't you mean tannis root and oleander—not oleo, Wanda?"

"Oh, yeah . . . oleander, not oleo . . . I thought it was awfully greasy."

"Well, it's a lovely thought that you could stop international terror with a stick of oleo," said Rhonda. Wanda seemed not to know that oleo was an old margarine that had surrendered to other swankier name brands. "But Wanda, are you sure these witches' covens are the best way to spend your time?"

"I think they're wonderful, and they dovetail so well with my *Left Behind* book. I found a reference to nuclear war on page 143 of *Left Behind*, and that's only 532 numbers off of 666. And you know what that means."

"It means you should read a little more of Jan Karon and a little less of whoever writes those books," Rhonda replied.

"Rhonda," said Wanda, wide-eyed in fear, "it's just that kind of liberal thinking that will trick you into worshipping the Beast . . . and then you'll wish you had listened to old Wanda.

"Anyhow," said Wanda, smiling broadly so that her snaggled teeth were on full display, "someday I believe when I get better at witchery I can at least give these old Iranian Antichrists a backache."

"But how would a backache stop their tyranny?" asked Rhonda.

"Well, it might not stop them, but it would sure slow them down. All I have to do is get my tannis root and oleo recipe right."

"Don't you mean oleander, dear?" asked Rhonda.

"All right, ladies," said Joanna, "let's talk about something else. How's Barney doing, Rhonda?"

The conversation turned to attendees' families as the women finished their feast. Eventually, Joanna invited them into the pastor's small study for tea, and the ladies continued to converse, until, when it was quite late, someone knocked on her door and entered—al-Haj Sistani.

Although put off by his abrupt entrance to the private event, Joanna was determined to be more civil to him than she had been at Jonathan's Catch.

Evidently, Al had similar intentions. "Hi, Joanna!" said Al, greeting her with an almost too friendly manner.

Joanna didn't like anyone to come on so familiarly, especially when she had a shaky friendship with him to begin with. She stood and positioned herself like a linebacker and said very distinctly, "That's *Sister* Joanna to you!"

"Very well," he said. "But in the name of Allah, I come in peace."

Joanna thawed a bit, smiled, and reminded herself to have manners. "Please have a seat, Al."

Her visitor smiled weakly, uncertain of what the hostess might do or say next. But he did take a chair directly opposite her in her pastor's study. The remaining attendees, with a curious look at Al, bade them both goodnight and left the office.

Al dove right in. "Sister Joanna, I want to ask you to help me talk to Carol and help her overcome her reluctance to accept me. I really love her, but I just can't seem to get our relationship off on good, solid footing. Could you possibly help me talk Carol into becoming a Muslim? She's just got to do it because I am in love with her and I can't marry her as she is."

Al had put the ball in Joanna's court. He knew of Carol's high regard for Joanna and if anyone could influence Carol toward marriage it was her.

"And why not?"

"Because I can't marry a Christian."

Joanna bristled. "And just what's wrong with marrying a Christian?"

"Well, they are just not Muslims. And as you know, it is a sin to marry outside the true faith."

Joanna remained defensive. "Let me ask you this, Al, what right do you have to demand that Carol become a Muslim?" Joanna paused, gathering her faculties for a formidable volley of logic. "Al, I wonder . . . have you ever considered trusting Jesus as your Savior? You know all of this mental anguish you've been going through could be solved if you'd just try Christ. After all, Islam isn't much of a woman's religion. A Christian woman who joins your faith has to give up both her femininity as well as her Christianity."

"Now, Joanna, we've been through all of this before. What you're asking of me is very hard."

"No harder for you than it would be for Carol."

"I think you're wrong there. It would be harder for me to convert. Islam is simply more ethnic than Christianity. All kinds and colors of people are Christian, but if you're Arab, you're Muslim.

It's like being a Jew—your race and religion are pretty much the same thing. Besides, what's so noble about Jesus?"

"Al, we've been through this before. Jesus is love. Jesus is out to renovate life but on terms that are good for the whole world. You can have a better life here and now, and you go to heaven for all the right reasons. Your life here and now and your eternity match. Both heaven and the here and now are all about being with Jesus. The Muslim heaven is a man's heaven for a man's personal indulgence. Can't you see that? We Christians want a foreverness that's about being with Christ. But a Muslim man wants to go to heaven to get a harem or enlarge the one he already has. Can you see how demeaning that is to any woman who would ever want to consider your faith? You don't even feel the same way about Mohammed that we feel about Jesus. For us, Christ is not just the founder of a masculine enterprise; he is the epitome of all grace and human redemption."

"Well, eternity's all very fine for there-and-then, but how about the here-and-now? I want Carol *now,* and I want her *here!*"

"Let's talk about the here-and-now. Tell me this, Al, what's so noble about Mohammed? What kind of prophet encourages his followers to go around blowing up things, and why does hurting and killing others seem to fit so snugly into your view of how to be people of faith and love?"

Suddenly Carol burst into Joanna's office. "What's this all about, Al? Why are you here?" she demanded.

"I thought you'd gone home, Carol," said Joanna calmly.

"No, I was helping to clean up after the banquet. But don't change the subject. What are you two up to now?"

"Tell her, Al," said Joanna.

"Carol, I can't live without you! I've tried imagining life without you, but I just can't." He fell silent.

Tears swam in Carol's eyes. "Al, I can't imagine life without you either, but I've got to know about how deeply you are involved with Scarlet Jihad. I cannot stand the idea that you are in any way connected with those who have such devious goals."

Al remained quiet.

"What is it, Al? Who are you, Al? You know something more than you are telling me, don't you?"

Carol turned her face away abruptly before turning back to Al again. "What a brave bunch of terrorists you must cavort with! Who could ever admire grown men who kill and destroy and torture innocent people?"

She paused and her tone softened. "How can you divide the world into two neat little categories of Muslims and infidels? I love you, Al, but I could never admire a religion that majors on torture and pain in the name of any god."

Carol's lip was quivering. Al was a man she both loved and questioned with revulsion.

"Carol," Al said, "I'm in love with you and you know it. But I just can't quit being a Muslim to allow our relationship to go further."

"And," said Joanna, "he came here specifically to ask me to help talk you into becoming a Muslim."

Al grew angry. "Joanna, you're not very gracious about other people's religions."

"*Gracious* is a Christian word, Al," Joanna snapped. "*Gracious* is built on the word *grace,* and grace isn't something that people who blow up things could ever understand. Did you really participate in blowing up the *U.S.S. Cole*? Did you, Al? A score of young Americans died on that ship. Don't talk to me about being gracious. No, Al, you may gather with the poor in the inner city, but you only do it to convert them, while the Pathway of Light soup kitchen goes on feeding them, never demanding that they be converted just to get a square meal. No, *grace* is a Christian word. *Vengeance* is a Muslim word."

"But you Christians are indulgent. You drink wine, go to lurid movies, and swear and take the name of God in vain."

"And you Muslims—especially you Yemeni Muslims—chew qat, buy pornography, and are sexually obsessed. And above all that, you kill and bomb and destroy all in the name of God."

"And you Christians tolerate homosexuality. You ordain gay bishops and sponsor gay marriages, and you even establish churches that are totally gay in their orientation. Whole gay churches! Even your heroes Jesus and Paul never married; and it sure makes them look suspicious to me."

Joanna stood. "Well, I'll tell you this, Mr. Muslim Smarty Pants, Mohammed married nearly everybody who would join his mulpaticity . . . his mulplacity . . . his . . . ," Joanna struggled to find the correct word.

"Multiplicity," offered Al sharply.

"Yes, his *mulpaticity* of wives. Well, even if I can't say the word, we both know what I mean."

Carol burst out laughing. Al broke into a grin, then a laugh. Then so did Joanna. Some of the vitriol drained from the atmosphere.

"You know," said Carol, "this conversation wasn't about me at all, was it? It was about two hard-headed religionists that both have such a need to win, neither of them can stand losing. When will the two of you learn that you rarely ever argue somebody toward your position; instead, you lead them by a kind of love that transcends argument? You are both religious legalists—lawyers who want to win your day in court."

Al was quiet. Carol's words convicted him. He was being too harsh in his religious tactic. One thing seemed to be growing clearer: if he hoped to win Carol, he was going to have to demonstrate his love in deeds and not argument. He had an idea. "How would it be if I began to help out in the soup kitchen, Joanna? How about it? Could you use an extra hand in the soup kitchen on Wednesday nights?"

Joanna was still fuming but after a long pause simply said, "Maybe."

For the first time in a long time, Carol looked at him with something approaching admiration.

"Well, I am certainly surprised," said Joanna, a little more moderately.

"You needn't be," said Al. "All Muslims are required by holy law of Sharia to give generously to the poor."

"Yeah! When they're not blowing up the poor," said Joanna heatedly.

"We don't blow up the poor—only the indulgent rich infidels." Al was getting agitated again.

"Yeah! Like those poor, innocent boys on the *U.S.S. Cole?*" shouted Joanna.

"If they were all that innocent, why were they on a warship parked in a Muslim harbor? They were hardly innocent! They were infidel snakes!"

"Mulpaticity!" shouted Carol.

Both Al and Joanna got quiet and managed a smile that soon erupted into a laugh.

"Can you be at the soup kitchen as early as 4:30 on Wednesday?" Joanna asked Al, attempting civility. "That's the time we start getting out the big pots and pans, and they are really too heavy for most of us women to lift."

"Sure," said Al. He turned toward Carol. "Can I drive you home?"

Carol nodded.

They left Joanna's office before further arguments could erupt and soon found themselves on the way home. In spite of the fact that Al had been riding in his little red Honda, he decided to drive it to the church, having no other real way to get there. They left Carol's car parked at the church, determined to pick it up after work on Thursday afternoon.

"Al," Carol began, "I know all about the Scarlet Jihad from Clarisse. I know we are from opposite worlds. And I know you love me, and I believe I love you. But this is one issue we have to get settled. I have no problem accepting you as a man of faith, even as a Muslim missionary of some sort, but I could never get involved with a terrorist. I've seen how Clarisse comes into the clinic all bruised and cut, and it makes me want to throw up. I could never go through that. And I can't imagine what devious acts her husband has up his sleeve. That would never be a life I could ever have anything to do with."

"Carol, darling, I am a hunted man. The answer is yes. I am in the Scarlet Jihad. We take an oath in blood when we join it that we will never quit, and if we do quit, we agree to give up our lives. Loyalty is a big deal in jihad. And right now my loyalty is under surveillance. They already suspect me as being complicit in the loss of the first batch of the RLDs. Now that the second batch has been stolen . . ."

Al grew quiet. The inside of the car became a womb of silence except for the gentle purring of the motor and the swish of the wipers.

Al methodically reached forward to increase the wiper speed; the soft rain was beginning to fall with even more determination. He glanced in the rearview mirror.

The near-silence was broken with his shout: "In the name of Allah, Carol, get down." Even as he yelled, he instinctively reached over and pushed Carol's head down toward the dashboard. At that moment, the back window shattered on her side, and a bullet passed above Carol's head. Al's worst fears had been realized; they had discovered his Honda. He despised himself for being so indiscreet, but this was no time for self-recrimination. Al shoved the accelerator to the floor.

The headlights of the car in the rear moved quickly up to Al's Honda. Al couldn't tell what kind of car it was or who was driving it. He was sure of one thing: there would be more bullets, and either he or Carol—if not both of them—would get hurt.

There was another shot and more shattered glass. This time the bullet took out almost all of the rear window and made a splintered daisy wheel in the front windshield, all but blinding Al from seeing the road ahead. He rammed his fist through the windshield, knocking the splintered shield out of the car completely. The sheet of cracked glass fell to the side of his car, flew up, and hung for a moment in the air, then fell across the windshield of the pursuers, obscuring their vision.

The sudden onrush of air and rain over the dash temporarily blinded Carol. Al shouted, "Carol, take the wheel and keep the car moving!"

Her vision cleared and she saw Al trying to crawl into the backseat. She grabbed the wheel and slid from her bucket seat over the console and into the driver's seat.

She stomped down on the accelerator, while Al whipped a concealed pistol out of his belt and fired it at the driver's side of the car behind them. The shot ripped through the already-shattered rear window of the Honda and sent it flying toward the pursuers' car. In the flash of a passing street light, Al realized it was a Spratton corporate car, a black Lincoln Town Car. It was Zalton's car of choice, but Al couldn't tell if Zalton was the driver. There was a fleet of black Town Cars at Spratton, so any member of Scarlet Jihad could be driving.

The Town Car lurched to one side after Al's shot. Al was almost sure he had injured the driver. But in a moment, the swerving car corrected its course and raced forward toward the Honda. The Honda was no match for the speed of the Town Car, and in a moment, the distance between them was closed.

"Faster, Carol! Can't you go any faster?" Al yelled.

"I'm going as fast as I can!" Carol shouted.

Two more pistol shots rang out from the pursuers' car but missed. Al fired at the left front tire of the Town Car. He missed. He steadied his wrist while two more bullets flew from the passenger's side of the Town Car. Then Al fired two more shots at the front left tire of the pursuing car, hoping they did the job since his magazine was empty. Suddenly, the rubber tire exploded. There was a volley of sparks cut by the rim of the Town Car, and the Lincoln nosed down sharply into the pavement, then flipped end over end and burst into a fireball that lit up the dark, wet night.

"Yahoo!" yelled Al. "Carol, we got 'em!"

But Carol didn't respond. She managed to get the Honda pulled off on the shoulder of the road and stopped.

Al looked at her. "Carol, why are you stopping? We still need to get out of here."

But Carol slumped over the wheel. Al leapt over the seat and lifted her head. There was blood everywhere.

"Oh, my darling," gasped Al. "Dear God, let this not be!"

The falling rain through the space left by the windshield mingled with the streams of blood.

"Carol, hold on, baby! Live so I can live! Die and the world ends for both of us!"

CHAPTER 20

A l-Haj Sistani shut down his mind to keep the pain he felt from bleeding into his heart. He held Carol so closely that her blood covered the both of them.

"Allah," he sobbed, "if there is any justice, any sense to the way I have lived my life, I beg you to make it clear now. If ever you gave the Prophet one ounce of your own being, I beg you give me back this beloved woman! If she dies, I die. If she lives, I live."

But Allah seemed not to answer at all.

A long time passed while Al held his beloved. He couldn't let her go. And for reasons he could not fathom, he said some very odd words that formed themselves into a very odd prayer: "Jesus Christ, Carol has loved you implicitly throughout her life, though I have never understood why. Oh Christ, does the name Carol Jones mean anything to you? Is she one of yours? Your blood was the business of every communion she ever attended. She actually believes it was your blood that redeemed her. Oh, if you are anywhere in the universe, anywhere within earshot, let Carol's dear blood redeem my willful stubbornness. Give her back to me, and I will serve you for as long as I live. I will call you Lord and master from this moment on."

Is there any power in a mantra of desperation? Al wondered.

Carol's blood felt warm as it soaked his own shirt and skin. Was it an illusion or was it something he really felt? It seemed there was fire all about him in the car.

Then through the rain-streamed headlight beams, Al saw the silhouette of a tall man and a dog—no, a silver wolf. It was Father Peter!

"I hear you've been looking for me and the missing RLDs. If you want them back, they are yours."

"Good God, man! How can you speak of RLDs at this moment?"

"But they were so important to you just a few hours ago. You were trying to hunt me down to get them back."

"Nothing matters. I have lost everything. Carol is gone."

"Oh, changed our value system, have we?"

Al said nothing. His tears mingled with the rain.

"Very well. Your value system needed changing."

He gently pushed Al's body away from Carol's. "Kinta," he said, "where's the healing that you own?"

The great wolf stretched upward through the open windshield, reached his forepaw out, and merely touched Carols naked arm and then collapsed.

In the same instant, Carol stirred. She gasped, caught her breath, then sat upright in the bucket seat.

"Carol, darling!" was all Al said.

They embraced.

"Al, what happened to you? You're all covered with blood . . . Good grief! So am I. Did we get the bad guys?"

"We sure did." Al was struck silent and sat mesmerized by a miracle Carol never saw. After a long silence Al smiled broadly then joy erupted as he laughed deliriously out loud, feeling as though he were in a dream.

"Carol, is that you?" asked the blind priest.

"Father Peter, what are you doing here?"

"Just passing by," said Father Peter.

"Passing by? Just passing by? Where's Kinta?"

The blind priest knelt down and picked up the wolf. Kinta was monstrously large, yet the old man seemed to pick him up with relative ease. "Here he is."

"Is he dead?" Carol asked.

"Not quite, but he'll be out of things for a while."

"Is it my fault, Father?" asked Al.

"No, it is nobody's fault. Kinta had a big job to do. When he got through imparting his strength to the weak, he took the weakness on himself, that's all. He'll be up and around in a bit. Carol is alive, and no redemption ever is free. It always costs the healer the price of the disease."

"What does that mean?" asked Carol.

"Al will tell you all about it," said Father Peter. Then he turned on his heel and walked away in the rain.

Both Carol and Al watched the thin priest carry away his great beast as they both disappeared into the night.

"Carol," Al said, "I am a Christian!"

CHAPTER 21

On that same night, Rhonda had left the banquet to head home and begin her favorite activity—watching TV until she dozed. She was extremely tired.

Paul was on an overnight AMA committee meeting in San Francisco on Sunday but would be catching the early-bird flight home on Monday, in time to be at his practice when it opened. They had talked of nothing these last few days except the theft of the RLDs and the wonderful priests of Holy Faith Abbey.

She mixed herself a drink of half sweet iced tea and half sour lemonade—an Arnold Palmer. It seemed just right for a rainy, muggy summer evening. Then she sat down to watch the H&G channel, as redecorating shows were her favorite.

On this particular evening she was especially eager to watch *Yarding and Gardening*, a one-hour bonanza on how to do your own landscaping. Rhonda had dreams of putting a new brick walkway along her beloved Snoqualmie riverfront home. She could visualize how it would look when she was finished but had not the fuzziest notion of how to do it. And she did so want to do it herself. She could afford a contractor, but they just never did things right.

Just before the program began, she pulled her cell phone from the pocket of her bathrobe and dialed Paul's room in San Francisco. No answer. Paul was obviously out late with some associates. He hated quitting a good conversation almost as much as Rhonda hated missing the house and garden shows.

She stuck her cell phone back into the pocket of her robe and began to watch *Yarding and Gardening*. Toward the end of the show, she found herself dozing off.

She roused herself from this mesmerizing lethargy at the sound of breaking glass. She came instantly awake and stumbled over the ottoman where her houseshoes still lay. Her vision made out heavy, tall silhouettes against the glass panes of her front door. The men caught between the porch light and her glass were shadowy monsters, made taller by the light than they actually were.

Rhonda was paralyzed with fear. Then she saw a hand reach through the broken panes and unlock the front door.

She bolted for the stairs. "Oh, Barney, Barney!" she cried.

She dashed up the stairs and into the nursery and picked up her sleeping baby. Wide-eyed with wonder, Barney yielded to her as she started down the rear stairs and darted out the back door to the rear deck. Shifting Barney to one arm, she reached into her pocket for the cell phone, pulled it out, and tried to dial 9-1-1. But the phone screen said "Low Battery" and then went black. She stumbled down the back steps of the deck and started for the woods, rebuking herself for forgetting to turn the security alarm on. There was no way the police knew of her predicament.

She had not run very far down the back walkway when she stumbled over a loose piece of flagging. She fell face forward onto the rain-soaked stone, managing to half-toss Barney into the soft weeds at the side of the walkway. She attempted to rise twice more on the slick mossy stones. Her third attempt to get up was her last. She felt a pair of large, rough hands slip a chloroform rag across her face. The oddly gagging substance was rancid and horrible. She was vaguely aware that a bag was being thrown over her head. And then she was in a fire of instantaneous dreams—mental collages of vipers and terrorists and demons. Then the hurried cinema of dreams came to a close and there was only blackness. Rhonda lost herself in an ocean of cold, dark nothingness.

■ ■ ■

After Rhonda was knocked unconscious, the two men carried her to the Shapiro garage and debated the fate of the baby who had been lifted from the grass and was still crying.

"What do we do with this half-breed Jewish kid?" asked Akbar. He turned toward the howling infant. "Shut up, you little brat!"

"Take him out to the sea and drown him in a box of concrete or take him up into the Rainier basin and bury him," said Ishaq. "I don't really care what you do with him, but we cannot take time to deal with a baby right now. Of course, we must let the parents and all who find out about the kid's abduction believe the baby is safe. We will hold no leverage if they discover that the baby is dead. As long as they believe he is a hostage, we can use the kid to serve our agenda. Maybe Shapiro himself can be brought around by threatening him with the death of his wife or child."

Akbar took Barney and threw him in the car.

Ishaq stopped him. "Better use his infant seat. If the police stopped you for such a minor infraction of safety, our plans could be blown."

Ishaq put Rhonda in the trunk of Jabril's Lexus and left.

Akbar yanked the infant seat out of the Shapiro's car, managed to get it in the backseat of his Jaguar, and shoved the baby into it. Barney continued wailing at the unkind treatment he was receiving.

Akbar got into the Jaguar and backed out onto Snoqualmie River Road. Soon he was driving toward the Cascade Mountains. When he found himself in a wilderness area, he stopped the car and eagerly yanked the baby out of the infant seat, weary of the child's constant crying throughout the car ride. He slung the baby under his arm and toted him to a barren spot in a tree grove.

He laid the child on the bare ground and shined his flashlight on him. He took out his pistol, aimed it at the baby, and cocked the hammer of the gun. He was about to squeeze the trigger when he was struck by a huge animal, throwing him onto his back. The flashlight was gone, and his gun had landed some distance away. He was trapped in the dark by an animal that the close darkness would not identify. But the animal's attack was relentless. Each time Akbar tried to stand up, he was knocked down yet again.

Finally, he managed to stumble back toward the car's headlights. He jumped into the car and closed the door just as the beast leapt at the glass. He cranked the engine, shoved the car into drive, and peeled out of the area. His flesh was torn and his clothes had been nearly shredded by claws and fangs. Miraculously his face and hands were not injured. Once back on the main road, he stopped to change clothes, then drove on. Eventually, he paused to sleep.

The next morning, he rendezvoused with Ishaq at a truck stop just off the I-5.

"Is the kid dead?" asked the albino.

"He's dead and so far out in the wilderness he will never be found," sneered Akbar.

Ishaq was pleased. "Watch the phone," he said. "I'm going to go have a talk with Melody Jarvis. I want to know just how much her husband knows about who we are and what we're up to." He left.

Akbar thought about the baby and the animal. He hoped the baby was dead; he knew the animal wasn't.

■ ■ ■

Rhonda awoke in a dimly lit place—a cavern or cellar of some sort. The bag was now off her head, but she clanked when she tried to move her arms. Her surroundings began to take shape. She was in a dank and ill-lit furnace room, chained to a pipe. "Help!" she yelled. "I'm down here, handcuffed to a pipe! Somebody!"

"We're all handcuffed to pipes, Rhonda," said a kind, deep voice.

She knew that voice. "Joanna," asked Rhonda, "Is it really you?"

"Yes, Rhonda, it's me!"

The world came into view all too suddenly. "Where's my baby? Where's Barney?" she shouted.

"Barney's not here," said Joanna.

"No, no!" shouted Rhonda. "I want my baby now."

"Listen, Rhonda, we're all praying. Barney will be found, but he's not here."

"I don't want to pray. I want my baby now!" She collapsed against the pipe and cried.

Joanna managed to talk her down from her hysteria. Eventually, she was again coherent enough to take stock of her surroundings.

"Well, Joanna," she sniffed, "what are you doing here? And why did they take the two of us, and where's my baby?"

"I'm sure your baby's OK. God will take care of him, and there's not just two of us."

"Hello, Rhonda," said another familiar female voice. "Carol Jones here."

"Clarisse, say hello to Rhonda," Joanna said.

"Hello, Rhonda," said Clarisse al-Zhabahni.

Carol broke in, "Oh, Rhonda, I'm so sorry. I was in a high-speed chase last night and would have died except for the old priest."

"Father Peter?" asked Rhonda. She struggled to make the faces of Carol, Clarisse, and Joanna come into focus. Still, her vision just wouldn't clear and the horrible taste in her mouth lingered. She remembered reading somewhere that the taste of chloroform could only be cleared by sipping straight lemon juice.

"Joanna, Carol, Clarisse," she said, peering into the darkness. "Anybody else?"

"I'm here," said Melody Jarvis.

"Me too," said Mary Muebles.

"That's Mary, Melody, Carol, Clarisse, me, and you, Rhonda," said Joanna. "That makes six of us."

"What time is it?"

"I have my watch on, but I can't read it," said Joanna. "But I believe it's sometime Thursday afternoon, August the second."

"What makes you think that?" asked Mary.

"There's a little patch of sunlight on the floor over there. And it's been moving for several hours, so it must be the afternoon."

"Joanna, you're a genius!" said Carol.

"If I were, I'd figure out how to get us out of here and even figure out where 'here' is." Joanna felt as though she should take charge of the situation.

"Are all of you handcuffed to pipes?" asked Rhonda.

Carol spoke up. "You seem to be the only one who's got actual handcuffs. The rest of us are cuffed by plastic lock strips to radiator

vents and zinc conduits of one sort or another. As for me, I'm cuffed
to a hot copper tube. I don't know what's running through this pipe,
but it must be hot water. I can hardly stand the heat. But I guess
for the foreseeable future none of us are going anywhere. We're all
cuffed behind our backs."

"But why us?" asked Rhonda.

It was Mrs. al-Zhabahni who answered. "Rhonda, I may be at
fault in all of this. They found out where Esther's Refuge was. I never
should have gone to your husband for help."

"Now, Clarisse," said Joanna, "don't take too much of this upon
yourself. You are no more to blame than the rest of us."

"Still, I know how my husband thinks. He knows I was going
to see Dr. Shapiro, and I am sure he believes that I shared critical
information about Scarlet . . ." Clarisse stopped, uncertain of what
her companions knew.

"Go ahead and say it, Señora al-Zhabahni," said Mary Muebles.
"We all know about Scarlet Jihad. For goodness' sake, I have been
sleeping with—I mean seeing—Jibril. I don't know exactly what they
do, but he has a red tattoo with Arabic letters that I am sure says
Scarlet Jihad. I thought Jibril loved me, but the rotten taste of chloroform has convinced me that our romance isn't going all that well."

"I suspect Clarisse is right," said Mary. "All six of us are here
because these Yemeni thugs believe we know too much to be left
free."

"I am going to pray, sisters, that somehow God will act to get us
out of here. God can do wonderful things, don't you agree?" Joanna
said.

All of them concurred except Mary. "I don't know if God is all
that good at handcuffs," she said.

"Well then, Mary, I suggest you keep your doubts to yourself."
Joanna felt a little better, having had it out with the Latina doubter.
When things were sufficiently quiet, she closed her eyes and said,
"God, this really is a predicament, but as you can see, we've only
got one doubter in the room. So if you don't mind, just ignore Mary
and answer our prayer for the sake of all of us who believe you're

the best of all possible friends to poor, helpless women in cuffs and a lot of pain. Amen!"

Just then there was a knock at the only door the women could see. The door opened.

A man dressed in a janitor's uniform entered. He looked Arabic, probably Yemeni, and was bearded. He carried a tray with a glass of water and a small dish of lemon slices.

"I can't undo your hands, for you would likely try to escape," he said. "I know I would. I know I look Yemeni, but I am actually Hispanic, and I work in corporate clean up."

"And what corporation would that be?" asked Joanna.

"Ah, ah, ah! I can't tell you everything you want to know. I am an illegal alien who was hired by this company only recently for *mojando los pisos*. How do you say it—to mop the floors? I wonder if there is anyone here who speaks Spanish."

"I do," said Mary.

"Ah, Maria."

"And how did you know my name, Señor?"

"All *mujeres lindas* seem to be named Maria. It was a good first guess. Look here, I have ice water and lemons. I will hold the lemon water to your lips and you can sip and get rid of that awful chloroform taste in your mouth. It will be like as *communio Catholico*, only it will be sweet and healing for your taste."

One by one the janitor faced them and offered them a cup of lemon water, which each of them held in their mouth as they swished it over their numb tongue and teeth, trying to clear away the chloroform aftertaste. Each woman thanked him. Finally he approached Mary Muebles. When she had rinsed her mouth out, she spat out the water.

"Look, Maria, I know you are the doubter, but *tengo algas palabras para ti en Español*." So saying, the Spanish janitor spoke several sentences in Spanish to Mary. Then he stood and left the room.

"What was that all about?" asked Joanna.

"I think this janitor is not a terrorist. He said this *sala* has *insecta*!" Mary looked up toward a single wire that dangled on a white cord from a concrete ceiling. The light was so scarce that the cord was barely visible.

Mary repeated the odd phrase again, looking to the ceiling. One by one, through squinted eyes they all began to see it. Taped to the wire was a very small cord that ended in a small microphone. *Bugged.* "Insecta!" they all repeated, being careful to whisper. The janitor had obviously warned them to be very discreet in their conversation, lest they clue in their captors as to what they knew.

They sat quietly for fifteen minutes or so.

Then Clarisse suddenly began to cry. "This is all my fault." She wept.

"It's not your fault, Clarisse. Now stop crying and stop saying that!" Joanna demanded.

"I'm not crying just because it's my fault. I'm crying because I'm tied up and I don't know what to do."

Suddenly Carol began to cry too. "I don't know what to do either," she cried.

Melody Jarvis also had tears in her eyes. "I feel like crying."

"None of you have done anything wrong," said Rhonda. "Certainly not you, Melody."

"I know, but I'm the only one of you who is pregnant. And I've got the jitters even when things are going well. And now they're not going well, and I have to go to the bathroom so bad." She bit her lip. "I have no reason to cry other than I feel like I'm gonna wet my pants."

"It's no sin to wet your pants," said Joanna. "Everybody that's tied up for a long time does it." Joanna realized that it was a stupid thing to say. "That's my helpful hint of the day." She started to laugh.

They all did, except Melody.

"Oh, please," said Melody. "If I laugh, I'll wet myself for sure."

But she did laugh.

"Oh, me!" cried Melody, "I did, but just a bit!"

Then they all laughed some more, but it was an odd laugh built of hopelessness and hysteria more than lightheartedness.

"Don't feel like you're all alone. We'll all be there by evening if Joanna's right—if it is afternoon now," Rhonda said.

Silence returned, along with worry. When it seemed like the women might dissolve again into tears, the door flew open.

It was the janitor. "There's a bathroom outside this door. I've been instructed to cut the plastic cuffs from your wrists, so you can come and go to the bathroom freely. I warn you, though, this bathroom is not very dainty and feminine. In fact, it makes a Texaco toilet look like the Hyatt. But you'll at least be free to go whenever you want to."

"*Tienes algas otras palabras?*" said Mary, hoping for more clues.

"No."

"*Puedes decirnos dónde estamos?*"

"No. *Pero eres en una sala muy lejos de sus casas.*"

The janitor stopped talking and walked to Rhonda, who required a key to liberate her from the cuffs. Then he took some scissors out of his blue coveralls and began to snip the plastic latch strips from behind the women. After he liberated Melody, she asked the other women if she could go pee first. They said yes and she flew to the bathroom.

For all her complaining, she was back in what seemed a very short time. One by one they left the room. "*Gracias, señor!*" said Mary.

"Yes, gracias, gracias," said Rhonda.

"Oh, yes, gracias, gracias, and evermore gracias," said Clarisse.

"I get the idea, *doñas*," said the amused custodian. "But a single *gracias* is enough and even that is not as necessary as you believe. I have permission from the boss to bring you an order of burgers from McDonald's. My mind is not so good, so you will have to order something simple like meal deal number one or number four."

"Is number four the *pollo frito* or *hamburgesa?*" asked Mary.

"I want a salad," said Clarisse. "The Mandarin salad!"

The custodian chuckled. "I cannot do all this. Who wants hamburgers and who wants nothing?"

With their choice narrowed, the ladies unanimously voted for burgers. He left and was back in a very short time with sacks of goodies for all. Clarisse dove into her bag and was about to take a bite when Joanna reminded them that they needed to offer thanks. They all agreed.

"Lord," Joanna said, "thank you for giving us burgers in this deplorable place. Lord, bless our captors. We don't think too much of them, Lord, but we know that you love everybody. I don't see how, but you do, so bless our enemies. They all seem to be Arabs. But bless them anyway. You told us to pray for our enemies, and so we just ask you to give them all good things. And if you want to kick them around a bit till they all act a little more like Jesus, well, that'd be all right too. But most of all we want to thank you for giving us a janitor who seems like an angel. We do like him a lot, Lord, but all things being equal, we'd all just as soon be out of here. Lord, could you give us a sign? In Jesus' name, amen."

The women devoured the burgers, amazed at Joanna's prayer. Her companions were in no mood to bless their captors. They ate without speaking much. What did Joanna mean when she asked God to give her a sign? What kind of sign could possibly come to them? Rhonda wondered most of all.

CHAPTER 22

On Thursday afternoon, two travelers arrived at their respective homes just minutes apart. Paul Shapiro knew he had not been able to get Rhonda on the phone all day long, but he didn't think much about it. She was either outside, working in the yard, or off on a lark for lunch and time with friends. But when he arrived home, his mood immediately changed. Rhonda was nowhere to be found, although both cars were home and the house was locked. The security system, however, was not engaged. The front door glass had been broken, and there was a note on the table.

■ ■ ■

When Gary Jarvis arrived at his apartment, he found the interior trashed and his wife gone. He also found a brief memo from Melody's captors. Stunned, he read the note.

> *Your wife is safe and will remain so as long as you do not interfere with the business of Scarlet Jihad. But rest assured if you make any attempt to find her or follow your presumptions about our faith or our intent, you will never see her again.*

> *The Will of Allah*

What might Melody be enduring even at this hour? His anxiety was in orbit. Melody was well into her third trimester with their first child. He knew that even the slightest pain in any area of her body was doubled by the stress of her late-term pregnancy.

"God," he prayed, "we must have a double serving of your grace. Keep my wife safe and I shall keep my mind." It was the kind of bargaining in prayer that he would not have prayed in his less needy moments. But there are moments of need that forget propriety.

When his mind had cleared a bit, Gary pulled out a finger-print detection kit. He dusted anywhere within the apartment that Melody's abductors might have laid a naked hand, but nothing turned up.

The phone rang.

The caller ID screen flashed "Paul Shapiro."

"Paul! What's wrong? Is Rhonda missing too?" Gary found himself saying without introduction.

"What do you mean 'too'?" Paul asked.

"Melody's gone!" Gary was quiet for a moment then added, "Our place was ransacked, and I found a brief note from the abductors."

"I have a note too!" said Paul.

"I keep a bit of forensic junk in my desk here at home," Gary said. "And I did enough dusting to realize there are no fingerprints either on the note or anywhere in the apartment."

"Gary, should we get the police involved—besides you?" asked Paul.

"Ordinarily I'd say so, but in this instance . . . Paul, could we meet at the Denny's on the interstate just north of downtown? By six o'clock?"

"Sure, let's go. Wait a minute. I wanted to tell you that my note mentioned that they were also detaining a client of mine. The wife of Zalton al-Zhabahni."

"The one Melody said Rhonda took to a refuge for battered women?"

"The same! Gary, I know our women would never have revealed the whereabouts of Clarisse al-Zhabahni unless they were forced to."

Both men were quiet.

"What are we waiting for?" Gary said. "Let's go! And bring your note."

In an hour and a half they were sitting at Denny's, comparing the kidnapper's notes to each of them. On Paul's was the following line: *Rhonda will remain unharmed as long as you do not reveal to the police what Mrs. al-Zhabahni may have told you in your private counseling sessions about Zalton or any of his dealings with the Scarlet Jihad.*

Gary then produced Akbar's little black phone book. He explained to Paul how he had come by it and then began to search through it for any clue as to where they could start their investigation. But in sorting through page after page of the tiny leather book, he was unable to come up with anything.

"Paul, I know you must be out of your mind about the fate of our wives, and you probably want to go to the police. But that would be the wrong thing right now. These Yemeni goons might kill the women! We must protect them—we must be sure of their safety until we can get them away from these brutes! I promise you that I will keep in constant telephone contact with you."

"Gary, we still don't know exactly what the Scarlet Jihad is up to. We may try to solve it somehow, but we're running out of time, and without knowing if Rhonda is secure . . . I don't even have the courage to think about it."

Paul's cell phone rang. He stared disbelievingly at the caller ID, then quickly picked up the call. Gary could hear a woman's voice on the other end.

"Pauly?"

"Ronnie?"

"Pauly! I can't believe it! Oh, Pauly, do something. We are captives of a desperate group of men. I was taken last night—if this is Thursday. We're in some sort of makeshift prison. My cell phone was in the pocket of the bathrobe I was wearing. And somehow, glory of glories, those who drugged me and took me from the house missed seeing it." Rhonda suddenly dropped her voice and seemed to be fighting the urge to exult or even to talk loud.

"Paul, oh, Paul!" she said. "Are you all right?"

"Yes, darling, I'm all right . . . so far!"

"Paul, do you have Barney?"

"No, darling, I was hoping he might be with you."

Rhonda broke into violent sobbing.

Paul kept the tears from his conversation by sheer willpower. "Ronnie, calm down and tell me what's going on."

Rhonda got control of herself and said, "The other women are with me."

"What other women?"

"Joanna, Carol, Clarisse, Melody, and Mary Muebles."

"Gary is with me, Rhonda."

"What? Gary is with you? Then please tell him Melody is all right too . . . but we have no idea where we are. We're in some kind of furnace room or basement . . . I know this—we're close to a McDonald's. They got our sandwiches to us in no time. We can't be more than a mile or so. Honey, I know that's not much to go on, but it's all I can tell you right now . . . Yes, I'll leave the cell phone on so you can trace the phone . . . yes, I'll hang on." Rhonda was ecstatically hopeful, and so were the rest of the women.

But Rhonda's ecstasy did not last long. "Oh, no!" she said, glancing at her phone. "The screen's blinking 'Low Battery' again. Oh, Pauly, I won't be able to keep the signal going till they trace the call. Paul, please find our baby!"

"I will," he said.

Then the phone went dead.

■ ■ ■

"Oh, no!" gasped Melody.

Just as she spoke, the door flew open. It was a white-haired Arab. An albino.

"Give me that phone!" he demanded. He wrestled it from Rhonda's hand.

"No, please!" she cried out, then felt his fist across her face. Rhonda collapsed in unconsciousness, and the albino threw the cell phone on the floor and stomped on it, crushing the women's hopes.

"Which one of you is married to Inspector Jarvis of the Seattle Police Department?"

"I'm Mrs. Jarvis," said Carol Jones.

"She's lying," said Mary Muebles. "I'm Mrs. Jarvis."

"Very well, I see your game. But it won't go on long. I'll be back with a rough little piece of detection equipment that will help you all quickly arrive at the truth." He left, slamming the door behind him.

"His name is Ishaq the Albino," Clarisse said. "I haven't seen him since I left Sanaa, but he is known far and wide as a man without conscience. We are to be pitied. We are here alone with Satan as our shepherd."

CHAPTER 23

With the fading of Rhonda's cell phone battery, Gary and Paul's hopes for a quick fix on the women's hiding place were lost. Gary and Paul then talked through clues as to how they could have intersected with Scarlet Jihad in the first place.

Gary was still befuddled about the elusive numbers in the back of Akbar's book, but no matter how hard he tried, he could not make sense of the code—if it were a code. What did it mean?

Eventually he and Paul decided to part and pursue their separate paths, attempting to find more clues to the women's whereabouts. Gary decided to hunt down Wanda the Wiccan—the only female acquainted with all parties who hadn't been kidnapped. He knew some of the homeless folks' favorite haunts and started checking them out.

Around 10 p.m., he found her. She was sitting on a curb under a street light, reading her favorite book.

"Ms. Williams," said Gary, "could I ask you a few questions?"

"Yes! Shoot!" she said.

"Do you know any of these teachers that came from the al-Jabar mosque?"

"Nope," said Wanda. "All I know is that they call Jesus 'Isa' and that makes Miss Joanna mad as a wet hen." Even Wanda realized it was an odd metaphor.

Gary decided to be more direct. "Joanna and Mary and almost all of the women who came to these Qur'an studies are missing."

"Where'd they go?" asked Wanda. "They can't have been whooshed away in the Rapture 'cause I'm still here."

"No," said Gary, "No Rapture—more like a capture than a rapture." He was wasting time.

"I got a map of Seattle here in my shopping cart—by the way, Inspector, in case of the Rapture, my shopping cart will be unmanned," Wanda rambled. "But I could take that map and do a candle-wax-and-flax-wort poultice. If you put the poultice on while you sing a Celtic rune at midnight, it can help you cure warts . . . I mean, find things you lost. You want me to try it? It might help. We learned how to do it after last week's Mystic Mass!"

"No, Wanda, thanks."

"That's OK," continued Wanda. "I put some flax-wort on a Muslim bible they gave us free, and I discovered that there is a hideaway in a huge warehouse that Al works at. It's big and nobody knows about it. It's where they keep lots of boxes full of Muslim bibles—boxes and boxes. They're exploding boxes. Jesus is coming again." She paused for breath. "You want me to read you some out of my book? You want some flax-wort? It helps you find things. Think the president of Iran is the Antichrist? Better get ready just in case."

"See you, Wanda," said Gary, walking away. She was weird. Her conversations went nowhere. And Gary had to find a group of hostages as soon as possible.

But it was now after 10 p.m. He was exhausted from worrying and searching and decided to go home and try again with renewed energy on the morrow.

■ ■ ■

After several hours of restless sleep, Gary drove to the Comfort 8 Suites Friday morning to go though Mary Muebles' things. He flashed his badge at the clerk, who gave him a key to 117. He put on some rubber gloves, entered the room, and began sorting and hunting. Nothing turned up until he got to her bureau.

In the lowest drawer behind her pantyhose, he found a strange manila envelope stamped with a Mexican postmark. Inside was a certificate of immigration. It looked fairly authentic, except for a whited-out area on the line marked "Admission for Citizenship." He took out his pocketknife and gently scraped off the paint. Underneath was a blue rubber-stamped word: DENIED. The date affixed was July 3, 2004.

Why had Mary been denied a chance at American citizenship?

He found a second envelope that contained some kind of Mexican parole papers. Interesting.

Gary began to wonder about Mary's story—that her father was supplying her with money for the motel room and bills. Was she telling the truth?

He found a small tin box full of photos. One was of a funeral, not in the United States but in Mexico. The coffin in the photo had some ribbons on top of it that were marked *Amamos Papa Muebles*. Was that for Mary's father?

Most condemning of all was a picture of Mary in a cabaret, laughing and having a beer with what appeared to be a very blonde— even white-haired—Arabian. Who in the world could this be? There was Arabic writing on the beer bottle and on the mirror over the bar. Had Mary ever been in an Arabic country? Who was she? She seemed to be more than a homeless artist with a rich father. Make that a dead father. But where could Gary go to discover the truth? He rubbed his forehead with a rubber glove and kept searching.

■ ■ ■

On Saturday morning, August 4, Gary and Paul met again at a roadside diner on the south edge of Seattle's business district to see if either of their addled brains could discover where their wives were being held. Gary had checked to see where all of the Seattle McDonald's restaurants were located, finding that there were more than fifty, mostly located in better neighborhoods and on prominent highways and intersections. Narrowing the search to where Scarlet Jihad might be holding captives seemed impossible.

Both men were clearly on edge, trying to make their brains work on any clue while tears gathered in their eyes.

"Sooner or later, this has to break to the news," said Paul. "Somebody is going to notice that these women are missing. Especially as tomorrow's Sunday and Joanna won't be in the pulpit."

"We need more time to get to the bottom of this," Gary said. "The citywide fear this news will bring will leave the media hounding us, vastly complicating our own work."

"But Gary, wouldn't we be smart to get this thing out into the open?" Paul paused for a moment. "I mean, wouldn't this go faster if we had the whole city out looking for them?"

"Paul, you read the notes. If we blow this thing wide open, our wives are as good as dead. I couldn't live with myself knowing my wife was . . ." Gary cleared his throat. "And all because of my indiscretion. Paul, have you gone through Rhonda's things? Maybe she left a clue. Maybe the kidnappers left some telltale mark that would help us find them."

"You mean, like a fingerprint?"

"Yeah, maybe a fingerprint." Gary stopped. "No, that probably wouldn't happen. I dusted our apartment for prints and found nothing. These guys are smart."

Gary was suddenly struck with an idea. "What kind of paper was your note written on?"

"I don't know . . . white."

"Like a notepad?"

"Yes, except it looked like it was torn off a notepad. Maybe like a hotel notepad, but the top of the paper was ripped off."

"Good paper or cheap paper?" Gary pursued.

"Good, I think, like a kind of stationery vellum. More like the notepads they leave in a Hyatt room than a Motel 6."

"Could I see it?"

Paul extracted the kidnapper's note from his shirt pocket.

Gary turned it over eagerly. "Oh, look at this—a watermark."

Paul could see it, though he had not noticed it before. It was a watermark of nearly invisible pine needles.

Gary sat back. "That's the logo of Vancouver Stationers."

"You're sure of it?" asked Paul.

"Dead sure," said Gary. "City hall orders a lot of their product. I've seen this very kind in the mayor's office. Call them, Paul, and see if it's possible to get a list of their Seattle customers."

"Wouldn't it be better if you talked to them?"

"I've got my own bit of forensics to work on this morning." Gary pulled an envelope out of his pocket and dumped its contents into his hand. A small, dried clod of red soil fell out.

"What's that?" Paul asked.

"This is a little bit of mud that was on our carpet after Melody's abductors left. It has to be from them. Neither Melody nor I go anywhere with this kind of mud."

"Where do you start looking for that kind of mud in a city the size of Seattle?" asked Paul.

"Well, somewhere in the country. Maybe around the Spratton warehouses."

"Sounds like a good starting place."

"I'll work on mud today. And if the Vancouver Stationers aren't helpful, we'll work on them later tonight."

"You mean break in?" Paul asked.

"Well, you don't need to make it sound like grand theft. I just want to look at their files for a little bit. Not a break-in; more like a moonlight requisition."

Paul smiled. But the gravity he wished he could brush aside was still with him. Rhonda and Barney were still gone, and he wasn't any closer to finding them.

Gary stood. "Let's get moving. Call me if you find anything."

"You too," Paul replied, getting up from his chair.

The men parted.

■ ■ ■

Gary drove toward Zalton al-Zhabahni's massive warehouse complex at the edge of the city. He had no hope of actually finding the women there. He knew al-Zhabahni was far too clever to hide the women in any place where his own reputation would be called into question if they were found.

Considering the huge security system of Spratton, Gary had not the slightest hope of getting inside the complex. He parked a half-mile away and assumed a surveillance stance in a clump of trees. Using a set of heavy binoculars, he scanned every part of the Spratton facility from the front entry to the docks, thankful for the good visibility of the sunny day.

He noticed a semi parked at the import side of the warehouse docks beside the main building. The truck was mud-splattered on its sides. The mud nearly covered the Spratton Laser Technologies logo.

As it was Saturday, there were hardly any cars parked in the main lot at the opposite end of the building. He got back in his unmarked police car and drove directly into the loading docks area where the huge muddy truck was parked. He could see a single workman with a dolly, moving some boxes back and forth on the warehouse docks.

Gary got out of the car, put a pencil behind his ear, and grabbed a clipboard, intending to look like a dispatcher. He walked directly up to the dock and was about to speak when the workman spoke to him. "Have we got three or four more trucks coming in from Frisco?" asked the workman.

"Three, I think," said Gary, glad for a multiple-choice question.

"Think? Don't you know? What kind of dispatcher are you?"

"Three, if we got the one yesterday." Gary knew he was on dangerous ground, but had little choice but to keep the game going.

"Yesterday? We never get trucks on Friday." The workman eyed him.

"I meant this week."

"Well, we did get one on Wednesday, so I guess that means three more."

"I guess so. These must not come directly from the docks in San Francisco."

"Well, that's what they say," said the dock worker. "I don't think I believe them, though. I don't know of any mud holes on the I-5 that would do this to a truck, do you?"

"Nope, they didn't pick this up anywhere along the way, unless they went off-road during a rainstorm."

"That's what I think too," said the worker.

"Gonna unload it on Monday?" Gary asked.

"No, now that's another funny thing. We're told never to unload a muddy truck. They send a group of special workers for that. They're all Yemenis, I think. They don't trust us white boys to unload the muddy trucks. To be honest, I think they're breaking teamster rules, allowing only Arabs to do the job. But I'm not going to be the whistle-blower. I need my job too badly, so I just look the other way. You been a dispatcher long?"

"Long enough," said Gary. "I'm afraid that I'm going to have to report this. We can't have nonunion people doing this. Yemeni or not—they can't get by with this."

"They say the NSA and the CIA know about this," said the dock worker, "and they're much bigger than the teamsters. So if they don't care, why should I?"

"Well, I mind," said Gary, making some notes on his clipboard. He kept his eyes on his writing. "Well, if you don't unload them, are they unloaded here?"

"Nope. These go to another warehouse somewhere out in the wilds."

Gary remembered Wanda Williams' odd words: "There's a secret warehouse that nobody knows about." Suddenly he wished he had let the snaggletoothed witch ramble on a bit more before he left her.

"I'm afraid I'm going to have to impound these trucks till the big boys at the union get a chance to look this over."

"Do what you gotta do; just don't mention my name."

"I won't," said Gary as he stuck the clipboard under his arm and walked away. "Thanks for your help. By the way, get your union badge out of your shirt pocket and clip it where it can be seen. You know the rules."

"Sorry," said the worker, reaching into his pocket and pulling out his badge.

Gary got back in his car and drove away, returning to the same small grove of trees he had previously occupied. He got out and sat down on a rock with his binoculars and began his watch.

Nothing occurred for three hours. Gary's thoughts again turned to Melody. He was so distraught that he almost missed a scene unfolding near the muddy truck a half-mile away.

He shook himself and focused his binoculars. A single car had just pulled up—a Honda Civic with missing front and rear windows. Al-Haj Sistani got out. What could he possibly be doing there? What could have put him back into the good graces of Scarlet Jihad? Or did they even know he was there? Gary was mesmerized.

Al climbed into the filthy truck and adeptly backed it away from the warehouse. Obviously, he had done this before. Gary put down his binoculars. He needed to start surveillance of a trickier kind: tailing a semi.

He jumped in his car, resolved to follow at such a discreet distance that the driver would not pick him up in a rearview mirror—a tough feat since there was zero traffic on the lonely red-soil road.

After three miles, the truck turned onto a graveled highway that led down a crude unmarked road in the direction of the Mount Rainier basin.

Here and there Gary saw pieces of road equipment, including a couple of bulldozers. This was no state highway. This road had been built—likely by night—to an undisclosed area that no one in the state of Washington even knew about.

The summer rains had left the roadway soft, and the big truck had some trouble negotiating between the soft shoulders of the raw earthen road.

Gary noticed a left turn signal flashing through the muddy back of the truck. He pulled off the road at a cattle crossing, partially hiding his car in a thin grove of trees.

An Arabian wearing a red prayer shawl greeted the truck.

Gary scrutinized the truck as it turned toward a rather large but makeshift steel building surrounded by fifteen or twenty open bay doors with attached docks. "Good grief, old Wanda," Gary whispered to himself, "could this be the warehouse full of exploding bibles or Qur'ans or whatever?"

The truck backed into the dock in front of an open bay, guided by another Arab. Then an Arab on a forklift began to unload it. When they finished, al-Haj Sistani got back in the truck and drove it back down the facility's entrance road.

Gary decided to let Al go and focus on the facility. He stealthily scampered toward a rear door and, finding it open, carefully entered the huge facility, aware that two of the men who had just unloaded the truck were still somewhere on the premises. He slipped behind the various stacks of boxes, each uniformly stacked in four large quadrants as though they had been unloaded from four trucks. The boxes were all unlabeled. If old Wanda's flax-wort hex could be trusted, the boxes should be filled with exploding Qur'ans. But what on earth could that mean? Gary reached for his pocketknife and slit the cardboard sides of one box, pulling out a gray, soft brick of plastic explosives.

"Whoa!" murmured Gary in the huge storage facility. "There must be tons of explosives here. What can these people have in mind?"

Suddenly he was hit from behind and sent spinning into a huge pyramid of the skids of boxes. He fell to his knees but was hit again and flew across a large alleyway of space between boxes. Before another blow came, he whipped out a Taser and lunged at his assailant, hitting the man in his groin. The assailant fell to the floor, writhing in pain.

Just as Gary was about to congratulate himself, he heard the report of a pistol shot. At the same moment, he felt the sudden rip of the bullet through his upper left shoulder. Dodging several more rounds, he waited for the sweet sound of a magazine being ejected from a pistol and falling to the floor. In the meantime, he tried to discern the source of the shots. Clink! There it was. In that split second, he was over and around the cardboard cases, flying onto the back of the man with the gun. Gary hit the shooter before the man could slip a second clip into the pistol. The shooter spun into a wall of cardboard cases.

Gary struck so hard that he went off-balance into some nearby boxes. In spite of his wounds, he quickly hauled himself upright and flew at the assailant still fumbling to reload his gun. He kicked the gun out of his hand and punched the shooter until the man crashed to the floor, unmoving.

Gary waited for a moment. All was quiet. There seemed to be no one else in the facility. He pulled out a can of mace from a holster on his belt and put the tasered assailant into dreamland. He dragged his two unconscious attackers to a steel pipe and handcuffed them on either side of it, then left the building.

He walked slowly back to his car and managed to turn it around in the soft earth, taking care to keep his left shoulder as still as possible. He carefully navigated the trip back over the soft, red road, feeling exquisite relief when his tires hit pavement again.

But his jacket and shirt were now lathered in his own blood. He drove as fast as he could to the Deaconess Hospital's emergency room. It was well after dark when he finally got treated. He sat back down in the waiting room and remembered to call the night chief and tell him he was wounded, asking permission to miss work in the morning.

"Of course, Gary. Go home to Melody."

Gary bit his lip.

He had such an urge to tell the chief the truth, but he didn't. Police involvement would only complicate the problem.

"But first, I'll come by and check on you," the night chief added. "'Bye."

"No, I'm fine. W—wait—," Gary stuttered, but the chief had hung up.

Instantly his cell rang. It was Paul.

"Hello, Paul. Look, I can't talk right now. I have to call back the . . ." He stopped, overwhelmed by Paul's upsetting information.

"What?" he erupted. "What do you mean it's in the papers . . . You mean the whole thing? Are all their names mentioned?"

Gary listened, remaining silent but restless while Paul shared the details. He forgot about the night chief until, minutes later, the chief strode up to him. Gary looked up.

There was a long pause then Gary said, "Yeah, Paul. Thanks for telling me. I have to attend to something. I'll call you back." He hung up.

"Was that Dr. Shapiro?" asked the night chief.

"Yes," said Gary.

"His wife is missing and your wife is missing?"

"Is that what the papers said?"

"That's what they said."

"How did they know?"

"It seems the janitor of the Pathway of Light Cathedral saw Joanna Nickerson get abducted. Then he got a friend to try and call her circle of friends—he himself is deaf, you know—and nobody they tried to contact ever showed up. You know something about this, Gary?"

"Maybe . . ."

"When were you going to trust the police department?"

"It isn't a matter of trusting and not trusting. I have a note from the men who took all of the women captive. They made it clear that if we went to the police, our women wouldn't be coming back . . ." He stopped as a sob rose in his chest.

The chief patted him on the back.

"Since you know everything," Gary resumed, "I'll check with Paul Shapiro in the morning and see if he's heard anything."

"A couple of blues went over earlier. They spent a long time questioning him. He doesn't know anything more than he did yesterday or even this morning when you left on your own private Hardy Boys adventure. When were you going to call the rest of us in?"

Gary just shook his head.

"Shapiro believes the women were taken by Scarlet Jihad," said the chief. "What do you think, Gary?"

Gary wasn't ready to tell the chief everything, and until he had sorted it all through, he decided to tell him nothing.

"Like I said, I'm going."

"OK," said the chief. "Play this game your way, but if they were taken by Scarlet Jihad, my friend, you're playing with fire."

Gary got up and walked toward the exit.

"By the way," yelled the chief after him, "how'd you get yourself shot?"

"It's a long story," said Gary over his shoulder.

"When you're feeling better, I want to hear the whole thing," shouted the chief.

Gary went home to sleep and fell into a dreamlike trance. Sometime in the middle of the night, he awoke, remembering the involvement of al-Haj Sistani. Two things struck him with hope: he knew where Al lived, and he was prepared to beat out of this two-timing, hypocrite convert all that he might know about the kidnappings. He had to find Melody.

CHAPTER 24

The Pathway of Light Cathedral was a place of despondency on Sunday, August 5. They had no preacher.

The front page of the Seattle paper showed pictures of Pastor Nickerson and listed the names of all the missing women under the headline "WHERE ARE THESE WOMEN?" The article said their mysterious disappearance was "baffling" to their husbands as well as to the entire Seattle Police Department.

Gary and Paul went to church to ask if anyone there other than the janitor had seen the abduction, knew who the kidnappers were, or had any idea where the women had been taken. All was fruitless.

They had lunch together at Jonathan's Catch. And while the sea bass served there was generally considered the best in the area, neither of them was in the mood to comment on the cuisine.

"I'm off till Tuesday," said Gary as he pushed his half-eaten dinner toward the center of the table. "I wonder if you would like to make a call on al-Haj Sistani with me?"

Paul nodded, still chewing.

"I'd be glad for the company," Gary continued, "but I warn you, things are likely to get a little rough if and when we find him. He's involved in the evil business of everything Scarlet Jihad has in mind."

They spoke little after Gary's warning but paid for their meal and left. Soon they found themselves on the way to Al's newly rented apartment. He was not there. Gary kicked the door in. It shot open without even splintering the jamb. When it was utterly clear that Al wasn't home, they searched for any shred of information that might contribute anything to the case, rifling through Al's spartan accommodations. But nothing pointed to Al's complicity in Scarlet Jihad or their wives.

They drove out to Spratton Laser Technologies and checked out the rural warehouse off the red dirt road. Finally, they drove by the Starbucks on Queen Anne Hill where Gary had twice before seen some of Zalton's thugs. But nothing and no one turned up.

It was getting dark when Gary finally dropped Paul back by the Pathway of Light Cathedral where Paul had left his car. Both men felt deflated.

Gary shut off the engine and they talked for a little while. Eventually, Paul, without prefacing or asking permission for what he was about to do, simply bowed his head and began to pray silently.

Gary studied his silent friend for a moment or so. He himself had prayed so often that he felt all prayed out, and he wondered if prayer really had any purpose in a senseless world where horrible things happened and blotted out any reasonable definition of a God who cared about what went on in Seattle. Even as he watched, Paul was lost in a kind of anguish that wouldn't define itself. Gary watched as the silent tears crossed his face.

Silent is how we pray, thought Gary, *and silent is how God remains while human heartache rages. There is no reason in an unreasonable world.* He had prayed so many times during recent days that God would protect Melody and keep her alive and help him find her. But God was as silent as Paul was in all his ripping, tearing entreaties for God to care and come and help.

Gary sat, growing angrier and angrier at God, and would have raged aloud had he no compassion for the feelings of this praying friend. But something happened that arrested his thoughts. He saw a flash of silver on the sidewalk, clearly visible in the early evening light. Was it there or not? Was it an illusion or what? No, it was there as steady as light on silver fur.

"Kinta!" he shouted.

Paul quit praying as though the word *Kinta* was benediction enough to any earthly prayer. Gary switched on the ignition to follow the wolf. But at that precise moment, Kinta left the sidewalk and turned into the darkened shrubs that formed a curtain between the church and the cheap houses that crowded the rear of the building.

Gary and Paul both got out of the car and followed Kinta. Kinta turned from the darkened yard into another set of sidewalks and then back across some more yards in a northwestern direction. Again they followed across the yards and through the hedges of private homes. Several times they saw the glare of people's televisions shine on residents' faces.

On they passed. Twice they lost sight of the wolf, but each time they did, he seemed to wait for them. Finally, Kinta walked up to a door and let off a kind of shallow bark. Father Peter appeared at the door to let him in. But feeling no brush of the wolf against his leg, he turned his head down in Kinta's direction and said, "What's the matter, friend? Why do you not come in? What are you waiting for?"

"For us," said the psychiatrist.

"Paul Shapiro!"

"Me too," said the inspector.

"Gary Jarvis?"

"That's right!" said the policeman.

"Anyone else?"

"Nope, just us." Gary smiled.

"Come in, come in," said the priest.

They followed him into the room.

Then Gary stopped in his tracks. Father Peter was not alone. There stood al-Haj Sistani. Gary's anger was instantly stirred, and he flew across the room and punched the young Arab against the wall till Al fell sprawled on the floor.

Kinta growled, but not at Al—at Gary, who backed away from Al momentarily.

While Al collected his thoughts and shook his head, Gary advanced toward him, ready to pounce again if he tried to rise.

"Gary," said Father Peter, "get a hold of yourself!"

"Father, do you know what this man has done? Do you know who he is?"

"Not altogether," said the old priest.

"He's a member of Scarlet Jihad! He's one of Zalton's goons."

"How do you know this?" asked the old priest.

"I tailed him when he unloaded a truckload of plastic explosives in Spratton's secret warehouse. He should be put away for life."

"Nonsense," said the priest. "He became a Christian last week."

"Well, he was a Muslim terrorist on Saturday night. He's a liar and a double agent," said Gary.

"Al, is this true?" asked the old priest of the young Yemeni, who had finally gathered enough composure to stand again.

Al shook his head.

"It is true! You lying son of hell!" Once again Gary advanced toward the young man.

Al threw up his hand to speak.

"Before you strike him again, let's hear what he has to say," said the priest.

Gary stepped back and unclenched his fist.

"I was taking a truckload of . . . no, I must go further back," said Al. "After I lost the RLDs, I was out of favor with Zalton's boys. That's why I shaved my head and tried to hide out as a skinhead. But after the second shipment was stolen at the airport . . . "

Paul Shapiro shuffled in his seat, knowing who the thief was, but apparently Father Peter hadn't revealed that fact to the young Yemeni.

"I received word from my former comrades," Al continued, "that all was forgiven on the previous theft since I had nothing to do with the second theft. They thought me innocent, and I was restored to their confidence. But I am not a part of their cause."

"Former comrades!" blurted Gary. "Former? How former? You were working for them this past Saturday."

"Inspector, please," said the priest. "Let the man talk and then you can take your turn."

"Yes, former!" insisted Al. "You see, last week, I became a Christian!"

"Not much of one!" shouted Gary.

"Please," said Father Peter.

"It is true that I took a load of plastic explosives to Spratton's secret warehouse, but I did so knowing fully what they had in mind for the Seahawks' stadium. So in one of the boxes I packed a benzene detonator. On Tuesday morning that whole warehouse is going up in flames, and the explosion will expose Scarlet Jihad and destroy their plans."

Gary suddenly settled down. "Is Carol Jones gone? I suppose she's with the rest of the women—with our wives."

"Yes," Al said. "I found that out when I read the morning papers. I can't get her on the cell phone, and she's clearly not at her condo. She must be with the rest of the women. That's the only explanation I can think of."

"So you're not privy to what Zalton has going?"

"No, of course not. He is the only one among the Scarlet Jihad who knows the whole scheme. I know he has a terrible distaste for you and Paul."

"Why us in particular?" asked Gary.

"I should think it would be obvious. Paul took his wife away from him, and you are too hot on their trail to be trusted. If he has your wives, he believes he controls you. It's a simple matter of staying in charge until those four truckloads of explosives are put in place Wednesday.

"They're going in on Wednesday with PEPSICO vendor signs on their semis and will unload what appears to be stadium food. That's how they're going to do it. They will kill the drivers of the real vendor trucks, take their trucks to the country warehouse, and load them up with the boxes."

"How do you know all this?"

"Well, as you discovered on Saturday, I'm eligible to be one of the drivers if Zalton wants me. But I doubt he will. He has plenty of Yemeni hopefuls who are eager to be martyrs. It won't ever get that far. What Zalton doesn't know is that the warehouse is going up in smoke on Tuesday."

"If what you are telling us is true," said Gary, "then you are a good man. No, you're a genius—a Christian genius!"

"Not really," said Al. "I just have this cold feeling in my gut that our women are being detained in that warehouse. So we have less than forty-eight hours to get them out before the whole thing blows."

Suddenly Gary saw the light. "Dear God! That's got to be where they are. It's the easiest place Zalton could keep them, because if anything happened to all those explosives, the women would be gone as well and nobody would ever make the connection between his devious plans for the stadium or the kidnappings."

After a bit of chit-chat, Gary and Paul walked outside, leaving Al and Father Peter in the house.

For a while they walked in silence, then Paul broke into the silence with some urgency. "Look, Gary, we've got to go through that warehouse and find that benzene detonator. We must."

"But how will we do it, Paul? There are a lot of boxes there. You and I could not get through them all on our own."

"I've got an idea. Let me work on it," said Paul. "I'll be in touch." He set off to walk back to his car at the church.

As for Gary, there was one more call he had to make. Al had made it clear that there was one person who knew where the women were. He knew everything, every twist and trick of Scarlet Jihad's business.

They had fewer than forty-eight hours. And having a brief talk with Zalton al-Zhabahni would take the first hour of his next forty-eight.

■ ■ ■

Paul knew he also must use the time wisely. His wife's life was at stake. His child . . . God knew where his Barney was. With Father Peter busy and Sister Joanna gone, Paul drove directly to Holy Faith Abbey on Old Bellingham Road.

CHAPTER 25

Gary Jarvis drove immediately to the al-Zhabahni mansion. He parked his car and knocked on the front door. No one answered so he kicked open the door—his second of the day. The security alarm went off, but Gary didn't worry about the police coming before he got in and out. He wandered almost casually through the immense house until he found Zalton's office. He heard distant pulsing of squad cars responding to the alarm system. Finding no clues, he strode out the huge front door he had kicked in. He was long gone by the time the police arrived.

He drove straight to the mosque, but it was locked up. By the time he got out to the Spratton corporate offices, it was nearly dawn. No one but the evening security crew was there, and they would be ill-informed and suspicious about any questions as to Zalton's location.

He left with no idea of where to look next. He decided to return home for the remainder of the night to get some rest. He didn't sleep well. He kept feeling that the important part of the time he had left to find the women was being squandered by his purely selfish need to rest.

■ ■ ■

At 5:00 a.m., Monday, August 6, Gary was up again. He decided to check the Starbucks where he'd seen the Yemenis on previous occasions, but they were not there. In fact, besides the two sleepy-eyed clerks behind the counter, there was no one there. Finding himself desperately in need of a caffeine jolt, he decided to have a cup of coffee himself.

As he sat sipping, he tried to think where the Yemeni terror group might possibly be hanging out so early in the morning. He finished one cup of coffee and then took another, nibbling on a dry biscotti while he drank. His mind was muddled with desperation and sleeplessness. He went to the small men's room around 7:00 a.m. to get rid of some of the coffee. While in the restroom, he heard two overly loud male voices in the coffee shop, and they weren't speaking English. He opened the restroom door to have a peek. There were Zalton and Rasul!

"If Mohammed will not go to the mountain, the mountain must come to Mohammed," he murmured happily.

He washed his hands, touched the handle of his pistol in its shoulder strap, and then left the bathroom, approaching the pair of men—who were now seated—from the rear. He slipped up behind Zalton, shoved the gun in his rib cage, and said, "Get up very slowly, you Arabian devil. Make one false move and I'm gonna pull this trigger and blow you straight to hell, and you can forget about those seventy-two virgins."

Gary kept one hand on the pistol, almost surgically inserted in Zalton's ribs, and the other on Zalton's collar to keep him from attempting to run.

Gary glanced at the other man. "Come along, Rasul, or I'll blow your head off too. You terrorists like to play rough, don't you? You love blowing up planes filled with innocent, unarmed people. Well, let's see how you do with a real, tough, hairy-legged, Christian man who's got a pistol at your head, you gutless Muslims."

Gary was too angry to worry about being politically correct. "Well, I'm gonna show you how one ordinary Seattle citizen gets even for all the young lives you took out on the *U.S.S. Cole*. Now, get up, Rasul, or you ain't gonna have a boss in about thirty seconds." He pressed the pistol. "Tell him, Zalton. Tell him to come on, or I'll blow you to kingdom come, so help me God—that's God, not Allah—you got that?"

"Come on, Rasul," said Zalton. "Do as he says."

Gary saw the startled Starbucks barrister pick up the phone as the three men exited. He knew the kid was calling 9-1-1 and knew he was working against the clock at this time. When they reached the outside of the coffee shop, Gary said, "Pay attention, Rasul. I'm only going to ask you once. What have you done with my wife?"

"You can go to hell!" shouted Rasul.

"Bad answer!" shouted Gary. Then he kicked Rasul in the groin. Rasul bent over in pain. Gary took the gun out of Zalton's ribs and pistol-whipped Rasul into unconsciousness. He fell silent at Gary's feet.

Gary quickly put the gun back into Zalton's ribs and said, "Now there's just the two of us. I'm gonna ask you only once, Mr. Z, where's my wife? Be careful how you answer because I'm currently having a wonderful time kicking big fat Arab derrieres. And I would like nothing more than to get my boot on yours."

Suddenly Gary felt a sharp blow to the side of his head.

"That's for you, Yankee infidel!"

Ishaq had come from out of nowhere, and Gary's enjoyable world of consciousness fell apart. He was faintly aware of being kicked in the stomach by Ishaq as the sound of sirens came racing up Queen Anne Hill. He had no idea that Ishaq had come very close to shooting him with his own pistol but was prevented by Zalton al-Zhabahni, who told him to throw the pistol back on the policeman and stick with the program. There was too much to be lost by letting Ishaq's anger get out of hand.

■ ■ ■

About an hour after Gary lost consciousness, Melody was sitting quietly in the circle of women whose will was slipping into murky weakness. The albino and Rasul entered the room.

"I am going to try this one more time," said Ishaq. "Which one of you is the inspector's wife? Before any of you get noble in shielding any other member of this party, let me point out the tongs I am holding in my hand. It's manicure time. If you continue lying, I am going to deal with your fingernails one at a time. Now who wants to be honest and who wants to be stupid?"

This time none of the women said anything. Melody felt that she could no longer let her sisters pretend and protect her. "I'm Mrs. Jarvis," she said.

"Do the rest of you agree to this?" Again, Ishaq's threats were met with silence.

"Well, come along, Mrs. Jarvis. We'll find out if you really are Melody Jarvis, one fingernail at a time."

Melody stood and then rolled up her sleeve, showing Ishaq the tattoo she and Gary had gotten on their honeymoon in the Caribbean. "Gary and Melody" was inked on a fuzzy blue arrow run through a bright red heart.

"Well, that's more like it, my little infidel," said Ishaq. "Come on. We're going to get your husband on the phone, and you're going to talk to him about calling off his surveillance of the warehouse."

"He won't listen. He never listens to bad men."

"So you think I'm a bad man, do you? Well, I guarantee you that your husband will listen. Every time we take off another finger-nail, he will listen to you scream and he will obey. American men are weak that way. They have such a respect for women they have become like women themselves."

"Unlike Muslim men, who have no respect for men or women," said Melody.

Ishaq cuffed her across the face. "I'd advise you to keep quiet. You can be more talkative when we get your man on the phone."

He led Melody from the room, shoving her through the door and then following her and slamming the door behind them.

Joanna gathered her little flock around her and they prayed for Melody.

Ishaq tried to dial Gary Jarvis but was unable to reach him, not realizing that Gary was still sitting on the sidewalk outside Starbucks, trying to get the fuzz out of his brain.

"Very well, Mrs. Jarvis, since your husband is busy, I'll save the interview for later. Right now I have some things to attend to in the city, and I just don't feel like having an alert woman with me." He seized her head and stuffed a chloroformed rag against her face. Her mind swam for a bit, then suddenly Ishaq disappeared and her entire world was gone.

■ ■ ■

She awoke with that dreadful taste in her mouth.

"I'm thirsty," she said.

"Give her something to drink," said a man's voice.

"What?" said another voice.

"Water," was the reply.

Soon Melody could see the shadowy face of a bearded man bringing her a drink of water. She gulped it eagerly. It tasted so cold and so good. But exhaustion overwhelmed her, and she fell unconscious again.

Some time later, she awoke again. This time she tried to look around. The room swam a bit. Her hands were tied behind her with a plastic cinch again, and she felt a stifling sensation from being forced to breathe unventilated air. She was not in the same room where she had been with the other women, but she was still in a room that had no windows.

Gradually her swimming vision found a solid place to stand, and she could see more clearly. The dimly lit room was full of trash—all kinds of boxes and other paraphernalia. She could see coils of wire and boxes labeled EXPLOSIVOS and PELIGROSO. Even though her knowledge of Spanish was remedial, she knew that whoever was detaining her was making improvised explosive devices. There was a benzene soldering torch aflame on a work bench and strange blocks of gray clay or something.

She heard the footfalls of two men approaching. They were speaking in a foreign language, probably Arabic. She decided to continue to appear unconscious.

They eventually entered and, after pausing to see if she appeared awake, continued their conversation and moved to the work table. Melody waited a while, then worked up the courage to open her eyes to watch what they were doing. Both men were clearly Arabic and occupied with inserting coils of copper wire into various sorts of rubber electrical fittings.

At one point in their conversation, the face of the older of the two men came fully into the low lamplight in the room. Where had she seen that man before? Then it came crashing through her dim consciousness—Zalton al-Zhabahni, the CEO of Spratton Laser Technologies. She had often seen his picture in the business section of the Seattle papers. She unintentionally gasped a bit. Instantly the heads of her captors swung in her direction. Both could see that she was conscious. They dropped what they were doing and ran in her direction.

One of the men belted her in the face, while the other crammed a wadded, chloroform-soaked cloth over her nose. Once more Melody lapsed into a limp existence, hearing Zalton say something angrily to his companion, whom he called "Ishaq."

CHAPTER 26

"All right, brothers," said Brother Lawrence, "we're almost there. Do you remember the plan?"

They all nodded.

"Don't lie unless you have to. And if you have to, there will be a mandatory confession at 8:00 a.m. on Tuesday. Keep track of your sins—all of your sins—especially you, Brother Anselm."

A shy priest in the middle of the bus looked as if he agreed fully.

Paul Shapiro sat silently in the middle of the bus, looking at all the brothers gathered around him. Dressed in Levis and white T-shirts, they didn't look like monks. With their beards and impeccable clothes, they looked more like old rock stars who had finally learned to do their own laundry.

But Paul knew they fully understood the danger of their mission. So it was with confidence that he watched them clip on their teamster badges, which they had produced in the wee hours of Monday morning on their monastery computer. Each badge had their picture and their pre-holy-order name. The badges looked very authentic—authentic enough to convince the three teamster security men who guarded the facility.

They drove past the Spratton office building and onto the red clay road that ran for four miles through the forest. The old monastery bus had never been labeled and was as white as the T-shirted occupants of the bus. Paul wasn't altogether sure that his plan would work, but if his wife was a prisoner at the remote warehouse, it was certainly worth a try.

The bus pulled up at the warehouse, and the men silently got off. When they filed up to the loading docks, they were met abruptly by one of the guards.

"What can I do for you gents?" said one of the guards with a foreign accent.

"I'm Father . . . Brother . . . Mr. Ned Baker. Teamster Union, Local 306." Brother Lawrence made a mental note: sin number one—lying to the guard. "And we're here to load the trucks when they get here."

"Well, which is it—Father or Brother or Mister?"

"Just call me Ned."

"These trucks are supposed to be unloaded only by nonunion workmen from Yemen," said the guard.

"New orders, pal. All boxes are union—loaded or unloaded— or we 'yellow tape' this warehouse and close its doors." Ned Baker was surprised at the believability he was putting into his lies.

"The trucks won't be here till tomorrow."

"Tomorrow!" said Brother Lawrence. "We were told the trucks would be here today!" He hadn't lied in a while, and even though he felt that he had done this one very convincingly, he knew he had to keep track: sin number two. "Well, if we could step into the dispatcher's office, I would like to see the manifest and order."

"Certainly," said the guard. "The rest of you, back into the bus. We'll see you in the morning. That's when the trucks come."

"Back into the bus, men," said Brother Lawrence.

Dutifully the men began to file back into the bus as Ned followed the guard into the dispatcher's office. Ned was glad the small office was empty.

The sentry picked up the dispatcher's book. "See? I'll show you right here. The date is August the seventh, and this is August the sixth. You'll have to go back into town and come back in the morning."

"Well, you're right. Does the manifest tell how many teamsters you'll need to do the loading?"

No sooner had the sentry turned back to look at the book than a sharp blow to the back of his head sent him sprawling into a steel post, which further deepened his concussion. He was clearly down for the count.

"Oh, Lord," said Ned Baker in a whisper, "that makes sin number three."

Just as he finished the prayer, two other sentries came running up to the dispatch office. "We thought we heard a noise," said one of them. "Where's Bahni?"

"Bahni?"

"The other guard?"

"Oh, he's probably lying around somewhere. Look, I'm Ned Baker, Teamster Local 306. I'm here with a crew to load the trucks when they come."

"They're not coming till tomorrow," said one of the two men.

"That's exactly what Bahni said. But would you just look at this manifest?" asked Brother Lawrence, holding it out to them. When their heads came close enough together to see the manifest at the same time, Ned quickly placed his hands on opposite sides of their heads and brought them crashing together with such force they both fell unconscious to the floor.

"Sins number four and five," admitted Brother Lawrence. He thought that all of the sentries on duty had shown up. But just to be sure, he picked up the dispatcher's microphone, pushed the speaker button, and said, "All employees of Spratton, please report to the dispatcher's office at once." The echo of the loud speakers ricocheted through the cavernous warehouse. Nobody showed up, so Brother Lawrence figured they were free of any trouble for the moment. He went back outside.

"Men," he said, "get off the bus. We're going in to begin our work. We're looking for a clock and a bottle of benzene in one of these boxes. There will also be a detonation device and a battery pack."

They all filed off the bus.

"Be careful with your morality!" said Brother Lawrence. "I was only in there ten minutes, and I told two lies and bludgeoned three bad guys."

The monks looked alarmed and crossed themselves.

"I think most of the dirty work is done, so you should be able to get by with a minimum of transgressions. I'll expect all of you to show up to the confessional tomorrow. Don't worry, Anselm. We'll be taking extra time, so you won't have to hurry. Now, men, to work! Let's get the job done and get out of here."

The monks crossed themselves again and entered the warehouse. Each of them was armed with box cutters.

Two hours later, they were back on the bus with a bottle of benzene, a timer, and a battery pack.

Paul was the last to exit the warehouse. He stepped up to the bus door. "I'll be back tomorrow to get my car. In the meantime, I am going to stay around the warehouse and do a little snooping of my own."

"OK," said Brother Lawrence, "but be careful, Paul. You know how these guys hate Jews."

"I know. Thanks, Brother Lawrence, for a job well done." He stepped back down into the red dirt. "By the way, which one of your men found the detonator?"

But he really needed no answer. Brother Anselm was smiling.

The bus pulled away.

■ ■ ■

"What happened to you?" asked Ishaq as he splashed a glass of cold water directly into the face of the sentry who had a huge bruise across the front of his forehead.

"I don't know. A bus full of teamsters came and said they were ready to load the trucks and then this one—"

"What makes you think they were teamsters?"

"They all had badges."

Ishaq gnashed his teeth. "Look at this!" he shouted. "Look what happened. What kind of security guards are you anyway?" He kicked one of the Yemeni men who was still lying on the floor to vent his anger. "Look at this place!"

The entire warehouse was strewn with opened cases around piles of plastic explosives. "Who were these people?" he shouted.

"I told you; they were Teamsters Local 306," said one of the sentries. "They all had badges. Call the union and find out who they were."

Ishaq took out his cell phone, pushed an automatic dial button, and placed the phone to his ear. "Is this Local 306? . . . Did you send a team of truckloaders out to Spratton Laser Technologies?"

Whoever was on the other end of the phone was clearly confused.

"No," Ishaq fumed, "not the main complex, the warehouse . . . What warehouse would that be? What kind of numbskull are you?" Ishaq realized that he was about to give away an important secret that Spratton had created at great expense. "Never mind," he said. "Thank you very much!"

Ishaq decided that it was time to take up dialogue with another of his detainees. He had no idea of how informed the police really were and worried that their plot would be exposed when he needed to keep it quiet for two more days. Then his attack on the infidels would destroy the hordes of indulgent sinners as Allah intended.

Most of all, he was troubled that his warehouse had been plundered by some group who had rifled through four truckloads of explosives looking for he knew not what. All of the explosives appeared to be present and accounted for—none of the boxes was empty. What were they looking for if not the explosives themselves?

And no one had discovered the female hostages still secreted away there.

Thinking of the women reminded him to head to their quarters to question them. So he left the warehouse's cavernous steel-ribbed vault and went down into the concrete subfloor to deal with them.

He called Jibril during his walk. Jibril was thirty minutes away, having a drink at a bar on Queen Anne Hill, but he promised he would drive as fast as he could so Ishaq would have some help with his hostage interrogation.

"Did you ever get that policeman's wife to talk about how much her husband might know?" asked Jibril.

But before Ishaq could answer, his cell phone crackled and the call dropped off.

At least Ishaq knew Jibril was on the way. The albino entered the small, dark hallway that led to the dingy concrete room where the women waited. He stuck his key in the door and turned it. There was a commotion on the other side of the door. The women had gotten used to the door flying open, and since it never afforded them any good news, they ran to the darkened corners of the room like frightened animals.

"I've got a few questions to ask you, Mrs. Shapiro," said Ishaq, approaching her and yanking her up by the arm. "You've got to know more than you let on. You're married to the man who has been Clarisse's counselor."

"Then ask me," said Clarisse. "Leave Mrs. Shapiro alone."

"Believe me, I would like to, you Yankee infidel dog. Unfortunately my boss hasn't given me permission. Why he loves you—why any good Muslim man of faith would love you—I'll never understand."

"Where's Melody—Melody Jarvis?" demanded Joanna.

"Let's just say she's in a very safe place and will be released as soon as she confesses to her husband's complicity with the police."

"Complicity with the police!" Joanna yelled. "He works for the police. He's a policeman. And you can bet that if he finds you, he'll kick your little Arab buttocks all the way back to Yemen."

"You're one mouthy Christian woman. Your kind of big-mouthed mama is why the Prophet told us to keep women in their place."

"You got some kind of prophet that tells all you hairy-chested terrorists to beat up on women. Must make all you men feel mighty proud, kicking around your women and children and acting like you're some high and mighty spiritual gurus. Ain't nothin' wrong with your prophet that wouldn't have been better if he'd started acting more like Jesus. Your so-called prophet is keeping the world in poverty and pain and causing millions of useless murders."

Rhonda could see Ishaq growing red with rage even in the dim light.

"Furthermore," said Joanna, "if he had thirteen wives, I should think that many good women could have strangled him themselves."

"Joanna, don't . . . ," said Rhonda.

But her warning came too late. Ishaq dropped Rhonda's arm and walked over to Joanna. He doubled up his fist and struck her in the jaw. The blow was so hard that Joanna spun into the concrete wall, then stumbled for a couple of steps and fell to the floor. She was down but not out. She shook her head as if to clear away the brutality and managed to get to her feet again.

"Listen up, you Christian prostitutes!" shouted Ishaq. "Let this be a lesson to you. Never say anything bad about the Prophet. Come on, Mrs. Shapiro, let's see how much you know."

He grabbed Rhonda by the arm again and shoved her toward the door.

Surprisingly quick, Joanna moved her large frame directly in Ishaq's path. "I can't let you do this," she said.

Ishaq once again dropped Rhonda's arm and drew back his fist as though to hit Joanna. And then the most amazing thing happened. Joanna caught his none-too-large fist in her ample palm and spun him around so fast that she wheeled her back against his abdomen before he even realized what was happening. Then she stomped her stiletto heel directly down on top of his foot. While he grimaced in pain, she drew her elbow forward and then sent it flying backward into his ribs. There was a sound of cracking. Once more the surprised Yemeni man bent even further forward at the pain. Then she spun around and brought her large knee directly into Ishaq's groin. He fell forward, and she moved quickly out of his way, punching the back of his neck so that the blow drove him to the floor. His head cracked the concrete, and he lay there completely unconscious.

"Next time you feel like beating up on women, you'll do better to get saved!"

The women in the room were stunned into silence.

"I'm sure glad I'm saved," said Clarisse. "I knew I got saved for some reason."

"Me too. I'll think twice before I get unsaved," said Mary Muebles quietly.

Joanna was breathing heavily.

"Joanna"—Carol smiled—"you are a very persuasive evangelist."

"Where did you learn how to do that?" asked Clarisse.

"Remember that old *Miss Congeniality* film with Sandra Bullock? She called it the S.I.N.G. maneuver."

"Sing?" asked Clarisse.

"Yeah, you know, that's where you hit the big, bad ones. S.I.N.G.: Side, Instep, Nostrils, and Groin. I always wondered if it would work. This seemed like a good time to try it out."

Clarisse walked up to the inert Muslim. "I've known you for a long time, you worthless, rotten terrorist, and I've always wanted to do *that* to you," she said, kicking him in the stomach.

Nobody else moved.

"Are you sure he's unconscious, Joanna?" Carol asked.

"I think he's out of it, girls."

"Well, then here's one for me!" Carol announced, walking up and giving him a swift kick in the rear.

"Girls, I hate to spoil your fun time, but we need to get out of here lest he should come to," said Joanna. She took Ishaq's hands and dragged him over to the pipe, then took the empty handcuffs that had been Rhonda's and bound him.

"Let's get out of here," said Joanna.

The women needed no further encouragement. They followed Joanna out the door.

Joanna stopped. "Look, he's got to have a gun. I'm going to go get it." She turned around, walked over to Ishaq, and removed the gun from his hip pocket. "We may need this. But one thing is for sure: he doesn't need it."

She started to leave again, then stopped and stooped down and began going through his pockets. "I'm taking his cell phone," she said. "That should keep him from calling out for help in case he gets the urge."

The women smiled.

"Joanna, you are just plain good at this espionage stuff," said Rhonda.

The women continued to watch her as she pulled a set of keys from his left front pocket. She smiled, stood, and rejoined her friends just outside the door. Experimenting with the key set, she finally found the one that locked the door. "Now I am ready to go," she said.

The other women followed her beyond the hallway into the cavernous warehouse. Joanna placed her index finger upright in the center of her lips to signal all the women to be quiet as they followed her along.

They could hear a radio playing somewhere on the far side of the warehouse. They kept to the wall where the lighting was poor, hoping that whatever guards or warehousemen were around would not see them.

As Joanna and her friends drew closer to the door, they spied three sentries drinking coffee from Styrofoam cups. They were squarely in the path the women needed to escape. The men were engrossed in a conversation, but they were also blocking the door to freedom.

"Girls," whispered Joanna, "I'm gonna create a diversion to let you leave through this door. Now, I've got to get to the opposite side of the warehouse to do it. But when I divert them, I expect you to *move*." Then for reasons that defied them all, she handed Rhonda Ishaq's cell phone.

"Wait," whispered Rhonda, as she took the phone from Joanna. "What kind of diversion?"

"Now, honey, there are some things you just don't need to know," whispered Joanna. "But now that I've given you Ishaq's phone, give me yours."

"But the battery won't work."

"What I want to use it for won't require batteries." She grabbed Rhonda's dead phone, turned, and left.

The women waited for almost ten minutes, then saw Joanna emerging from the shadows fifty yards from them. What was she doing? She was walking right under a bright light. Right out into the open.

"Yoo hoo, all Yemenis! It's me, Joanna the Christian."

Rhonda couldn't believe how utterly brazen she was. The moment Joanna called, the three men dropped their cups and ran toward her, drawing their pistols. Simultaneously, Rhonda shoved the stunned women hurriedly toward the exit.

"Now, boys," said Joanna, "I wouldn't get rough. I've got a pistol, too, but more important than that, I've got my cell phone." She pulled Rhonda's phone out of her pocket. "See, fellas, I've already dialed the number to a timer right out here in the middle of all these boxes. All I've gotta do is push the Send button to the detonator and then, well . . . You'd be amazed at how one dedicated Christian woman can make Muslim terrorists look weak."

By the time she finished her threat, the exit door onto the docks was swinging wide open and all the women were gone. Joanna, however, did not fare as well. The three men rushed her and one of them struck her with the butt of his pistol. She was knocked unconscious. But even as she fell, Isaiah caught her.

"Thou hast done a wonderful thing, Joanna," said the prophet.

"Yea verily thou hast!" said Spotty, "I don't know that I agree with all of thy tactics, but what thou didst for your terrified friends was wonderful. But I don't mind telling thee that things are going to be tough for thee when Ishaq gets free."

It was the first time Joanna could remember Spotty speaking in King James. She wanted to say thanks, but she slipped into a coma before she could get it said.

■ ■ ■

Paul Shapiro's cell phone rang. He looked at the dashboard of his car and then picked up the phone from an empty beverage holder.

"Hello," he said.

"Pauly! It's Rhonda! We're all at a McDonald's that's just a mile from the offices of Spratton Laser Technologies, but we had to walk more than four miles to get here. We were all imprisoned in the hidden warehouse off a dirt road. I don't think even the police know about this one."

"Oh, Ronnie, it is so wonderful to hear from you! Are you OK? What happened?"

"Listen, I'll tell you when we meet. Just get here. We're going to wait down the road in a grove of trees. When we see our car, we'll all come out. We think we're being followed, so we're taking precautions. Oh, Paul, is there any word on Barney?"

"No—now don't cry. Everybody's praying. We'll all start looking as soon as we know where to look."

"Paul, I love you," Rhonda said, her voice momentarily quivering. "We've had some trouble too. Joanna didn't make it out, and we haven't seen Melody Jarvis in three days. But the rest of us are here."

"I'll be right there. Stay safe," Paul said and hung up.

Neither Melody nor Joanna could be accounted for. Paul wondered what might have become of them.

■ ■ ■

When Paul and Rhonda met, they were overjoyed to see each other. Paul notified Gary in a very brief phone call to give him an update on Melody. Gary could ask for back-up or whatever he needed to do to get the police involved. The rescued women were ecstatic to see Paul, and their joy erupted in tears and hugs and a kind of delirious mayhem.

When this mutual hubbub subsided, Rhonda began to cry, and Paul, who wanted to be strong for her, found himself crying as well. They held each other for the longest time, and while relieved to be together, both were thinking of their baby.

Suddenly, Paul's cell phone rang.

"Paul Shapiro here." He tried to sound professional.

Silence. Then: "Mama, Papa, Mama, Papa!" said a small voice.

Paul trembled and handed the phone to Rhonda.

"Mama, Papa!" said the tiny voice.

Rhonda fell against Paul, shedding tears of delirium.

Paul took the phone again.

"Paul," said a friendly, familiar male voice, "I'm having a great time with Barney. We're up at your cabin outside of Carnation, Washington. Wanna come see us?"

"Father Peter! Bless you, bless you! We'll be right there."

Once Gary had assured the others they were about to be rescued, Paul and Rhonda drove recklessly fast and were at the cabin's driveway within the hour. Paul pulled up to the cabin and shut off the engine. Then he and Rhonda saw a wonderful sight. Barney was toddling through the low shrubs with his chubby hand locked in the silver fur of the great wolf. On came the beast and the child, like the lion and lamb, like love and power, like all that have meaning with all who give meaning.

Heaven was real.

Earth was its promise of substance.

Barney was alive.

CHAPTER 27

Melody Jarvis awoke in the darkness with a tiny thread of light coming through a long tube. She struggled and found that while her bindings were gone, she was tightly enclosed in some sort of box.

Horror-stricken, she realized she had been buried alive.

After the initial terror of her discovery, she willed herself to think of other things, so as not to focus on her predicament. She thought of how her hands and feet were no longer bound. She decided to practice some very shallow isometric exercises. They would not preserve her muscular movements if her imprisonment lasted a long time, but if her incarceration turned out to be short, they would help.

She was maddeningly thirsty. Her free hands groped around inside her coffin-sized box. Her right hand fell upon a rather large flask. She moved it carefully to her mouth, and while there was barely room to tilt the bottle, she felt a trickle of water hit her tongue. She drank it carefully and then set it back down within reach. She felt her pregnant belly pressed against the top of the coffin and suddenly wondered what time it was.

She drew her left hand toward her face, thankful for the cheap watch Gary had bought her in Acapulco from a street vendor years earlier. It was gaudy, but she had kept it out of regard for him. Now it was invaluable to her. It had an illuminated dial. She pressed the light button. It was 9:43.

But it couldn't be evening; there was light coming through the breathing tube. Two or three times she thought she heard birds singing. That meant that she had slept through the whole night without moving. So it had to be 9:43 a.m. the next day.

She lay there thinking about how to keep her sanity when a voice came through the tube. "Melody, can you hear me? I have an assignment for you."

"Get me out of here!" she screamed. "They're trying to kill me. Help! Help!"

"Melody, please settle down," said the reassuring voice. "Stay calm. Panic is not going to help right now."

Melody desperately worked at controlling her hysteria, and when she was calmer, she asked, "Who are you?"

"Never mind that right now. I am used to living in darkness and it is negotiable."

Melody knew immediately who it was. "Father Peter! Thank God it's you!"

"Melody, don't worry. I'm going to figure a way to get you out of here."

"Oh, Father Peter. I'm so thankful you've come."

"I'm going to give you two assignments: the first is to take these sleeping pills. Do you have any water down there?"

"Yes, Father."

"I'm going to drop a couple of these pills down this tube. Tell me if you get them."

There was a pause. Melody could tell there were shadows passing through the tube, and the pills fell fairly near her chin. She picked up the pills, put them in her mouth, and swallowed them.

Father Peter spoke again, "I'm going to drop two more of them, but don't take them for a while. It's broad daylight out here. And I can hear a lot of people out beyond this section of trees. Where you are is awfully close to the remote Spratton warehouse. I don't believe anybody has seen me yet. At least Kinta hasn't let on, but

I'm going to have to leave you for a while. I'll get somebody, locate a shovel, and get you out of there. But I can't do it right now. I promise you, though, that I'll be back."

"Wait! When are you coming back? And what's my second assignment?" Melody shouted.

"Well, it ought to be keeping quiet. Try not to scream or make any noise, as sooner or later this section will be passed by someone. But your second assignment is to memorize these words from Psalm 116. Whenever you're awake, work on these."

"What are they? Go ahead."

"'Return to your rest, my soul,'" began Father Peter, "'for the Lord has been good to you. For you rescued me from death, my eyes from tears, my feet from stumbling. I will walk before the Lord in the land of the living.'"

Suddenly the world was quiet. Melody felt a wonder in knowing that someone knew where she was and, like the everlasting God, he had given her assurance that he would be back. She believed the priest and the wolf were servants of the most high God. She had little to do but to trust them and memorize a passage of Scripture. She wondered if it would come back to her. But she tried the words in faint whispers and they were hers. And she knew the priest would tell her husband where she was.

"Return to your rest, my soul," Melody said, "for the Lord has been good to you. For you rescued me from death, my eyes from tears, my feet from stumbling. I will walk before the Lord in the land of the living." The light from the tube fell with a blinding splendor as she replayed the words. At last she fell asleep with the rich words on her tongue.

■ ■ ■

When Gary awoke late on Tuesday, August 7, he somehow sensed it was going to be the longest day of his life. He still had a huge lump on his head from being struck by a pistol handle yesterday. Now Zalton and his boys knew he was on to them, but he still didn't know where to look for them. Worst of all was having no idea where to look for Melody.

Paul called to tell him that only four of the six women hostages had escaped. He was plunged into agony when he learned that Melody was not among the escapees. He had no idea what had happened to her. His despair only deepened when he checked his e-mail. There was an anonymous message.

> *Inspector Jarvis: Your wife has been buried alive.*
> *She should live for a while, if she can stand the close*
> *quarters, but she will remain safe only so long as*
> *you make no attempt to rescue her. Her position is*
> *unknown by anyone but those to whom her safekeeping*
> *is a matter of little concern. Try to rescue her and we*
> *will introduce a small blast of cyanide gas down her*
> *breathing tube.*
>
> *We suspect that your friends at the police office have*
> *already been tampering with the contents of our*
> *warehouse. Leave us alone till the weekend is passed,*
> *and your wife will be returned to you unharmed.*
> *Interfere with any of our plans and the retribution of*
> *Scarlet Jihad will be swift. Your wife's life is not in our*
> *hands but yours.*

Rhonda had told Paul where Ishaq was chained, and Paul had told Gary. Naturally, Gary—ignoring the kidnappers' note—made straight for the very warehouse he had earlier discovered. It was late afternoon by the time he drew near to the hidden warehouse.

His fatigue was exacerbated by a dull throbbing headache from Ishaq's pistol handle. But the adrenalin of finding Melody and the hope that she was still alive kept driving him forward.

He decided that he would park his car a long way back from the second warehouse and walk around behind the complex. Maybe when it was dark he could find a way into the highly secured facility from the back.

By the time he was situated, it was almost seven o'clock, and the overcast sky was bringing on an early darkness. Gary pulled out his pistol and his flashlight and walked the mile of country road that abutted the barbed-wire fence around the back of the property. The first lights of evening were popping on all along the back wall of the warehouse. Should he break in or not? Was she even in there? And if so, she could be in any dark corner of it, and he might still not find her for a long time.

"What should I do, God?" It was a prayer of frustration; he was sure God would not take the time to answer it.

But just at that time, he saw a flash of silver in the forest behind the warehouse. He moved toward it and saw the flash again. It was a wolf. Had he been hit on the head so hard he was seeing things? No, it really was there. And there was a man, a tall man who looked like . . . "Oh, God," prayed Gary, "let it be Father Peter."

Gary slipped up very close to Father Peter and said nothing. Nor did Kinta make a noise. Not a single rumble passed his throat.

"Gary Jarvis," said Father Peter.

"Yes! Yes! But how did you know it was me?"

"It's the Chrome Azzaro, remember? Kinta, don't attack him, even if he's got on that foul smelling stuff."

Gary smiled.

"Gary, look around. Can you see a shovel anywhere?"

Gary's heart skipped a beat. "Father Peter, I've been going mad looking for Melody. Do you have any idea where she is?"

"But of course. Fifty feet more and you'll be four feet above where she is."

"Four feet above? She's buried alive around here?"

"Yes, and has spent the day memorizing Psalm 116. Do you know it, Gary?"

Gary ignored the question. "But where is she?"

"Kinta," said the old man, "take us to her."

The old priest grabbed the wolf's harness and followed him into the woods. They soon came to a standpipe. "Melody," said Father Peter, "how is your work going on the psalm?"

Gary could hear the faint strains of his wife's voice coming calmly from the breathing tube: "Return to your rest, my soul, for the Lord has been good to you. For you rescued me from death, my eyes from tears, my feet from stumbling. I will walk before the Lord in the land of the living."

Gary was mad with joy.

"Melody, darling, it's me! I'll have you out of there in no time."

Melody became so excited she tried to raise her head and bumped it against the top of the coffin.

Gary shone his flashlight around in the gloom of what appeared to be a thousand tree trunks. Leaning against a nearby trunk was a shovel. Whoever buried Melody had left it there.

He began digging furiously. In a few minutes, his shovel hit the wooden box. The shovel flew, and within moments Gary saw a crude rope hasp binding the coffin lid. He yanked the rope free and drew the wooden door back with no effort at all. There Melanie lay, almost blinded at first by the flashlight. Gary extended his hand. She was so weak, she could barely lift her hand to take his, but she managed to get it up slightly. Gary got carefully into the box with her and lifted her out of the box. She could barely sit up on the ledge of the hole, but her face was alight with joy.

"Gary, oh, Gary, darling! I thought I would never live to see you again." Melody was weaving as though she might actually fall back into the hole. Gary steadied her a bit.

"Gary, I'm scared to death! These men hate you! They said they wanted to kill you."

"Nobody's gonna kill me. And if anybody does, it won't be that punk Ishaq."

Gary was so firm in his reply that it shut off all conversation for a while. Finally Melody spoke into the darkness, while she still held very firmly to Gary's hand.

"Gary, darling, my back hurts something awful. Take me home so I can prop up my legs. I want to carry our baby to term."

"Melody, listen, I'm not gonna take you home. That's the last place I would ever take you because it's the first place Ishaq and his goons might look. But I will keep you safe. Now we've got to get out of here. The guy who put you in the box might come looking for you. I know you can't walk to the car. I'm going to drive down that unpaved lane until I get to that little knoll over there, and then I will carry you the rest of the way to the car. Wait right here with Father Peter and Kinta. I'll be right back."

With some reluctance, Gary took off into the darkness, using the flashlight to navigate the woods.

Father Peter said nothing for a while. Then he said, "Melody, these are dangerous times, and it would be in your best interest to be very careful . . . shhh."

Melody hadn't been saying anything, but Father Peter could hear a distinct rumble in Kinta's throat. In a moment, a tall figure appeared at the edge of the clearing, clearly silhouetted against the distant light of the warehouse.

As he got closer, Melody could tell that it was one of the two men who had been assembling bombs in the warehouse. When he reached the edge of the clearing, he switched on a very powerful flashlight and entered the little clump of trees where she and Father Peter were hiding with Kinta.

When the man spotted the open grave, he gave a startled, angry yell. But it was cut off by two hundred pounds of fur and fangs. Kinta pounced, spinning the man into the hole. He dropped the flashlight when he fell, and when he tried to reach up and grab it, the wolf lunged at his hand, lacerating it.

Suddenly the assassin reached into his shoulder holster and pulled out his gun. There was enough light issuing from the idle flashlight to help him aim at the animal about to lunge at his throat. He fired two shots and powder blaze illuminated his torn hand and angry face.

Suddenly, Gary launched into the hole, pinning the man and wrenching the pistol from his hand. "This one's for you, Akbar!" Gary belted him in the face so hard that Akbar fell back into the box, silent and unconscious.

"Gary, I'm so glad you're back!" Melody breathed.

"Kinta," said Gary, reaching over to pet the unharmed animal, "you're a good dog . . . er, wolf. Anytime you want to apply for the K-9 force, I'll be glad to get you an application. You know you can make a lot more money in police work than you can working for Father Peter."

"Now, Gary," Father Peter remonstrated, "Kinta and I are glad to help the police whenever we can, but we have our own work to do."

"True," said Gary. "Come on, let's get back to the car." He hoisted Melody in his arms and huffed and puffed his way up a shallow incline, carrying her.

"Father Peter," Gary panted, "you are an angel. What would we have done without you?"

"It wasn't me," said the old priest. "It was Kinta."

"If you are one of the angels of deliverance, surely Kinta is one of the beasts of the Apocalypse, on loan to earth to pave the way for the Second Coming," Gary said, stopping to catch his breath and peer intently at them. Then he turned back toward the car and carried Melody to the passenger's seat.

After getting her comfortable, he said, "I'm going back to that box. There's something I forgot to do. If anybody comes around this car, just honk the horn and I'll come running."

"Wait a minute, Gary," Melody said. "What happened to the other women?"

"You don't know?"

"No, tell me!"

"They're all right!"

"Thank God, thank God! All?"

"All . . . except for . . ."

"Except for who?"

"Melody, Sister Joanna hasn't been found yet."

"What?"

"She didn't make it out of the warehouse with the other hostages."

"Warehouse? What warehouse?"

"That one," said Gary pointing through the darkness to the dimly lit steel fortress.

"Is that where we were?" asked Melody.

"When you were with them—yes, that's where you were. The women described how heroically Joanna acted to save them, but that she herself never made it out."

"Do you think she could be buried alive too?" asked Melody.

"It's possible. I'm going to start working on that just as soon as you're safe."

Melody's eyes welled up with tears.

Gary couldn't stand to see her cry. She had been brave for all she had been through. He stopped for a moment and held her and kissed her tears away.

"Darling," he said, "I must go back to that grave and do one final thing. Like I said, if anything occurs, just honk the horn and I'll be back. Father Peter and Kinta will keep you safe. God protect you!"

Fifteen minutes later, he returned.

"Why did you go back?" asked Melody.

"I had a man who I needed to 'box up' until the police come." Gary said nothing else for a while then added, "You'd be surprised what you can find, rifling through a man's wallet and then going through his pockets."

Gary extended his right hand, showing a little book full of names and telephone numbers. A few of the numbers were American-based, but most appeared to be Yemeni contacts.

"These guys are dirty, and they're in Seattle for the long haul, Melody."

"But there are a lot of women's names."

"I recognize some of these names. They've often been booked by the police—they're hookers. And I hate to tell you this, but among the many names is that of Mary Muebles."

Melody shuddered. Was Mary some kind of double agent?

Gary felt the swift passage of time—it must be near midnight by now. "Let's go Melody!" he said, closing her car door. "Can we drop you somewhere, Father?" he asked.

But there was no answer. The old man and the animal were gone.

Gary looked around, then shrugged and walked to the driver's door. He drove back down the unpaved road with the lights off until he was a safe distance from the plant.

Back in the woods the standpipe stood erect in the darkness. Akbar's coat was there, lying on the ground, but where was Akbar? All was quiet for the longest time. Then there was the sound of someone inside the box pounding the dull, unresponsive wood and screaming.

CHAPTER 28

Gary checked Melody into a small motel under a pseudonym.

"This is almost romantic," said Melody. "I know the situation is desperate and that you're only trying to hide me out till the tempest is passed. But to be at the center of some horrendous espionage attempt makes me feel like a significant player in life."

She smiled weakly.

Gary's answer made Melody remember just how desperate their circumstances were. "Put on your dead bolt and do not open that door for anyone. Here's Akbar's cell phone. I took it from him before I boxed him up. Check the caller ID to make sure it's me when it rings. If there's any knock at the door, call me on this cell phone. Do not use the hotel phone."

"Where are you going, darling?"

"I'm gonna pick up a friend and see what I can do about locating Joanna."

"Gary, be careful."

They kissed good-bye, and Gary ran back to his car.

Gary drove as fast as he could toward another hotel where al-Haj Sistani had also checked in under a false name. Al was ready when Gary knocked on his door, and they set off toward the warehouse where the women had been imprisoned.

Al was full of questions: "What do you expect to find when you get there? What will you do first? What is to be gained by all this, in terms of finding Joanna?"

Gary cleared his throat and answered methodically, "Rhonda gave me the keys to the cuffs and the door where Sister Joanna left Ishaq chained to a pipe. I think we'll start with him and show him some of the things the Geneva Convention hasn't thought of yet. Maybe we can loosen his tongue, if he knows anything about where Sister Joanna is. Once we find her, then I'll have no reason not to call the Seattle Police Department and get them to throw a cordon around the warehouse to keep every bit of the explosives bound up in that place."

Al mulled over Gary's plan. "I'm not sure about your plan. You don't know Ishaq all that well. He's a tough man. I saw him behead a dozen Afghan loyalists. He's a devil."

"Al," said Gary, "I need to ask you this. I know you were close to this man. Are you OK with confronting him as an enemy when he still thinks you're his friend? I know your life is void if he discovers you're a Christian. Are you sure you're up to this?"

"I'm not afraid," said Al. He thought for a moment and said, "That's really not true. I'm terrified. But I have come to see that all I have ever stood for is wrong. What I have done for Scarlet Jihad in Yemen was diabolical. My part in the *U.S.S. Cole* disaster should earn me the judgment of God, but I have come to see God in a whole new way than I ever saw Allah. Since God was gracious enough to forgive me for the whole of my wrong life, I must stand against my fears. If I die, I die. But I will not live knowing I did nothing to prevent the murder of thousands of innocent people—every one of whom God loves."

Gary only listened. Al was silent. Then as the pavement gave way to red, soft shale, Gary said, "There's the beastly building up ahead."

He switched off his lights and let the car roll quietly along in the ample starlight. It rolled into the familiar clump of trees and stopped. Gary handed a cold, dark flashlight to Al and took one himself. "Got your rod?" he asked Al.

Al said nothing, indicating the bulging shoulder holster under his thin Windbreaker. They walked in silence over the dark sod until they came to the dock area of the warehouse. Two sentries were standing in the darkness. One of them lit a cigarette and handed it to his friend. Then he lit his own cigarette. Both guards faces glowed faintly from the cigarette's orange light.

"Which of these two guys is yours?" asked Gary in the darkness.

"If you don't mind, I think I'll take the little one. His name is Tawhid. He's a pansy; I used to beat him up at qat parties in the old country."

In a moment, Gary and Al rushed upon the two men and clubbed them into silence. Caught off guard, the sentries were toppled easily and fell first into the steel walls of the warehouse then forward onto the concrete dock. Gary and Al heard the guards' heads crack.

"Ouch!" said Al. "I told you Tawhid was a pansy. If all terrorists were like him, Hezbollah would be selling rugs in Tehran."

"Get their hats, jackets, and badges. Don't forget their pistols and nightsticks," said Gary. "Let's go inside and see what we can find."

The lights were weak inside the building, making it hard to see in the distance. But both men could tell the warehouse was empty.

"Oh, no," said Al. "The explosives are gone."

"Shh," said Gary. "First, we check for Joanna and Ishaq."

They quickly made their way to a stairway that led to a cavernous honeycomb of concrete passages. "This looks like a bunker to me," said Gary.

Al nodded.

Here and there throughout the passages, they would come to a television camera. Gary knocked the tiny security cameras out of their brackets with his nightstick.

At the end of the honeycomb they found the room Melody had described to Gary. An abundance of McDonald's wrappers and boxes were in its trash can. But Ishaq was gone. And there was no evidence of Joanna.

Both men instantly turned on their heels and sped back through the maze of corridors and up the stairs into the warehouse, focused on the absence of boxes of explosives. They moved across the floor to the great truck bays.

Somehow Ishaq and Zalton had managed to get the explosives out of the warehouse and back into trucks. But where could those trucks be?

Without the RLDs, Ishaq could make no strategized attack on the stadium, but four of those trucks parked at strategic locations would still kill a great many people.

"We don't have much time to act," Gary said, breaking into a run.

"Act how? What do we do when we act? How do you locate the missing trucks? They were all supposed to be in trailers marked with stadium vendor signs on the sides of the truck vans," said Al, running alongside Gary.

"Yeah, but they won't be that way anymore. Ishaq would never declare himself by using the truck we might be on the lookout for. It's only sixteen hours till the Promise Keepers reunion celebration begins. They could go off even during the first speaker. By the way, who is the first speaker? Do you know?"

"Yeah. It's the attorney general of the United States."

■ ■ ■

"Are you sure you have this right?" Paul asked Brother Lawrence.

"I have asked Brother Anselm several times. He's the only one here at the monastery who can read Arabic, so we have to trust him."

"Then there's no mistaking it. These will be the trucks the Scarlet Jihad will be using. These are the labels that appear on the sides and backs of the vans. This is where those trucks are currently parked, and these are the routes they will take into the city from their marked locations. Brothers, be sure you watch the trucks as they are parked. Get out ahead of them on their marked routes and be sure they don't get around you. You know what to do after that. The moment you've done your thing, leave the trucks and run. The police should be there soon after you go. Do you understand?"

The monks, dressed in truck driver's overalls, nodded.

Paul Shapiro had intercepted the informative note when he rescued the women at the McDonald's. It was the same note Mary Muebles had taken from Jibril's pocket before the encounter at the Comfort 8 Suites. But Paul felt like it must be the official plan and was worth putting everything they had into it.

Joanna had scratched a new note on the back of the captured memo saying she would die when truck four exploded. The problem was that the memo didn't say which truck was number four. Further, Mary had told Paul that she had seen both Akbar and Jibril reading a Muslim book of martyrs. Mary believed both men would be wearing suicide belts when they began the drive into the city and that they would detonate the trucks after they had parked by the stadium in the assigned positions. It would be the easiest—and most glorious way—for the Scarlet Jihad plan to be pulled off.

It was almost daybreak Wednesday when Paul left Brother Lawrence and the other monks and went to his car. It was time to call Gary.

"Paul," said Gary, reading his name off the caller ID screen.

"Gary, time is of the essence. And as of right now, there are four semis filled with explosives that will be detonated during the Promise Keepers reunion rally tonight. We know the route the trucks will take into the city, and we know where they are parked right now. We're going to do our best to blockade the trucks on the isolated state highways they will each be taking on their way to the I-5, where they will then drive to the stadium."

"Who's we?"

"Me and the monks of Holy Faith Abbey in Bellingham."

"Paul, this thing is bigger than you, and it's way out of the monks' league. You should leave this to the Seattle Police Department."

"Sorry, friend, we can't do that. We all believe that at the first sight of any police helicopter or squad car, these guys have instructions to commit suicide by detonating their own explosive vests, which will turn their payload into a destructive fireball. If we are successful in blockading the trucks, you'll be the first to know."

"Whatever risk you think the Seattle police will be, believe me, you're taking a lot into your own hands to think you can do it better. Paul, listen to me. I—"

Click.

Paul had hung up.

Seconds later Paul's phone rang. The caller ID screen showed Gary's name and number.

Paul ignored the phone and walked back into the council of monks.

"Men, start your engines," he said. "Let's roll!"

CHAPTER 29

Joanna Nickerson had been beaten so badly, she hardly looked human.

"Come on, you infidel cow," said Ishaq, "into this truck. You have only a few hours left to live, so I suggest you get about renouncing Christ and begging Allah to let you in the kingdom of peace."

"I will gladly get in the truck, for I shall be free to feel the love of Christ without your horrible brutality. But I will never renounce my Savior, Ishaq. How could I ever renounce him who is my light and my salvation? No, I renounce all who brutalize and kill the weak and undefended in the name of a god who is not worthy of the throne you say he holds. Allah is not merciful enough to call himself a god for me. Am I so afraid of pain that I would call such a being my god? The God I love is unlike Allah. He is the Father who longs to call all men and women his children. I spit on every god who would order the likes of you to brutalize and kill the innocent."

The words were barely out of her mouth when Ishaq's fist caught her full in the face and she staggered to her knees. Her face was bleeding where his heavy diamond ring had cut savagely into her jaw.

Joanna's lip was trembling, but she rose to her feet and stiffened her spine. "Like Esther," she said, "I face you in the name of the true God, and if I perish, I perish."

"Have it your way, infidel!" he said. "But for now, get up in that truck!"

Joanna climbed up slowly into the trailer of the semi. She slumped against the metal wall as the double doors swung shut behind her.

In the darkness, she did what she had not permitted herself to do in front of her Muslim captors. She cried. Then she beat the walls of her confinement. "God," she cried, "I love you, but I do not understand the purpose you must find in my pain. God, let me die now. I have been so brutalized that I almost prefer to die."

She realized that when she did die, it would be sudden. She would not have time to feel flames or pain before she found herself awake and safe in the arms of Jesus.

She felt the generous vibration of the truck as the motor engaged, and then the truck was moving. She had no idea where she was going, but she knew that the dark cavern of the trailer was full of boxed explosives of some sort. She found herself absent-mindedly quoting the Lord's Prayer, and then Isaiah 40:31—"Those who trust in the Lord will renew their strength; they will soar on wings like eagles; they will run and not grow weary; they will walk and not faint."

At some point she switched to quoting Joshua 1:9—"Haven't I commanded you: be strong and courageous? Do not be afraid or discouraged, for the Lord your God is with you wherever you go."

She was halfway through Philippians 4:19 when she was interrupted by a strange sight—two sets of eyes. One set was kind and small and none too bright for the darkness that threatened to swallow them up. But the other set was blue and feral and penetrating. They drew their light from the night stars and threatened to obliterate the darkness of the van.

Joanna rubbed her eyes to try to make the other eyes disappear or reappear with a firmness she couldn't doubt.

"Joanna, thou hast been faithful over a few things. He will make thee ruler over many things."

"Father Peter?"

"It is I, Joanna, and your suffering has been seen and recorded by the God of all love. Kinta, speak!" commanded the old priest.

Kinta came as close to a bark as Joanna had ever heard.

"Oh, Father! How wonderful that you should be here with me!"

"I don't know. I love being with you, but this truck is on a one-way trip to the heart of hell."

"That's what Ishaq said too," said Joanna. "Ishaq is so mean. He is a white jackal."

"I know how you must have suffered."

"It was no picnic. I'm a bloody mass of cuts and bruises. I don't think I've ever seen anybody as ugly as I must appear."

"Nobody ever got ugly serving Jesus. He did a lot of suffering himself, you know? But I want to give you a medallion. You may not have long to wear it, but it was given to me by a brother priest in Aden."

Father Peter walked to Joanna and slipped the chain and medallion around her neck. In the darkness the medal felt cold at first and then strangely warm.

"What does the medallion say?" asked Joanna.

"It says, 'I have tested you in the furnace of affliction.'"

"Maybe on the edge of perdition as well as affliction, if Ishaq is right about this truck," said Joanna.

"I hardly ever agree with the White Jackal, but this time I think he is right."

"Father Peter, can there be any worse chauffeur to the heart of hell than the albino?"

"Joanna, he's not doing the driving. He's not even on this sixteen-wheel bomb."

"Where is he?"

"He's got a briefcase bomb—a radiation bomb. They're made out of nuclear junk from a power plant dump and a detonator. They don't kill a lot of people when they go off, but the radiation sickness they produce does. A lot of people are going to get sick. When this truck pulled out, he left for the stadium. If none of these trucks gets through, he will still make it past security and, well . . ."

"Can he be stopped?"

"I don't know."

"Since when don't you know?" Joanna bellowed. "You know everything! Why don't you know when and where and how we're going to get out of this truck?"

"The man who is driving this rig is wearing a suicide vest. I might be able to stop this van from exploding, but I cannot stop him from doing his thing."

"Well, let's work on one problem at a time. How would you keep this van from exploding?"

All of a sudden a blinding beam of light came on in the van. Father Peter had a flashlight.

"Why in the world didn't you turn that thing on earlier?"

"I see as well without a flashlight as I do with one. And darkness is friendlier to the kind of talk we really needed to have."

Joanna winced as she saw the shadowy cargo of death that was stacked all around them. "I guess I've got what I always asked the good Lord for: I always wanted to die fast and not linger in my passing. When it happens, it will happen fast, I'm guessing. Funny thing about it, Father—I used to sing 'Shall We Gather at the River?' like the whole congregation was about to go on a picnic at a state park. Now that I can see the river we're about to gather at, I'm not so sure I want to gather there right now. Not that I'd mind seein' Jesus and my mama, and I for sure wanna go to heaven, but I just don't know if I wanna be on the next load. And most of all, there's my little Janie. Who's gonna love her and take care of her?"

Joanna paused. "You know, Father, I think every God-fearin' believer wants to go to heaven and maybe spend eternity there. It ain't the bein' there that's so distasteful, it's the gettin' there."

"Reverend Nickerson," he said, "I know you must have borne a world of pain from being in the presence of these hoodlums who call themselves sons of Allah. And I don't want to interrupt your monologue on heaven, but for my part I'd like to see you go there a little later. And we might manage it if you'd quit being so determined about getting there so fast."

He tossed her a little black tool kit. "Open this up. There are some wire cutters in it. Take them out and then take this flashlight and start looking for a detonator."

Joanna opened the pouch up. "You mean the little black pliers with the blades close to the pivot of the grips?"

"Well, I don't know what color they are, but the rest of your description sounds right. Now take the flashlight and begin looking for that detonator."

"With the truck wobbling like it is, how will I ever find it?"

"I'd start at the front of this van. That's where the explosives would be most stable while in transit, and stability would be very important before the driver decides to blow this truck—and us—to smithereens."

"Stop it, Father Peter. I hate that word—especially if I'm one of the 'smithers.' Where do I start looking in the front of this van?"

"My hunch is it will be outside of the stacks of cased explosives. The detonator is the last thing they hook up, so it would be done after all the explosives were loaded. Remember, plastic explosives are very sensitive to any sudden jarring. So don't stumble into any-thing or kick anything in the dark, or we could get back into your heaven monologues in a big way.

"My guess also is that the whole detonator will be pretty make-shift—a shoe-box apparatus with a system of wires and a receiver of some sort. The receiver will probably also be primitive—could be a wired-in cellular phone. Could look like a garage-door opener."

"I don't know if I can do this."

"You've got to do it. I can't see, and Kinta doesn't know what we're talking about. While I don't mind having you as a fellow traveler toward heaven, Kinta and I have some things to do before we take off. So think about little Janie and get to looking for that detonator."

Joanna took the flashlight and shone it on the floor as she moved around the periphery of the explosives. She felt her way toward the front and rounded the corner of the cargo. Bingo. She spied the detonator.

"Here it is, Father Peter," she said jubilantly.

"Good! Good work, Joanna! What's the receiver?"

"It is a cell phone," she exulted. "You were dead right!"

"Bad metaphor," said Peter. "Now, the first thing I want you to do is to be very careful. The second thing I want you to do is to turn the cell phone over and use your fingernails to open it and remove the battery."

There was a moment of silence, then Joanna said, "There, it's done!"

"Describe the rest of the apparatus," said Father Peter.

"Well, there is a single wire running from the cell phone into a secondary mechanism that has a huge battery pack, and this pack has an additional three wires—two of which are attached to a gray brick. I'm guessin' that is a small block of the plastic explosives."

"This secondary battery pack is the real culprit. It's the one that will detonate the truck. For the moment, focus on the wires that run from that battery pack into that brick."

"This is kinda exciting!"

"Well, it's nice you're feeling some enthusiasm for your work. You could be appointed to the bomb squad any day now."

"Thanks, but I'd just as soon go to work in a beauty parlor."

"Now, be very careful and use your wire cutter to cut the wires that run from the main battery source . . . not the dead wire that connects to the cell phone. Got that?"

Joanna turned her flashlight down the side of the van and it fell on the great wolf. He was sleeping as though the entire odyssey fraught with death had somehow bored him. His demeanor spoke to Joanna, who suddenly felt as though she would live. With a kind of abandon in the middle of a new calm she had never felt before, she capriciously clipped the two wires just above where they disappeared into the brick.

Gloriously nothing happened. She was delighted. "I just clipped them," she said, "and we're all here. What next?"

"Fold the clipped wires back to keep them away from the explosives."

She did. It was easy. "What next?"

"Pull the inserted bare wires slowly away from the brick and then put the whole apparatus as far from the explosives as you can get it."

There was another brief pause.

"All done," said Joanna exuberantly. "Is there anything else I can do while I'm saving our lives and destinies?"

"Now I'm afraid we'll just wait and see where the driver may be taking us. He probably isn't wearing a detonator belt, since he was counting on the cell phone detonator to do the job. Come back and practice your Scripture until the truck stops. That will be the next place we'll have to figure out what to do. But that could be ten or fifteen minutes from now, so we'll have time to worry or pray or however you choose to fill your time. But, please, no more talk of heaven. I don't think I could live through any more of your theological cheering up."

"Well, for my part, I'm glad I'm going to heaven."

"Nice confidence, but as I said, God still has a lot of stuff to get done in Seattle."

Joanna settled down beside Kinta. He was still asleep.

Joanna could not be totally at ease. She knew that at any minute the truck would stop and the doors would fly open, revealing an angry driver who couldn't get his cell call to set off his truckload of explosives.

She turned the flashlight on her new medallion. It bore her memory work for the day: "I have tested you in the furnace of affliction." It was a reminder that God worked best where the furnace flamed with fire.

She remembered the story of three Old Testament heroes who had been thrown into a fiery furnace, and she smiled at their confidence. Shadrach, Meshach, and Abednego had answered, "The God we serve . . . can rescue us from the furnace of blazing fire, and he can rescue us from the power of you, the king. But even if he does not . . ." It was the *if nots* of life where confidence most counted.

Joanna could see that God was as much in charge of the *if nots* as he was the certainties. The doors would open, her enemies would be at the gates, but her enemies were not in charge of her personal peace. That peace was locked in a better place. "God," she prayed, "be with me in the darkness and when my enemies come. The time—I fear—is not far distant. My trust is in you. I rest in your peace."

"I heard that," said Father Peter. "It's a better prayer than you previously prayed. Worrying in God's presence is not praying. On the other hand, quoting the Bible in a truck full of TNT—now, that's what I consider confident praying."

Joanna decided to let the remark pass. She closed her eyes to focus on her little Janie and of all the good reasons she had to go on living.

Kinta was sleeping.

The truck roared on.

The rubber tires thundered on the pavement.

Or was it gravel?

CHAPTER 30

Paul Shapiro remained in contact with the courageous eight monks who had vowed to do whatever it took to stop the trucks from reaching central Seattle. All four terrorist semis would be coming from small towns east of the metropolitan area—one from a truck stop in Carnation, another from Ravensdale, a third from Greenwater, and the fourth from Graham.

These trucks would enter the city on state highways 202, 169, 162, and 161, respectively, moving into downtown from these rural radial spokes. They were set to come together on the stadium exit.

The eight monks were each driving a dump truck to blockade the vending trucks driven by the terrorists. Miraculously, the monks got their dump trucks to the originating point of each vendor semi on time. Unfortunately, the dump trucks behind the semis followed too closely, allowing the Yemeni drivers to easily spot the dump trucks in their rearview mirrors.

What the terrorist drivers didn't know was that a second dump truck—filled with gravel—was also preceding each semi in order to dump a truckload of gravel at their preplanned section of the rural highway where the bar ditches, like medieval moats, would prevent the large trucks from turning around. In this secluded section the dump trucks in front would dump a huge load of rock directly in the path of their particular truck, and the dump trucks in rear could also dump a barricade to keep the Yemenis from backing up.

In the first three scenarios, the blockades of the huge trucks went according to plan. The monks unloaded their trucks in the path of the semis. They dumped them as the semis approached and then sped away from the semis. In each case, the individual Muslim drivers picked up their cell phones and dialed up a receiving cell phone detonator in the plastic explosives in their trailers. It was a martyr's commitment to the faith. The three fireballs mushroomed into light and thunder that rocked the countryside, seen as far away as Puget Sound. In every case, the monks were able to escape injury.

Paul had been waiting on the south road, Highway 169, coming in from Buckley. He had seen the first three fireballs through his binoculars and was convinced that the southernmost truck held the best chance of having Joanna Nickerson on board. In the first place, she was to be in truck number four, and, assuming the terrorists began numbering the trucks from the northernmost route, number four would most likely be the southernmost truck. He also knew that the albino had been seen at the Buckley service station on the 169 closest to the southernmost truck.

It was Anselm who had caught sight of Ishaq forcing a black woman into the back of the stadium vendor truck. He immediately called Paul and was grateful to hear that he was with Brother Lawrence on the dump truck set to blockade the southernmost truck of explosives. It was no problem for Anselm to identify the terrorist who had, five months earlier, almost beheaded him while he was a Peace Corps worker.

He would never forget Ishaq's demeanor and fierce red eyes. But through the haze of his horrific memory, he saw that, in the present, Ishaq did not get into the semi that he had forced the black woman to enter. He handed the keys to a short man. The short man embraced the Jackal, and the two of them triple-kissed and parted.

But before Ishaq took off, he grabbed a fairly large suitcase out of the passenger's side of the truck cab, patted it, and pumped his fist in triumph.

Ishaq jumped into a Ford 500 and took off for the city, taking the main interstate. When he had not been gone long, the Yemeni driver, whom Al would've recognized as Tawhid, swung himself up into the cab of his truck and started the engine. Brother Anselm, dressed in trucker overalls, also swung up into the cab of his truck. They drove off.

When they had not gotten very far into the country, Tawhid saw an uncanny thing. In the narrowest portion of 169, at a place where a small concrete bridge passed over a nameless creek, there was a truck dumping a huge pile of rocks right in the center of the highway. He applied his brakes and brought the semi to a screaming stop. He looked in his rearview mirror as he began to back up. It was then that he saw a second truck not a hundred yards behind him had stopped and was raising his bed to dump its load of rocks as well.

Tawhid picked up the cell phone to call into his cache of explosives, but his screen showed a "No Connect" message. The gravel and rock poured out of the truck behind him. He pulled out his pistol, placed the barrel into the roof of his mouth, and was about to pull the trigger when he saw two men, neither of whom he knew—Paul Shapiro and Brother Lawrence—run past the bridge to the back of his trailer. He leapt out of the cab and followed them to the back of the truck. But before he could prevent it, Paul tore open the huge doors to the trailer.

Tawhid aimed his pistol at Paul but was struck in the chest by a huge wolf, toppling him and dislodging the pistol from his hand. Brother Lawrence grabbed the gun and threw it into the rough at the side of the road.

"I don't want to hurt you, dear Muslim friend," Brother Lawrence said, bending down over Tawhid and nudging Kinta aside, "but having denied you of your glorious homecoming in heaven, it would be better for all of us if you would fall asleep for a while."

He punched the terrorist, rendering him completely unconscious. It would have seemed oddly compassionate had he not immediately added, "No seventy-two virgins for you, buddy boy!"

Paul turned his attention from Tawhid and Brother Lawrence into the darkened interior of the trailer. "Anybody in here? Father Peter?" he called.

"I'll get him," said Joanna, rising to her feet. "He's been napping. He's an amazing man, you know. He can lay down in a truck full of TNT and go to sleep."

Paul was amazed but hid his emotion. But Joanna's sudden coming into the light made him want to weep. Her face was a mass of deep cuts and bruises. Her arms and legs showed clear signs of torture.

"Dear God," cried Paul. "What happened? What have they done to you, Joanna?"

"Nothing much, just a group of Muslim boys on a little outing. If the good Lord has his way, where they're going they won't be yelling for more virgins; they'll be crying out for ice water."

Father Peter emerged at the end of her speech. Paul and Brother Lawrence helped Joanna off the truck. The old priest managed to get down from the truck by himself. "Paul, I've got to get to the men's rally. Could you drive Kinta and me there?"

"Yes," Paul answered. He turned to Joanna. "Can you and Brother Lawrence take charge of the prisoner? We'll send out the Seattle Police Department to take charge of all these plastic explosives."

"It would be my pleasure," said Joanna. "Lucky for this terrorist, I believe in turning the other cheek."

"Good for you, Sister Joanna," said Father Peter, taking hold of Kinta's harness. "It took just as much blood on Good Friday to arrange for your eternity as it did Tawhid's."

"I know all the doctrine, Father Peter, but at the moment, I don't want to be reminded just how much I ought to love my enemies. I promise not to kick him around while he is unconscious, but I would love the pleasure of resenting him for a little while, if you don't mind. You go on and take care of things at the Promise Keepers rally. Brother Lawrence and I will watch 'lovingly' over this comatose terrorist."

Paul smiled. "This way, Kinta and Father Peter," he said, as he dialed Gary to share the latest news.

CHAPTER 31

At 2:00 p.m., Gary, Paul, and Father Peter met at the entrance to the men's room on the east side of the stadium. Some of the attendees had already arrived.

"We may be sure Ishaq won't open the suitcase until the stadium is packed. But I believe he is already here, waiting for his big moment," said Gary.

"Any idea of where he might be?" asked Paul.

"No, and that's what troubles me," said Gary. "I believe he would avoid the open seating on the field, since the radiation unleashed in an explosion there would go up and out the top. He would likely find a place where the explosion would be shut in by the concave sections of the roof. This would not only secure more instantaneous deaths from the bomb; it would also cause greater residual infection of the radiation. Still, he's going to try to avoid discovery. He will likely pick a broom closet or some shut-in place near a concourse."

"It's a big stadium, and there are only three of us," Paul said. "And one of us is blind."

"I resemble that remark," said Father Peter, smiling. "And I have Kinta—he's really good at finding bombs—especially if it has a TNT primary detonator, which I believe it will have. Still, you're right about this being a very big stadium."

Gary cleared his throat. "That's why I've invited the Seattle bomb squad." He cleared his throat once again. "Here they come now."

Twelve men walked up, each leading a German shepherd. "Paul, Father Peter, meet the men of the bomb squad. Lieutenant Jeffries"— Gary indicated one of the men—"is the head of the department."

"Gentlemen," began Jeffries, addressing Paul and Father Peter, "I'm sure you realize that this is a very delicate operation. It has to be pulled off very fast and with a great deal of precision. What we don't need is a lot of pointless searching by people who don't understand the terrorist mind-set. Each of these men knows what to do to render the bomb impotent if it should be found. We're going to search for the terrorist by examining every part of the stadium according to the blueprints furnished to us by the city. If we haven't found the man in two hours, the rally will be cancelled for tonight, and those already gathered will be asked to leave the stadium."

Paul believed Gary was right to bring in the bomb squad, but Father Peter felt a little thwarted by the lieutenant's announcement. Gary would be allowed to stay in any area of the stadium he wished and could maintain walkie-talkie communication with Lieutenant Jeffries at all times. But Paul and Father Peter were being nudged out of the plan. They walked away.

On their way out of the stadium, Father Peter said he had to go to the men's room and turned abruptly into one of the stadium's huge facilities. Paul waited for him for five minutes. When he didn't come out, Paul went in to look for him. He looked under the stainless steel urinals that seemed to stretch halfway to Tacoma and checked the floor area under the stalls but saw nothing. Paul smiled. The priest was up to something.

■ ■ ■

When Father Peter and Kinta emerged from the opposite end of the men's room, next to tier G, the old priest knelt down and took Kinta's shaggy head in his hands. "There's a very bad man loose in this place, and you've always been very good at finding very bad men. Go to it. I would only slow you down, so I'll wait here till you get back."

Father Peter drew a red prayer shawl from his pocket. "I took this from the albino," he said. "This head rag is the official uniform of Scarlet Jihad. You're looking for a man carrying a suitcase, and he will smell like this head rag. Be careful when you do find him, but take him down." Father Peter removed Kinta's harness. "Go, my friend, and if you run into any of those police dogs, don't let them pull you into a quarrel. Stay focused."

If Kinta understood anything, it was that he was looking for a man who smelled like Ishaq's prayer shawl. He moved to the outside of the corridors around the stadium labyrinth. In thirty seconds he had raced down out of the stands. He crossed the Astroturf to the makeshift steel stage set up for the evening program. He sprung up onto the stage and stopped in clear view of the few early attendees who had already entered the stadium. He sat and then rocked back on his haunches and lifted his proud head in the afternoon sun. He howled a desolate, entrancing howl that alarmed those who had begun to gather.

Deep within the stadium, a dozen police dogs stopped to listen to the howl. The feral wail somehow recalled the primitive days of their unity with all canine beasts.

The great dogs heard with ancient ears and responded. The canines of the Seattle bomb squad tore themselves from their fidelity to their masters and ran toward the lonesome howl.

Down, down they ran, out into the open field and then onto the stage. Gary heard Kinta's howl and ran out onto the Astroturf at the fifty-yard line. Spying the pack of gathered dogs with a wolf in their center, he pulled out his cell phone, switched it to the camera mode, and shot a photo of the spectacle.

Thirteen brothers gathered to howl in a chorus of longing brotherhood. And as soon as the howling concord satisfied them, Kinta rushed off the stage and his comrades followed him.

The early attendees were bewildered and frightened. They scattered toward the exits to flee from the pack. No person was attacked, but the chase had done its job. The stadium was empty.

Then the pack separated into individual sentries. Each fled at top speed into the various galleries that opened into the yawning labyrinths of the Seahawk stadium. Then all was bewilderingly quiet. Gary stood waiting, still gazing down at the phenomenal photo he had just taken.

Then he heard the baying of a lone animal. He presumed it to be Kinta. The baying seemed to come from the goal post at the far end of the stadium. He ran down the field, past the end zone, and up into the stands. The baying paused then sounded a second time. He was definitely headed in the right direction. He dashed into the interior of the stadium. Others on the bomb squad had also heard the sound. One by one they arrived at the same scene that Gary himself encountered.

It was Kinta.

The wolf now stood facing an elevated space among the support beams. The stout form of the albino could be seen hanging from this flawed hiding place.

Ishaq's situation was desperate. He had not only Kinta to reckon with but a whole council of fangs that had gathered around underneath him, snapping viciously.

Gary had the sense to get another cell phone photo of the half-hidden terrorist, even while looking for the suitcase. Eventually, he saw it lodged nearby among an octopus of iron girders, buttressing a main arm of the stadium.

Gary also saw a rifle with a scope near the suitcase. Perhaps the albino had intended to shoot some important Christian personage before detonating the radiation bomb. But now his whole dream of suicide and terror seemed to be evaporating before his eyes.

This thought must have occurred to Ishaq as well as he surveyed the gathering of policemen, whose circle lay just beyond the animals. Desperate, Ishaq did an insane thing. He leapt from his hiding place as though to make a dash for the suitcase and the rifle. But his feet had barely hit the floor when he was grabbed by thirteen sets of jaws. The brotherhood of beasts worked together to spread his arms and legs away from his torso, so that he lay sprawled on the floor. The police stood dumbfounded. Gary, however, snapped yet another cell phone picture.

Satisfied, Gary moved among the snarling captors to reach Ishaq. He clamped a set of cuffs on Ishaq's right hand. The dogs were reluctant to let go of Ishaq even for Gary to roll him over to lock his left hand to his right behind his back. Gary patted him down to check for other weapons. When convinced Ishaq was clean, Gary said, "OK, men. Call off your partners and let's get this suitcase out of the city. Take it out to the Mount Baker Wilderness and deal with it."

Gary suddenly felt as though he was overstepping his authority and stepped back from the albino still writhing on the floor.

The police summoned their dogs back. At Lieutenant Jeffries' nod, a couple of the bomb squad veterans walked forward and picked up the suitcase.

Paul, who had watched from a distance, walked up to Gary. He patted him on the back. "Good job, Gary," he said.

"Good job, yourself," said Gary. "You know where Father Peter is?"

"I know right where he is. He's waiting just outside the men's room, holding the harness to his seeing-eye wolf. Let's get the two of them together."

But no sooner was Ishaq in cuffs than Kinta was off toward the men's room. He didn't like harnesses, but he did love Father Peter.

Gary and Paul met up with Father Peter and the wolf. The foursome were walking out of the stadium when Gary said, "Well, hopefully the ordeal is over. We've just got to round up Zalton and the rest of his goons who didn't blow themselves up."

"There may be a problem," said Paul. "I haven't seen Mary Muebles since she gave me the lowdown on the semi schedule she took from Jibril."

"Do you think she left Seattle to protect herself?"

"Worse than that," said Paul. "I think she might have been in the second truck this morning. She was with Jibril at breakfast, and I think she might have been in the cab or maybe in the van when it detonated. It seemed odd that Mary would have had anything to do with Jibril after her incarceration in the warehouse. Yet Jibril convinced her that it was his intention to return for her and rescue her from the fate she would have shared with the other women. She believed him, and thus he reentered her trust. And Clarisse has broken all contact with Rhonda and her friends at Esther's Refuge."

"Oh, dear God, I hope she's safe."

"I fear she may have been on truck one," Paul said. "Zalton, I am sure, was on truck one, and I'm afraid he captured her and . . . he would not have let her live, knowing that he had to die."

Suddenly the victory they all felt with the capture of Ishaq was blunted by huge feelings of loss.

They were silent. Father Peter and Kinta walked behind a car in the parking lot but did not reappear on its other side. Neither Gary nor Paul knew where the priest and wolf went or when they might show up again. But they knew the two would likely be back. There are times when it takes a man and a wolf to make the world sensibly whole.

CHAPTER 32

The Promise Keepers reunion rally was shut out of the stadium Wednesday evening by the Seattle Police Department and the National Security Agency. But the national leadership of the men's group was not paralyzed by the problem of having a convention canceled. In only four hours the word went out: "We came to Seattle to rehearse our role of leadership in a confused time. Let us gather by the thousands in whatever location will give us space. Let us say to our nation that fear in a troubled time is never an option to men who believe in God and are unafraid to put their hand to confidence."

The word spread from leaflets and cell phones, from hotel bulletin boards to bullhorns. And the Promise Keepers heard and responded. And it wasn't just the Promise Keepers—thousands of men of every faith or none joined in. The entire world, it seemed, joined their hearts to the cause.

They met at the Seattle Center, with huge spillover crowds stretching from the Center to Queen Anne Hill. Rallies spread as far as the Cultural Center. The open quadrangle of Seattle Pacific University became the chief gathering place and hosted numerous sermons and testimonies. A spirit of purpose spread downtown with an instantaneous approval of the city.

The terrorist attempt on the rally brought national coverage. The information was too sketchy for full five o'clock reports on the

West Coast, but by the eleven o'clock news on the East Coast, the national buzz caught up with the incredible story of thwarted terror.

The segmented rally held throughout the city bore a strange and positive message. It had been a very fearsome day. Yet believers and nonbelievers nationwide tuned into the positive worship services of the Promise Keepers. The wide shots of thousands of men singing hymns and contemporary choruses in the vast spaces of the city's beautiful sights seemed to declare a kind of national messianism that obliterated all talk of dangerous moves toward theocracy or of the "kooks on the far right." America needed a symbol of hope, and the singing of so many thousands of her citizens portrayed that symbol.

And questions flew. Who was the blind man Father Peter? His name had been whispered ever since Joanna's Exodus a year earlier. Was his seeing-eye dog really a wolf? Adding color to the story were Brothers Anselm and Lawrence and all the other brothers of Holy Faith Abbey. The eight brave truck drivers from the monastery were heralded as macho monks who barricaded the city in a time of terror.

The most replicated images of the event were the cell photos taken by Gary Jarvis, showing the gloriously odd and surreal tale of a wolf and twelve dogs and of the Albino of Aden, trapped beyond reach of a suitcase bomb and sprawled among the canines. The Seattle bomb squad also received praise for removing the deadly device. Had it gone off, thousands would have died—not just from a single explosion but after weeks of agonized suffering.

Still missing were two women who had helped the Seattle police. A woman of Spanish descent named Mary Muebles and Clarisse al-Zhabahni, the wife of Zalton al-Zhabahni. The head of Spratton was thought to be either dead or escaped from Seattle to avoid prosecution. Still, as the echoes of Wednesday afternoon wore on through the weekend, neither the women nor the Spratton CEO could be found.

Gary and Paul were on *Larry King Live* on Monday night, and Joanna was on *Oprah* by Thursday of the following week. Neither Gary nor Paul liked being seen as national celebrities. Both of them constantly celebrated Father Peter and Kinta—neither of whom had been seen since the rally. Nor were they likely to be.

Joanna was not so camera-shy as the men and seemed to be in rare form as she joked and volleyed comments with Oprah. Her bruises were covered with heavy makeup. She easily fell into a long discussion on whether terrorists would go to a martyr's bed or a bed of hot coals. She had no intention of being funny, but her conversations just tended in that direction.

"Did you actually strike a terrorist in your escape attempt?" asked Oprah.

"Yes, honey, I did! And I'd do it again. 'Course, I know Jesus loves everybody, but these terrorists catch on a little slower with me. I know we should pray for our enemies, but I think we should hit 'em first and pray for their healing later."

The following Saturday found Joanna in the kitchen after a special banquet being held at the Pathway of Light Cathedral.

"There are elements of every story that must remain hidden," said Joanna, after the tables had been cleared. Al-Haj Sistani was still in the kitchen, putting away the larger pots and pans.

"I do declare," said Joanna, "the way he waits on us women is truly phenomenal. You know he gave Carol an engagement ring after church on Sunday! Carol's the first Methodist I'd ever say was lucky to win the hand of a retreaded terrorist. Al's the best Christian man I ever met, and probably the only convert I'll ever have from Islam . . . but as I was saying, there are elements of every story that will forever remain hidden. I just wish I knew what happened to Mary Muebles and Clarisse."

No sooner had she gotten the words out of her mouth than her mouth dropped open. Jibril walked into the dining hall. The women looked alarmed and started to move backward from the approaching Yemeni.

When he saw their looks of fear, he dropped to his knees and held his bearded face in his hands. "Please, Joanna and all gathered here, I must tell you, you have nothing to fear from me. In the morning I will make my way to the FBI and surrender myself to prison for life. But I must tell you this: I did not detonate my truck from the cab. I left the cab, and when I called in the cell-phone detonator, I was a long way off. I did not want to die as a Muslim martyr. I want to know more about Christianity. I have watched two of your sisters in their final hour, and while they had no desire to be martyrs, they did the right thing right up to the hour of their deaths, and did it for reasons that were less selfish than what I had been taught."

The group listened in amazement.

"I know what happened to Clarisse al-Zhabahni. She died at the detonation of truck number one. I did not drive it." He paused, his shoulders momentarily shaking.

"And Mary. When I inadvertently left the plans on Mary Muebles' nightstand, she felt terrible guilt about serving me as a consort. She was conflicted, as your psychiatrist would say.

"But her personal pain never reached its zenith until she gave Dr. Shapiro the plans for our trucks . . ." Jibril stopped. He bit his lip and remained silent for an embarrassingly long minute.

Finally he seemed in control of his emotions and spoke again. "For our trucks—the trucks of Scarlet Jihad—to enter the stadium complex. So she gave them to the psychiatrist and sealed her fate, I'm afraid. I never discovered her duplicity. That's why the trucks rolled according to plan. She was supposed to get into the cab with me, but she didn't do it. She could be alive. She could be hiding out to escape arrest. I only wish I could see her again to tell her how wrong I was. I fell in love with her, you know. She's the reason I couldn't kill myself. My love for her turned me from my covenant with the Martyrs' Brigade. I know she admired you Christians so much she felt guilty both about her lifestyle and her support of Scarlet Jihad."

"But what happened to Clarisse?" asked Joanna.

"She was tied and bound in the back of the truck. I watched Mary as she saw Clarisse taken away. This was another reason for Mary's grief. Mary was torn in her soul because she could think of no way to save Clarisse from the ruthlessness of her husband."

Once again Jibril stopped talking. "I think it was in seeing those women broken and torn, yet oddly at peace with the notion of dying, that I became broken in spirit. I suddenly understood that to be in the Martyrs' Brigade takes little courage. What requires courage is to die trying to save others not destroying them. I've been living in hiding for the past several days. Whoever finds me will take my life. I'm a dead man. I'll be lucky if the American courts get to me before my fellow Muslims.

"I cannot ask you for your forgiveness. It is too much to ask." He stood and walked outside the Pathway of Light Cathedral, passing Brother Lawrence, who was going in.

They didn't speak but looked straight ahead.

Brother Lawrence entered the dining hall and laid a case of RLDs on a clean table. "I kept one of the shipments of these RLDs," he said. "I sold mine this morning for $300,000."

"But aren't they part of destructive weaponry?" asked Joanna.

"They can be," Brother Lawrence answered, "but they have lots of uses in high-tech industries—like fiber optics and hospital laser programs. I sold mine to the Humana Hospital Health chain. They said they'd take yours too, but I figured that was up to you. So here they are. We're going to use our money to fix up Holy Faith Abbey; you can use yours to buy some new pews or hymnals or anything else."

Joanna was about to speak when the phone rang. It was Gary, calling from Deaconess Hospital's neonatal ward. Melody had just had her baby—a girl named Rhonda Joanna Jarvis.

EPILOGUE 36

Jibril was sitting alone on the damp sidewalk, staring at his pistol. He had twice put it into his mouth. He had nowhere to go. In one direction lay prison and maybe state execution. In the other was certain death from those he once called his brothers in the Martyrs' Brigade. Life held nothing that could lift his spirit. He sat with his head down for a long time and only gradually became aware that he was not alone.

"Don't do what you are thinking of doing," said Father Peter.

"What else is there? I don't have a home. There's no place to go."

"Me neither. At least, no place that's really asked for me. But there is always so much to be done. And frankly, suicide is a waste of good resources God put in your life. There's a lot more to live for than you think!"

"What do you mean?"

"Well, take me. Like I said, I can't think of a soul that's off to see me, but I'm off to Darfur and could use some help. Twenty thousand people died there this week—most of them children. When you show up with a bag of rice, they don't ask you about your religious background. In fact, where human life is in extremes, a criminal with rice is better than a lawyer with a court docket. In my opinion, it's an awfully good place to start over. And let's face it, Jibril, you really do need to start over."

"It sounds like you are advising me to flee the scene to escape prosecution," said Jibril. "I can't do that, and I can't return to Yemen."

"What you can do is turn state's evidence. You will be cutting all ties with Scarlet Jihad, but then that's what conversion means. It means you can't go home again—at least to old homes where old prejudices run deep and old resentments kill."

"How do I ever turn state's evidence?"

"I brought a friend with me," said Father Peter.

A well-dressed man stepped out of the shadows.

"Hello," he said. "My name is Eric Compton." He extended his right hand and between his first and middle fingers was a business card. "I'm an attorney, and, if I do say so myself, a good one."

"He is a good one," admitted Rhonda Shapiro, stepping out of the shadows with her boy cradled on her hip.

Suddenly Jibril saw a gathering of his old Christian enemies coming into the evening light.

Joanna Nickerson spoke first. "I sold the RLDs and got almost $400,000. I was going to use it to do some fixin' up at the Pathway of Light Cathedral. But honestly, I'd rather use it to fix up a life. Whatever it costs to get you through the courts, I want to put my money where my mouth is. Whatever money you need, Eric, this money is yours."

"Well, Joanna, I personally don't want any of it, but it will take a little to fund the project. And I promise I'll do it as cheaply as I can."

"Don't you get cheap on me, Eric Compton. Jesus hasn't ever been cheap when he passes out grace, so this isn't the time to get the cheap thing started. Jibril, are you really at the edge of grace? Did you really mean it when you said you wanted to start life over with a new passion for a new center to make it all work?

"Yes," said Jibril. "If the good Lord will have me, I'm gonna start over. But I'm stained with walking through a field of blood and don't think I can ever be clean."

"Well, Jibril, blood is the stuff of a new start. And here's the team that's gonna make sure you get the same chances we had."

"But I have hated you—all of you—and I've been your enemy."

"Well, we're all God's friends, so you're just gonna have to learn to think of yourself in a brand new way."

Father Peter leaned toward Jibril. "To start, Jibril, hand me that pistol. Your days of killing anyone—including yourself—are over."

Tears streamed down Jibril's face. "I have hated so long, and the lessons of love are so requiring."

He handed the pistol to Father Peter.

"I'm leaving for Darfur now, Jibril. Come, Kinta! Watch me as I walk away, Jibril. Search the darkness that swallows me. Then enter the darkness; the light is just beyond it. There are more reasons to live than you have ever guessed."

Father Peter walked into the shadows and his form was swallowed. There was a spasm in the night and just enough light to see that out of the whirlwind of emptiness stepped a form of someone else who had been forgiven: Mary Muebles.

Jibril ran to her.

"I did not die in the truck as you supposed," she said. "While you believed me dead, I yet lived. Tonight, I know the reason why."

■ ■ ■

The next morning an old priest and a silver wolf moved through an endless sea of tents and prayed with the starving and the dying while they waited for the United Nations relief trucks to bring them life.

And at the very same time, halfway around the world where it was still night, another pageant of life began. A Latina woman walked with a Yemeni man and his lawyer into a police station.

"I am Jibril," the Yemeni said. "I have the names of all those you need to arrest to make the city completely safe."

"I am his lawyer," said Eric Compton.

"I am his *mujer*," said Mary Muebles.

Jibril was clapped in handcuffs.

An hour later they were before the bailiff. "His bail is set at $1 million," said the official as he rapped the gavel. "The earnest deposit is set at $100,000."

"I'm good for that," said a voice from the back of the court.

"And your name, madam?"

"That's Reverend—the Reverend Joanna Nickerson."

The hearing went well for Jibril. His work as an informant was cited as the main reason Scarlet Jihad was stopped. He was given no sentence at all and released to the custody of Gary Jarvis as his probation counselor for a period of six months.

When Jibril's probation was ended, he and Mary Muebles were married at the Pathway of Light Cathedral in the company of those they knew so well.

And thus in one very small place, there was joy, for there were Jews and Arabs, Latinos and blacks, and a few Caucasians—God's children all. The wedding guests were not many but they were all significant. For those who change the world must first be changed themselves. As Father Peter might have said, "Whole continents are renovated one neighborhood at a time."